FREAKY FRANKY

by

I0673985

William Blackwell

FREAK FRANKY

Cover designed by Telemachus Press LLC
Published by Telemachus Press LLC
Paperback ISBN: 978-1-0697318-6-9
Version: 2017.11.01

Acknowledgements

I would like to thank the following: R. Andrew Chesnut, for writing *Devoted to Death, Santa Muerte, the Skeleton Saint.* One of the most scholarly books written on the subject of Saint Death, it was an invaluable source of information. Heartfelt thanks as well to my loyal readers and supporters, the hardworking staff at Telemachus Press, and my editor, Winslow Eliot.

Observe constantly that all things take place by change, and accustom thyself to consider that the nature of the universe loves nothing so much as to change things which are and to make things new like them. For everything that exists is in a manner the seed of that which will be.

—Marcus Aurelius

WILLIAM BLACKWELL

Religion is the sigh of the oppressed creature, the heart of a heartless world, and the soul of soulless conditions. It is the opium of the people.

—Karl Marx

For Tim Graber, a profoundly loyal and supportive brother.

FREAKY FRANKY

PROLOGUE

I'm sick of being poor. Estella Mendoza peered out the misshapen window of her ramshackle home on the outskirts of the small city of Nacozari in Sonora, Mexico. All she saw was a barren and scorched landscape, the sun setting in the distant, bleak horizon. Her stomach was knotted by more than just hunger pangs. A sense of frustration and hopelessness was giving birth to desperation. A fly buzzed around her head and landed on her cheek, which was leathered, lined, and pock-marked by the cruelty of Mother Nature. Time had not been kind to her.

She smacked her face hard, squashing the pesky fly and smearing its blood and guts across her face and hand.

"Got you, you son of a bitch," she said in Spanish, wiping her palm on the knee of her dirt-stained, torn jeans. She ignored the fly remains on her cheek, moving away from the screenless and paneless window and rummaging through dusty cupboards for a morsel of food. Nothing. A grease-stained, dented fridge door hung open, a small bowl of rice the only thing resembling nourishment on the otherwise empty shelves. Flies circled the rice, at times dive-bombing in for a small stale snack. Bending down, she reached inside, waved the flies away, and picked up the small bowl. Looking around the cluttered kitchen counter, she found a dirty spoon, wiped it on her tattered white t-shirt and, sidestepping debris littering the dirt floor, walked over to a green plastic lawn chair, weathered by the elements and cracking in various spots.

As she sat down, a brittle leg snapped, catapulting her headfirst into a wooden wall. The rice bowl flew out of her hands, shattering against the wall and showering her head with rice and shards of glazed earthenware. She hit the ground ass-first and groaned. "You son of a bitch." Dazed, she rubbed a small goose egg beginning to sprout on her forehead. Realizing she still clutched the spoon, she flushed and flung it against the door. With a metallic clang, it bounced off the door and skipped along the floor, stopping a few inches from her outstretched feet. Her face tightened and she reached for it, with the intention of throwing it clear out the window.

A knock on the door stopped the arc of her arm. "Who is it?"

From the other side, she heard a female voice say in Spanish, "It's me. Are you busy?"

Estella recognized the voice. Alejandra Rivera, her friend for over twenty years. Alejandra lived a few blocks away and in Estella's view, she had everything. A middle-class home, a wonderful working husband, and a ten-year-old devoted and well-behaved son. Where Estella had famine, poverty, and despair, Alejandra had an abundant food supply, an income stream, love, and hope. Poison tentacles of jealousy and resentment coursed through Estella's dazed mind. "What do you want?"

"I brought you refried beans. And rice."

Estella got to her feet. "Come in."

The door opened and Alejandra entered. "What happened?" she asked, concern furrowing her brow as she examined Estella and the accident scene.

Estella pointed to the shattered remains of the plastic chair leg. "It broke and sent me flying."

"I'm sorry," Alejandra said, putting the white bowl of beans and rice on a cluttered kitchen table and rushing to her friend's aid. She escorted Estella to a nearby wooden chair, which looked slightly less dangerous than the offending plastic one, and sat her down. The chair creaked and groaned, but held.

Alejandra produced a plastic spoon from a blue apron attached to her white dress and handed it to Estella. "Eat. It'll do you good."

Estella peeled the plastic wrap from the spoon, tossed it on the floor apathetically, and stabbed the spoon into the food. A wave of dizziness swept over her and she waited a moment for her head to clear before digging in. She quickly shoveled three spoonfuls into her mouth and swallowed them, hardly chewing.

Alejandra looked at the bump on Estella's head and searched her friend's eyes concernedly. "Are you okay?"

Between mouthfuls, Estella said, "Yeah, just a little bump."

"Well, be careful."

As Estella ate, Alejandra approached the kitchen counter and began cleaning up, throwing food wrappings into a nearby wastebasket and neatly piling dirty dishes next to the sink. It wasn't the first time she'd helped her starving friend by bringing her food and cleaning her humble abode.

"You don't have to do that."

Alejandra spun around and looked at Estella cheerily. "It's not a problem. And look at you, you're in no shape to do it right now." She resumed cleaning, turning her back to Estella.

A blind rage—a dark and hateful energy—seethed through Estella's veins. *My chance. Now's my chance.* Before she even realized what she was doing, she leapt from the chair with a vitality and vigor she never knew she possessed, grabbed a hatchet, and rushed toward Alejandra. As Estella swung the hatchet, Alejandra turned around. Her jaw dropped in shock and horror as she looked at Estella with fear-filled brown eyes.

The hatchet sliced into Alejandra's throat, blood spraying Estella's face and body. Two more swings and she'd chopped Alejandra's head clean off. The decapitated head dropped to the floor, rolled into the front door, and stopped. Almost as if she were pursuing her head, Alejandra's headless body convulsed and, spewing blood like a lawn sprinkler, staggered to the door. She crashed into it and slumped to the ground, outstretched hands frantically reaching for her head for a second or two before growing still.

Estella put the hatchet on the kitchen counter and wiped her bloody face with a soiled dishrag. She sat down at the kitchen table and continued eating. She glanced at the lifeless head and body of her one-time friend. "By the way, thanks for the food."

Two hours later, when night had blanketed the day, Estella clutched Alejandra's head in both hands. She danced around a small skeleton statue, sprinkling blood on and around the shrine. Satisfied with her efforts, she put the head next to the statue, lit a candle, and placed it next to the skeleton. She knelt down and began praying for abundance. In the suffused candlelight, the skeleton saint's hollow eye sockets glittered and glowed. Its grin seemed to mock her efforts and she realized there was more work to be done.

In the month that followed, Estella beheaded two ten-year-old boys, one of them her grandson, and sacrificed their blood to the skeleton saint. At the end of that month, she was convinced she had finally won the favor of her Goddess. On that day the police raided her home and discovered the bodies of all three victims buried beneath her dirt floor. She was sentenced to life imprisonment, showed no remorse for the killings, and authorities labelled her a serial killer.

CHAPTER ONE

"I'm sorry, he's dying."

Anisa Worthington put her hands over her face and knelt down on the floor next to the bed. She spread her fingers and peered at her five-year-old son Connor, watching his labored breathing. His face flushed as red as the satin bedspread covering his sweating body. His eyes were closed and he appeared to have drifted off into sleep, or a coma.

A lone tear snaked down her cheek and she brushed it away, turning to the doctor standing behind her. "He can't be dying. He was healthy three hours ago."

"That was three hours ago," Doctor Manuel Ricardo said, his brow furrowed with worry. "I've checked his vitals repeatedly. His systems are shutting down. His heart rate is sporadic. He's not getting enough oxygen to the brain. We need to get him to a hospital, and fast."

"No hospitals." They had been down that path before, soon after the doctor had rushed to the scene. Anisa had adamantly refused to have her ailing son taken to the hospital. Not long ago, her friend Melissa had died in the hospital after a heart surgery had gone awry. The heart surgery was apparently a success, but the towel left inside Melissa's chest cavity was not. It had caused an infection that ultimately resulted in her untimely death. There was still a lawsuit pending. *No hospitals. Definitely no hospitals.*

Connor precipitously jerked, arched his back, and clutched Anisa's wrist. His sea-blue, tear-filled eyes bored into hers, pleading. "Help me, Mommy. What's happening to me?"

Anisa put a comforting hand on his chest. "You're gonna be fine, honey. It's probably just an allergic reaction to something in the forest."

Earlier Connor had been outside playing in the large garden surrounding the small bungalow in Montague, Prince Edward Island. He had left the house as chipper as usual, excited about the prospect of being outside on this sunny June day, the first day of summer. He played happily on the grass, somersaulting around. At one point he leapt up and chased a butterfly, making funny faces that almost made his mother laugh. Then everything went wrong. He disappeared into the tree-line for a few minutes and when he emerged he was panting and puffing, red as a beet and his breathing so labored it appeared as if he were on the verge of a massive cardiac arrest.

Why do I hate the first day of summer? Why do I hate all the seasons? Anisa thought.

Connor's breathing became more labored. He released his mother's wrist and slumped back into the bed. His panicked expression slowly morphed into one of a strange, resigned dread.

Anisa stood and swung around to face Doctor Ricardo. Her hands were twitching, her face now wet with fresh tears. "Do something. You're the doctor. Fix him, for God's sake."

Doctor Ricardo moved in with his stethoscope and began listening to the erratic heartbeat. Connor's eyes had closed again and his head tilted toward the bedside window, where a spear of light poked in, illuminating what appeared to be a yellow scythe swiping across the child's throat.

Doctor Ricardo's eyes bulged with recognition and he leaped back, turning to Anisa and wrapping his big arms around her in a bear hug, squeezing the breath from her lungs. "Santa Muerte... Santa Muerte."

He finally released her. She gasped for breath. "What did you say? What is Santa Muerte?"

"Not what, *who*. Santa Muerte is Saint Death, or Holy Death. She is the personification of death. But she is also a great healer of many ailments. I believe she can save your son."

Before Anisa could respond, Doctor Ricardo rushed from the bedroom.

Anisa hurried to the window and watched him snap open the trunk of his Audi Quattro, fumble around for a moment, and then carefully lift out a small statue—perhaps two feet tall—of a skeleton draped in a red tunic. He also removed a purple jar candle and tucked it into his jacket pocket. As he walked swiftly toward the house, she noticed the black scythe in the skeleton saint's outstretched left hand, a small globe of the world clutched firmly in its right. *What the hell is this? The Grim Reapress?*

Inside the bedroom, Doctor Ricardo put the statue on a bedside table. He placed the candle in front of the grinning statue and lit it. Flickering flames cast jagged yellow lines across its hollow black eye sockets.

"What's with the purple candle?" she asked, clasping her hands together in an attempt to contain her nervousness.

"It's the votive candle for supernatural healing and health."

"Do you think it's gonna work? I don't believe in hocus-pocus."

Doctor Ricardo's face tightened. "Of course it'll work. It always does. Please don't use blasphemous words around this all-powerful saint. She might get angry."

"I'll be angry if it doesn't work."

"Calm down. Do you have any tequila?"

Fear and panic coursed through Anisa's body, an unstoppable debilitating tide. She clenched her hands tighter as the color drained from her face. A wave of dizziness washed over her. Her vision blurred. She put her hand on the wall. *Don't pass out. Connor needs you.* "No."

"Do you have any alcohol at all? To petition Santa Muerte to save your son, we need an offering."

"Rum."

"Go get it, quickly. And bring three glasses."

Connor opened his eyes, turned to them, and started convulsing. Spittle sprayed from his mouth like a tiny erupting geyser, a grim picture of a boy who looked like he was possessed by a demon.

Turning to Connor, Anisa froze, finally overcome.

"Not now," the doctor said. "Bring the rum."

She stood motionless, now chalky white.

Doctor Ricardo shook her violently. "Don't go catatonic. Get the booze. Now!"

Her eyes focused on the man in front of her, and she saw the deep concern etched into his sharp gray eyes. Snapping out of the panic and fear-induced catatonia, she rushed from the room and returned quickly with a bottle of Bacardi white rum and three glasses. She set the glasses on the makeshift altar to Santa Muerte. Doctor Ricardo took the bottle and splashed a little rum on the skeleton's face. He then filled all three glasses. He picked two up, leaving the bottle and a glass of rum on the shrine in front of the Skinny Lady. He offered a glass to Anisa. With an unsteady hand she took it.

"Drink it," he said.

Connor's convulsions became more violent. "Mooommmmy! Help me!"

Doctor Ricardo raised his glass to Anisa. "Drink."

They clinked glasses and took large swills. He took her glass and set it on the altar. Then he gently took her arm and pulled her down to a kneeling position in front of Saint Death. "I need you to pray with me. I need you to believe."

She studied her son. *He's getting worse.* She looked at Doctor Ricardo. "O-okay."

He clasped his hands in prayer, turned to the statue, bowed his head, and closed his eyes. "Repeat after me, okay? Most Holy Death, protector and restorer of bodily ailments."

In a voice suddenly soft and calm, she repeated his words.

He continued. "Angel of death. Angel of life, whom our Father created to help and serve. I implore and beseech you to restore the life and health of Connor Worthington. May he live long and may his body and mind recover fully its youthful energy and vigor..."

Anisa repeated his words, her tone now pleading.

The child's movements grew less frantic, but he still twitched slightly.

Outside, a gray bank of clouds descended over the house and it began to rain, torrential.

Thunder rumbled from the heavens. A fork of lightning cracked the sky, struck the ground, and exploded, fanning out mounds of red PEI dirt.

The boy's convulsions slowed, then stopped. He dropped his arms to his sides and splayed his legs out on the bed, lifeless. He closed his eyes. His expression grew calm.

Anisa stopped praying. She opened her eyes and glanced out the window at the torrential rain. She saw the mound of dirt exploding into the air a few feet away and looked back at Connor, his deathly stillness unnerving her once again.

Doctor Ricardo opened his eyes and followed her gaze. He touched her arm. "Please, we must finish the prayer."

Against her better judgment, she continued praying.

Once again, he continued. "I implore you, Most Holy Death, restore Connor's health. For the sake of Jesus Christ, who died on the cross to save our sins, answer our pleas and bring him back. Amen."

"Amen," Anisa said. She opened her eyes and turned to Conner. Both his hands were crossed on his chest, over his heart. His expression was calm and serene. His breathing was no longer labored.

He had stopped breathing.

Screaming bloody murder, Anisa sprang to her feet and rushed out of the room.

Doctor Ricardo heard the front door slam as the echoes of her grief-stricken screams were swallowed up by the old house.

He knocked back his glass of rum, bowed his head, and calmly continued praying to the saint of death.

CHAPTER TWO

Cofresi Beach, Dominican Republic, Sunday, 1:36 am. In the black of night, a million stars illuminated the sky and the full moon glowed ominously. Waves lapped gently on the shore. The beach along the shore was quiet and still, the surrounding grassy park strewn with empty rum bottles, beer bottles, and other debris. A motorcycle roared down the two-lane street fronting the beach, cracking the silence with the loud thumping sound of a broken muffler. Six small dogs dashed out from a two-story oceanfront apartment building, barking furiously. Two of them gave chase. The male driver kicked at the attacking canines as he slowed and they grew silent, retreating to the security of the apartment building front parking lot.

A light went on in a main-floor apartment behind them. A sliding-glass door squeaked open and out staggered a thin, dark-skinned man wearing only white underwear, a half-full rum bottle in his left hand. He shouted obscenities in Spanish at the dogs and they scattered. Then he face-planted the concrete parking lot, smashing his head hard. A tiny river of dark red blood poured out of his injured head, zig-zagging a path to the road. A small, black, mangy, mixed-breed dog returned, stopped at the man's head, and began slurping up the red river. A Chihuahua hopped up—favoring its injured left hind leg—to survey the scene, sniffed at the blood, barked twice, and hobbled down the street. Its barks slowly faded into the night.

A six-seater white motorized golf cart, also with a broken muffler that split the silence like thunder, roared up and skidded to a stop. It was occupied by four tourists, drinks in hand, laughing and slurring.

Seeing the fallen man, a fat man climbed out of the driver's seat and promptly dropped his drink-filled plastic cup, splattering its contents on the road. He turned to the others. "We gotta help him."

A woman with a cackling voice said, "Holy shit. That dog's drinking human blood."

"We gotta help him," the man repeated.

"Screw that, Herman. He might have AIDS or something. We don't know who he is."

But Herman ignored her. He staggered up to the face-planted man, knelt down, and hoisted him up, the half-full rum bottle still clinging to his blood-drenched hand. The dog that had been drinking fresh warm blood reared back and barked three times threateningly. Herman kicked it in the ribs, not too hard, but not too soft either. It yelped, turned, and ran down the street.

Dragging the bleeding man like a rag doll, Herman leaned him against a white car and slapped him gently in the face. "Are you okay? Wake up."

"Let's go, Herman," Cackling Voice said. "I wanna get to Ocean World casino." The other couple occupying the back seats of the golf cart sat watching in stunned silence.

The bleeding man opened his eyes, muttered something incomprehensible, and closed them again. With one hand, Herman propped the accident victim's head up. "Wake up."

The bleeding man opened his eyes. "Al... Alfredo."

"Is that your name?" Herman asked.

Alfredo nodded.

A white and blue cop truck rolled down the street and stopped in front of the scene. Flashing red lights illuminated the neighborhood. Two Dominican cops got out.

A young woman wearing a pink low-cut blouse, red hot pants, and impossibly high heels ambled past, led by her flashing smartphone. She glanced briefly at Alfredo and Herman and the two cops; then, click-clacking past, she quickly refocused on the drama contained inside her smartphone, electronic virtual reality taking precedence over real-life drama.

Some conversation and pointing ensued. Herman peeled off his white t-shirt, *Trust In Guns* emblazoned on the front in black. He handed it to one of the cops, a tall, lanky man who looked unsteady on his feet. Lanky Cop wrapped it around Alfredo's bleeding head. It took only a moment for them to help Alfredo, now slipping in and out of consciousness, his hand still clutching the rum bottle, into the back seat of the truck. Before they pulled away, Lanky Cop eyed Herman inquisitively and stuck his hand out the window, rubbing his belly with the other. Herman produced a US twenty-dollar bill and handed it to Lanky Cop. Lanky Cop grinned, rolled up the window, and sped away.

As Herman climbed into the golf cart, Cackling Voice said, "What are you doing giving the cops money? They're all fucking corrupt around here. You gotta pay for saving someone's life?"

Herman nodded. "Where's the rum?"

"Oh no," Cackling Voice said. "Turn this thing around and go back to Lifestyles hotel. We gotta get you cleaned up first. You're covered in blood. And no shirt."

Herman U-turned the golf cart and sped away, the metallic rattling sound of the ruptured exhaust pipe fading in the distance.

But for the gentle lapping of waves, silence once again prevailed. Blackness enveloped the night, broken only by the faint illumination of the moonlight and stars.

Above the bloodstained parking lot, a light flashed on in a second-floor apartment, directly above the suite from which the unfortunate Alfredo had emerged earlier.

Franklin Reiger slid the balcony door open and stepped out. For the last half hour or so, wrapped in the protective cloak of darkness, he'd been watching Alfredo with unbridled glee. He rubbed his clean-shaven chin, rolled his hand across his six-pack stomach muscles and studied the bloodstream below, marveling at how it glistened diamond-like in the glint of the moon. Looking down at his bare foot, his rapture was swept out to sea in the receding waves. Franklin tensed, veins swelling in his neck and forehead. He had stepped in fresh, steamy-warm dog shit. That wasn't the first time. Nor would it be the last. As long as Alfredo kept collecting street dogs (he called it "rescuing"), which he couldn't afford to feed or properly care for, Franklin's upper balcony would continue to be a minefield of doggy dung. The dogs wouldn't shit on Alfredo's balcony. Oh no. Don't do-do on the hand that feeds you, or at least the hand that tries to feed you.

"You fucking piece of shit," Franklin said, referring to Alfredo. He bent down and scooped up a handful of the moist fecal matter. "I hope you fucking die from that concussion."

With lightning speed, he dashed down the stairs and, using the handful of feces as a crude writing instrument, scrawled *FUCK YOU* on Alfredo's sliding-glass window in large capital letters. As he examined his handiwork, his frown slowly morphed into a grin, showing perfectly aligned white teeth. He swung around, walked a few paces, and picked up a small garden hose lying next to a steel cage. The cage was draped with brown shower curtains; the caretaker, Niamia Fernandez, had fashioned it as an outdoor shower and rented it out to beachgoers for fifty pesos a pop on the weekends. Hundreds of partiers, locals and foreigners alike, descended on the beach during the weekends, often playing unbearably loud, awful music and getting merrily pie-eyed and out of control. *Fucking stupid bitch,* Franklin thought as he washed the crap from his hands and then trained the nozzle on his shit-stained foot. *She's a piece of shit. She's just a fucking caretaker here and gets free rent for that. But that's not enough for her. Working every angle she can to make a buck, all behind the owner's back. Using their water, that they pay for, and making a business out of it.*

The makeshift beach shower was one of many of Niamia's business ventures. During the day, and sometimes even during evening hours, there was a steady stream of people calling for her. She sold sandwiches, tourist trinkets from a makeshift shack in front of the apartment building, as well as after-hours alcohol and cigarettes. She'd even hired a Haitian man to rent out parking stalls (ostensibly belonging to tenants of the six-suite apartment building) during the busy weekends.

Franklin couldn't remember how many times he'd blasted Niamia and the Haitian for renting out his parking stall to beach-goers during his absence. And each time, he was met with the same calm response: "Sorry about that. I won't do it again, I promise." But every weekend, either from his balcony, or when returning home from a sex-filled evening of debauchery, he would see the dark Haitian standing in the middle of the road, waving in oncoming traffic with a smile. Niamia would be standing nearby, smiling, as calm as a glassy sea, counting her coins, thinking up new ways to exploit the property, exploit the property owners, and exploit the foreigners. Franklin had counted sixteen business ventures that she ran from the comfort of her tiny main-floor, rent-free apartment. But he knew he had missed a few, knew there were more and there would be more. *Fuck it. Forget about her for now. She's next, but not now.*

He rinsed his foot clean, tossed the hose haphazardly on the pock-marked lawn, turned it off, and made his way back up to his apartment. *What a fucking gong show around here. Insane asylum, this building. I hate this country.* He stepped inside his living room, slid the door closed, flicked the light off, and sank into the plush brown sofa. He reached for a fresh black votive candle, a symbol paradoxically of protection from harm, vengeance, and death in the cult worship of Santa Muerte. He lit it with a match and placed it in front of a two-foot high skeleton statue, cloaked in black and gripping a silver scythe that glinted in the candle's glow. He studied the skeleton saint's hollow black eye sockets. Her mocking grin seemed to widen with the flickering of the candle.

It took a few minutes of closed-eyed silence before Franklin felt calm enough to continue. He shouldn't be angry. Shouldn't be disappointed. Shouldn't be sad. After all, Santa Muerte had answered at least part of his prayer of last night. Wishing to rid the building of its insane inhabitants, he'd prayed to the saint of death for the untimely death of Alfredo. And he had snickered as he watched Alfredo slam his stupid head into the concrete and bleed like a stuck pig. It was true that Alfredo had seemed somewhat alive as the cops had driven off with him. But that didn't mean he would last the night. Maybe he would slip into a coma overnight and die. Maybe he would even die before he arrived at the hospital. *That's it, think positive.* Now was not the time for negative emotion. It was a time to give thanks to Santa Muerte for answering his prayer.

He picked up the bottle of Brugal Anejo rum he had placed beside the ominously glowing statue and replenished the powerful saint's empty glass. Then he closed his black eyes, and began praying. "Oh Holy Death, Sacred Death, Saint Death, thank you for answering my prayers. Thank you for causing the head injury to Alfredo. I pray that you finish the job. Saint of all saints, I am deeply in your debt. Amen."

He picked up the bottle of rum again. Franklin was not much of a drinker. He prided himself on never getting drunk in the three years he had lived in the DR. But surely a little nip wouldn't hurt now. It was what Saint Death would want. They now had a contract. She had done his bidding, or at least part of it, and she would want something in return. He was prepared to do anything she asked of him.

This was a time for celebration, a time for rejoicing, a time to join with the venerated saint in the revelry that surely must accompany the answering of a prayer, the very first time he had ever asked the Skinny Lady for anything. And she had delivered. Delivered in spades. Well, maybe in hearts, meaning Alfredo's heart would be returned to a stillness richly deserved. Franklin allowed himself a long swill of the bottle, swallowing a good four ounces of the potent rum. He enjoyed the stinging sensation in his esophagus as it settled into his stomach. A pleasant buzz slowly began to envelop and dull his senses.

He closed his eyes, shut his mouth, and sank into the plush couch, allowing his mind to wander. He drifted back to a happier time, a time when his psyche wasn't constantly engaged in a tumultuous battle between the forces of good and evil. But try as he might, the panoptic tragedy of his early life pervaded his troubled mind.

Growing up in small-town Montague, PEI, Franklin was the youngest of four siblings: he had two brothers, Caleb and Nelson, and one sister, Anisa. He had a healthy relationship and a close bond with his brothers and sister. His father, Cole, was a dedicated husband, a good father, and a hard-working fisherman. His mother, Marina, was a consummate caregiver and a devoted and loving wife. They were a Catholic, God-fearing, church-going family. Picture perfect. Or so it was for a while. When Franklin was eight, and he was thirty-four now, his father died at sea, the victim of a ferocious storm that plunged him and his fishing vessel into the depths of the ocean, never to be recovered.

Franklin was Cole's favorite son, although Cole would never admit it. After his father's death, Franklin went on a voluntary hunger strike, refusing to leave his bedroom—except for Mother Nature's callings—for almost three weeks. Finally, when he was as thin as a rail, and sick as a dog, it was his older brother Caleb who convinced him to eat. "It's what Daddy would've wanted, brother. He would've wanted you to be happy and healthy. Please, eat something. Snap out of this or Mom will have you committed to a care facility for your own good."

Three years later, the tsunami wave of tragedy swelled and unleashed its fury. On a bright, sunny day, Caleb and Franklin were playing soccer on the expansive front lawn. Franklin guarded a net improvised with old tires and Caleb kicked the ball. Franklin dove, but missed. The ball went through the goal posts and bounced across the lawn toward the two-lane highway.

"He shoots, he scores. You get it, Franky," Caleb said.

But Franklin had become frustrated chasing balls. It was the third goal in three shots. "I'm tired. You get it for a change."

"Suit yourself." Before Franklin could change his mind, Caleb raced after the ball. As it bounced into the middle of the highway, he reached it. He picked it up and spun around, ready to return. But it was too late. A speeding pickup truck driven by an impaired driver hit him square on, catapulting him airborne for thirty feet, before he smashed into asphalt, dead on impact.

Franklin never got over the guilt. *It should have been me. Should have been me.*

Exactly three years later, the tsunami wave of destruction reared its devastating head again, unleashing another wave of tragedy. Franklin's eldest brother Nelson was out in the garage, repairing a 1971 Mustang Shelby Cobra convertible. Nelson was underneath the vehicle, installing a right front shock absorber, when Franklin entered the garage. All the tires had been removed and the car perched precariously on four metal jacks.

"Adjust that right side jack, will you, bro," Nelson said as Franklin, down on all fours, watched his brother work. "It needs to go up a notch."

Franklin had never been mechanically inclined. "What do I do?"

Nelson pointed. "Just take that red handle, stick it in there and pump it up a bit. I'll tell you when to stop."

"Don't you want to slide out first?"

"No, no, it's secure. Hurry, I'm dying under here. Hardly any room. My shoulder's killing me."

Franklin moved around to the front right side of the vehicle and picked up a small red hollow pipe.

"In there," Nelson said, pointing.

"Okay." Franklin put the handle in place and began cranking. The vehicle began to rise.

"Almost," Nelson said. "Another inch or so."

Franklin continued cranking.

"Right there is good."

"Okay." As Franklin got to his feet, he heard a whooshing sound. The hydraulic jack sprayed oil on his brother's face and, with lightning speed, descended and tipped over, sending the front axle crashing onto Nelson's neck, snapping it with a horrifying pop and killing him instantly.

A police investigation ruled the death an accident and Franklin was cleared of any wrongdoing. But the poison ivy tentacles of guilt ravaged him mercilessly from the inside out.

He leaned back into the couch, opened his eyes, and took another swill of rum, hoping to dull the pain of his tragic past. He wanted desperately to escape the grim images haunting his mind day and night—especially night. He gazed at the face of Saint Death, studied her menacing grin. Lit intermittently yellow-orange by the flickering candle flame, it seemed to mock his descent into his tragic past.

With a mountainous effort, he willed his mind away from the three horrifying deaths, although they had changed his life irrevocably—*No, nothing is forever*—and plummeted him into sociopathic tendencies. *No, I'm not crazy, everyone around me is*. Suddenly restless, he got up and strode through the dungeon-like quarters. Most of the windows were sealed with tinfoil and a thick black blanket covered the sliding-glass door. He pulled the curtain aside and studied the snake-like stream of Alfredo's blood in the dark street below. A motorcycle roared past, its headlights momentarily bathing Alfredo's blood in a twinkling silver glow. Franklin scratched his head stubble and a grin slowly replaced the frown. *That little shit Alfredo is gonna die. Saint Death answered my prayer.*

As he returned to the sofa, now relishing his third glass of rum, the grief was once again replaced by glee. As he commenced another prayer, the dark irony of his situation was missed on Franklin. As a die-hard Christian, in his youth, he had prayed for the resurrection of his siblings. Prayed for life.

Now, he prayed exclusively for death.

CHAPTER THREE

The next afternoon, less than a block away, Natalie Smithers lounged comfortably on a plush bed constructed on a grassy hill overlooking the beach and the ocean. A gentle sea breeze along with a strawberry margarita cooled her in the hot sun. *What an awesome spot. I love it here.* She gazed out to sea and watched a small boat with an outboard motor tug joyful tourists on a long, yellow, banana-shaped inflatable device. As the boat angled over a large wave, the banana suddenly flipped over, tipping six tourists into the ocean. She tapped her fiancé's arm. "Look, honey, they flipped over."

Terry Anderson opened his eyes. He had almost fallen asleep in the shade. He reached for his margarita and took a sip. "They've got lifejackets. They'll be fine."

"I know they'll be fine, baby. And so will we."

Natalie had every reason to be optimistic. She couldn't be happier. They had arrived at Cofresi Palm Beach & Spa Resort a few days ago for a celebration of their new made-on-the-internet union. They had only been dating for just over three months before Terry proposed in dramatic fashion: he'd hired a small Cessna to fly over her Toronto backyard on a sunny Sunday afternoon. The plane towed a large banner that said MARRY ME PLEASE NATALIE, I LOVE YOU SO MUCH. The banner, along with the euphoric yet sedative effects of white wine and the glittering diamond-and-gold engagement ring, brought tears of joy to Natalie's eyes. She'd looked at Terry, down on one knee with an expectant smile and a hopeful look in his deep green eyes. "Of course I will, baby," she had responded. "I love you, too."

The joyful image evaporated and she snuggled closer to Terry and planted a wet kiss on his lips. "Don't you think so, sweetie?"

"I don't think so... I *know* so."

She raised her crystal goblet, decorated with a pretty pink plastic umbrella, to Terry. "To us... to lifelong happiness, love, and loyalty."

Raising his green-umbrella-adorned goblet, he smiled, revealing a perfect set of white teeth. "To all that, together, as one, until death do us part."

They clinked, kissed, and returned to watching the yellow banana rescue effort. By now, the boat had circled and the driver had righted the inflatable vessel. The passengers helped each other and it wasn't long before all six were firmly seated, tightly clenching rubber hand grips and giving the thumbs-up to the boat driver. He acknowledged with a grin, revved up the motor and sped off, slower this time, slicing through the oncoming waves head-on, perhaps in an effort to mitigate the chances of another tourist splash-down.

Natalie ran a hand through her long auburn hair and with a final gulp, polished off her margarita. It was her third and she was starting to feel a pleasing buzz. She set the glass down and watched Terry as he closed his eyes and tilted his head back on the white plush pillow, evidently deciding to resume his afternoon siesta. It didn't bother her that at twenty-five, she was ten years Terry's junior. Age was just a number. With Terry, it had been love at first sight. His magnetic green eyes, neatly cropped ash-blonde hair, trim and fit build, along with his easy, relaxed manner, sense of humor, quick wit, energy, and zest for life had endeared him to her from day one. Although as a certified general accountant she was a success in her own right, it didn't hurt that Terry had recently announced he'd been promoted to bank manager at a Scotiabank branch in Toronto. As well as being goal-oriented financially, he was goal-oriented on a personal and spiritual level. He had laid the brickwork for a solid foundation to achieve financial and personal success. She thought his fastidious, proactive, and organized approach to life would compliment her sometimes lackadaisical and unorganized approach to goal setting.

More than that, Terry was an optimist and Natalie's attitudes occasionally stumbled down the pot-hole laden path of negativity. But, that was then. Then, she had still been reeling from the unceremonious break-up with her long-time ex-boyfriend Rex Fisher. Their three-year union had included plenty of passion, marriage plans, and a bond of trust and loyalty Natalie believed was as hard as rock and could not be shattered. But shattered it was, by a simple text message. The infidelity-prone piece of shit didn't even have the balls to break up in person. He had sent her a simple text: *I don't think this is working out anymore. It's true what they say about accountants. You're all boring. Lose my number, bitch.*

She had tried calling Rex for an explanation, or at least some closure. The calls went unanswered. Eventually they were blocked entirely. He unfriended her on Facebook. And, try as she might to figure out what had prompted the nasty text, Natalie couldn't. It had driven her into a funk that lasted almost a year. Some of her friends and her mother Melinda had encouraged her to find a hobby or something else to stimulate her. "You can't live like this for the rest of your life," Melinda had said. And after two days of thoughtful consideration, and a case of Vivo white wine, almost as if to spite her mother, she combined her hobby-search with her hunt for a new man. She volunteered at the local food bank, hoping to net a humanitarian man. When that didn't produce fruit, she began attending church and loitering around coffee shops. Still a big goose egg. Finally, she joined three dating sites in an effort to stem the tide of loneliness and desperation. Bingo. On *Plenty of Fish,* she'd reeled in the man who lay next to her now, gently snoring.

With a frown, she eyeballed him. Insecurity lanced her heart like a knife. *Serene and peaceful. Is he the same as all the rest? Will he dump me without telling me why?* She ran a hand across her moist red lips and realized she was beginning to frown. *Come on. That was then. This is now. This should be the happiest time of my life.* She remembered her last heated carnal encounter with Terry—perhaps two hours ago—and the frown quickly morphed into a delicious smile. He had been so tender, considerate, and damn talented in the hotel suite king-sized bed. He had brought her to the height of physical pleasure. Never had she experienced orgasms that intensely satisfying. They'd catapulted her to an ineffably high plane of existence. *That's it, girl. You can do it. Get yourself out of the funk.*

She waved over a waiter dressed in a penguin suit and ordered two more margaritas. He returned promptly with the drinks and a smile. Terry turned over on the bed, his back to her, and snored. Natalie thought briefly about waking him, and then changed her mind. Drink in hand, she wandered down to the beach, her red dental-floss bikini accentuating her finely tanned body: long, slender legs, well-rounded, tight derriere, and perfectly shaped mango-sized breasts peeking out slightly to offer a tantalizing view of cleavage. A few heads turned—that didn't go unappreciated—as she reached the water's edge and poked a glossy red, pedicured toenail into the water. *Nice and warm.* She sipped her margarita through the straw and surveyed the scene. It was a small beach, semi-crowded. Tourists leisurely strolled by, most with drinks in hand. Nearby, three children splashed each other in the water, yelling and screaming. An assortment of blue bed-style lawn chairs dotted the sand, occupied by tourists in various stages of repose. Some slept; some drank and talked amicably; others read; still others frittered away the hours doing crossword puzzles or playing Sudoku.

Thinking a swim might refresh her and help relieve the recent descent into negativity, she glanced around for somewhere to place her drink. Close to her was a tanned, toned man wearing a camouflage knee-length bathing suit. He was clean cut, with dark eyes, a black buzz-cut, high cheek bones, a chiseled, pointy nose, and sculptured abs. *A fine specimen.* He sat upright in a bed-style lawn chair, a full bottle of water on a plastic table beside him, inattentively flipping through the pages of a book.

He looked up and caught her staring. "Can I help you?"

Natalie felt her cheeks flush red. With an embarrassed grin, she raised her glass. "Sorry, I'm looking for a temporary home for this."

The man waved a hand over the plastic table. "Leave it here. Not a problem."

She approached and set the drink on the table. "Thanks. I wanna go for a swim. It's hot."

"I'll guard it with my life."

"I appreciate that. What're you reading?"

The man dog-eared and closed the book. "It's called *Further Along The Road Less Traveled.* M. Scott Peck. It teaches you how to achieve personal and spiritual growth."

"I could use something like that. Is it working?"

"I think so. The author has some brilliant insights into the complexities of life, spirituality, forgiveness, and relationships."

Natalie flashed her engagement ring with a smile. "I like the last part." She pointed to her fiancé sleeping fifty feet away, halfway up a grassy embankment. "I'm engaged to be married."

The man glanced back briefly at Terry. "Congratulations." But his expression was neutral and his dark eyes said something else. Natalie suddenly felt butterflies dancing in the pit of her stomach.

She turned toward the water and started walking. Before diving in, she glanced back. "Thanks again. I won't be long."

Licking his lips, the man eyeballed her shapely ass. "Take as long as you want."

Deep in the ocean a few minutes later, making good progress with a smooth breast stroke, Natalie tried to make sense of the sudden nervousness and fear that had knotted her stomach and started her heart pounding to beat the band: a single glance from those dark and mysterious eyes. It was as though he were looking right into her soul and in some perverted and devilish way scheming to make it his. A small wave broke over her head and she swallowed a mouthful of water. Bobbing her head to the surface as she swam, she spit it out effortlessly—without coughing—and quickly found the rhythm of her smooth stroke. She tried to calm herself. *It's your imagination. Nothing else.* But, no, that explanation simply didn't hold water. She had to admit she didn't know much about the Dominican Republic; it was her first time here. A DR virgin. But she had heard stories. Foreigners came here to hide from the law. Pedophiles, murderers, scum-sucking sickos shopping for prostitutes. Better not take any chances. In that instant, she decided to swim toward Ocean World, go to shore, and make her way back to the Lifestyles resort on foot. She'd forget about her margarita, and give that strange man a wide berth. For all she knew, he could be a serial killer.

Keeping a close eye on Natalie, Franklin absently closed his book. Even though a paragraph or two had caught his interest, there was no point in fooling himself. He hadn't bought it to find spiritual enlightenment. He had already found his version of that with Saint Death. No, the book had been purchased as a conversation starter, a decoy of sorts. Nothing more.

He watched her swim toward Ocean World and then turn, smoothly making her way to the shoreline. He eyeballed the margarita and, for a moment, almost gave in to the temptation to polish it off. *No. Mustn't do that.* Last night was bad enough. Wallowing in his tragic past, he had let himself slide off the cliff of sobriety. When he'd woken up that morning, three-quarters of the rum bottle were gone. Sprawled out on the couch, he noticed the candle had burned down to nothing and gone out. If it hadn't been for its protective glass, he might have started a fire and burned the whole building down. He reached for his water instead, unscrewed the cap, and drained half of it, still a little headachy and dehydrated from the night before.

Checking the time on the gold wristwatch he had inherited from his late father—2:36 pm—he wondered what to do next. He had arrived at the beach about an hour ago with the intention of satiating his sexual desire with the favors of a prostitute, but his attention had been diverted by the beauty and sexy smile of the woman—*damn, I didn't even get her name*—who had been lounging with her lover on the plush bed behind him.

"Did you see a woman in a red bikini?"

The male voice caught Franklin off guard. He glanced up and saw the red knee-length bathing suit first. His eyes roamed up the muscular stomach and chest and eventually stopped at the man's worried face. Obviously the woman's fiancé. The man's concerned gaze fixed not on Franklin but on the strawberry margarita on the table beside him. Franklin followed the man's eyes down to the drink and knew instantly there was no point in lying, as much as he would have liked to brush this clown off and say he never saw the woman. Besides, they would probably have a conversation about it later.

He met the man's gaze. "She left her drink here about twenty minutes ago and went for a swim." Franklin pointed toward Ocean World. "I saw her go that way."

There was a hint of jealousy in the man's eyes. "You offered to watch her drink?"

Franklin opened his palms and shrugged. "Hey buddy, she *asked* me to watch her drink."

"Sorry." The man extended a hand. "It's Terry, by the way."

Franklin took the hand and squeezed a little too tightly. "Franklin." He stifled a small smirk as he watched Terry struggle—for just a fraction of a second—and finally free himself from the vice-like grip. Terry opened and closed his fist quickly, trying to hide the pain and attempting unsuccessfully to keep his expression calm and composed. But it was too little, too late. Franklin saw the hint of fear and knew he had left an impression, a not so subtle *Don't fuck with me.*

Terry turned to leave. "I'm gonna go look for her. Thanks for watching the drink."

Franklin acknowledged Terry with a grin. *You better thank me, asshole.* "I'm sure she's not gonna drown. Swims like a dolphin. Damn fine form."

Terry frowned, turned, and headed down the beach, his gait increasing with every step.

It wasn't long before Franklin found the object of his desire. A slender young Dominican woman sauntered along the beach and gave him a seductive smile. He waved her over immediately and sized her up as she approached. Red bikini. *That's a coincidence. She'll do. For now.* Frilly black afro hair, a Swiffer, really. *Something I could use to mop the floor with.* Dark, passionate eyes. A sexy smile. Maybe ninety-eight pounds. Maybe twenty years old. Just how Franklin liked them.

He stood up and, in perfect Spanish, introduced himself. A moment later, Valentina Martinez lounged next to Franklin in another chair he'd kindly dragged over. She took a sip of Natalie's margarita, set it down, and grinned at Franklin. "What do you want from me?" she asked in Spanish.

"I want to fuck you."

"What are we doing here then? Let's go to your room."

CHAPTER FOUR

"That creep seriously gave me the *creeps*."

"You're not the only one," Terry said to Natalie as they lounged in bed with room service in the early evening, two medium-rare sirloin steaks with mashed potatoes, and a colorful assortment of stir-fried vegetables. The food, along with an open bottle of champagne, sat on a silver tray on their large plush white bed. Red curtains adorning the sliding-glass doors gave way to an expansive oval-shaped balcony overlooking the ocean. "He's a control freak. I can tell. He squeezed my hand way too hard. I felt like smashing him in his smug little freaky face."

Natalie sipped her champagne and poked at her vegetables apathetically. "That's not the right approach, Terry. Guys like him need to be ignored and forgotten about." It was easy to say, but after meeting him briefly on the beach, she had to admit to herself she was having a hard time getting Franklin off her mind. More than that, it was the feeling of dread that brief encounter had left her with. *Freaky Franky.*

"Well, I wanted to smash his face in."

Something in Terry's tone was irritating her perhaps more than it should. And the notion of violence was so unlike Terry. Wasn't he supposed to be Mr. Positive Upbeat guy? At least, thus far, that was what he had led her to believe. Was he really something else, a monster like that fuck Rex?

"You can't go around smashing everyone's face in just because they're rude to you," she said.

"I know, honey, but there was a bit more to it than that. He squeezed my hand so hard my knuckles cracked. He was challenging me, baiting me to retaliate. Isn't that physical abuse?"

"Maybe that's just how he shakes hands. You know, a manly shake, all that macho bullshit."

"If that's how he shakes hands, someone should knock some sense into him." Terry gave her a look and slid off the bed. He walked over to the balcony and slipped through the curtains, disappearing outside.

Natalie, about to cut into her steak, dropped the fork and knife on the silver tray. She picked up a glass of champagne, slid the tray to the foot of the bed, stood up, and took a pull on the bubbly. *Our first fight. What am I doing, defending that creep? Lecturing Terry on how he should conduct himself? What's wrong with me?* She gazed at the deep red curtains, fluttering gently in the cool evening breeze, and contemplated going outside and apologizing. But other thoughts invaded her mind, replacing the guilt. *What, he can't stay and discuss this? He has to disappear? Is that how he'll react when we fight? Run away, instead of talking it through and resolving it?*

She finished her drink and refilled the champagne flute. Yet another voice, the moderator, stopped her in her tracks just as she was about to spin around and confront him on the balcony: *Wait a minute, maybe he's right. He's obviously pissed off. He needs cool-down time, that's all. So, in the heat of the moment, he won't say something really offensive, something that may leave a permanent scar on our relationship. That's smart, actually. Isn't that also a mature way to handle disagreements? Speak when you're calm, not angry?*

A few minutes later, his expression tight, Terry slipped through the curtain, walked toward her, and stopped on the other side of the bed. "I'm sorry, honey. I needed time to think of what to say. I don't want to talk to you in anger, but I can't believe you would defend Franklin."

Natalie couldn't believe her own tone. "I wasn't defending fucking Franklin. All I'm saying is more violence is not the answer to violence. Or more aggression is not the answer to instigative aggression."

The color draining from his face, Terry's eyes narrowed. "You said a little more than that. You said, 'maybe that's just how he shakes hands.' I'm sorry, I'm in pretty good shape, have a good fucking grip of my own, and I know the difference between a firm handshake and one that's intended not only to intimidate, but to cause harm." He extended his right hand, showing her his knuckles. They were discolored, starting to turn a dark purple with bruising. "You call that a firm grip? It's a little more than that."

Shit, this really is turning into our first fight. But she couldn't stop herself. "Don't be such a fucking baby, Terry. If you didn't like it, why didn't you say something to him?"

A large vein sprouted in his neck and began pulsating. He squinted at her. "What? That's the mother of all contradictions. You just said earlier that people like him need to be ignored and forgotten about. More violence is not the answer to violence, however you put it. Now you're telling me I should've said something to him. Like what? 'Go fuck yourself,' or something politically correct like that?"

Natalie felt her face flush and her eyes moisten. This was supposed to be the best time of her life. What was happening?

Give it up. But a morbid curiosity, a demented desire to see if this speeding train of turmoil would crash and burn, fueled her fire. "You were the one who said you wanted to smash his face in. I was just trying to calm you down."

Clenching his fists, Terry advanced one step, then two steps, and stopped. "I like the way you try to calm me down. First tell me to ignore and forget that fuck, then say that's how he shakes hands, and then tell me to say something to him. Now you've lowered yourself to name-calling. I'm a fucking baby now, am I? Have you listened to yourself, Natalie? If you're gonna argue, at least you should start by making sense, not contradicting yourself. And by the way, if you want an intelligent response to your arguments, don't resort to the lowest of the low, name-calling."

"What are you talking about? You just called Franklin a fuck."

"Well, I'm not arguing with him, am I? And, in case you don't remember, you called him a creep."

"I'm not the one who said name-calling is the lowest of the low."

"I was talking about name-calling in the context of an argument." Terry retreated suddenly, sat on the bed, and put his hands over his face.

Natalie was about to blurt out another insult, more name-calling to be precise, but stopped herself, put her drink down, and sat on the other side of the bed, back facing Terry.

After a long and uncomfortable silence, Terry removed his hands from his face and looked at Natalie's back. "Honey, do we even know what we're arguing about anymore?"

She slowly turned around and met his concerned eyes. "Not really. It started with that Freaky Franky fuck."

Terry burst out laughing. "No, it's that Franklin creep. Remember?"

Wiping her moist eyes, Natalie grinned. "He's a freaky fuck, you ask me."

"No, a creep."

Natalie stood up, her silk white robe slipping open slightly to reveal half of her left breast, stopping tantalizingly close to the nipple, which was beginning to protrude through the sheer fabric. "How about a fucking creep? Or, if you don't like the profanity, just Freaky Franky?"

Terry rose, approached her, and hugged her passionately. He pulled back and kissed her on the cheek. "I'm sorry for my outburst, sweetie. I don't know what got into me."

She kissed him again. "No, I'm the one who needs to apologize. For defending that fucking creep and calling you a baby. You're not a baby. You're my baby."

"Well, I shouldn't talk about smashing people in the face. That doesn't exactly set the mood for romance."

Natalie's eyes glittered. "But I know what will."

Terry didn't need an explanation. "What's she doing in the closet anyway? Maybe that's why this friction started."

Silently, Natalie removed the eight-inch statuette of the skeleton saint from the closet while Terry cleared the bedside tray for the makeshift altar. A few minutes later, they kneeled on the carpet in darkness, looking up at Saint Death perched on the silver tray on the foot of the bed. She was clad in a red robe, a globe in her right hand, a blood-red scythe with a silver blade in the other. Her hollow eyes regarded them vacantly, but the powerful lady appeared to grin in appreciation for being summoned to help her devotees in matters of the heart. A red jar candle, a symbol of love, passion, and retrieving wayward lovers, burned brightly by her side. A shot glass full of tequila sat in front of her, along with the nearly full bottle. Terry and Natalie had shot glasses of tequila sitting beside them on the sumptuous carpet.

In accordance with the ritual, Terry took the bottle and splashed some tequila on Saint Death's face. He also lit a cigar, took a few puffs, and blew smoke into the Skinny Lady's face. Paradoxically, tobacco is believed to have great healing qualities in conjunction with the veneration of the saint of death.

Outside, the wind whipped up, fluttering the balcony curtains and whistling around the room. The candle's flame fluttered, nearly extinguishing, but found new life as the wind died down.

Natalie picked up her shot glass and motioned for Terry to do the same. He placed his cigar in an ashtray in front of Saint Death and, as the smoke swirled about her skull, picked up the shot glass of tequila, the skeleton saint's drink of choice. Natalie raised her glass and brought it forward until it touched his. "First, I want to drink to our longevity. But that's not all. I want to toast in the hope that our love is everlasting and that we learn how to fight in a healthy way instead of using insults that might permanently harm our forward progress."

"I'll drink to that."

They did.

"Do you want me to start?" Natalie asked, after making a face and setting her empty glass down.

"Go for it."

"Should we pray for protection from Franklin?"

"Nah. I don't think he's a threat. If we run into him again and get bad vibes, maybe."

"Okay. Then you know what I'm gonna pray for?"

"Yeah, just like last time, right?"

"Something like that." Natalie bowed her head, clasped her hands together, and began. Her tone rose steadily as she spoke. Terry dutifully repeated the words after her.

"Oh Lord Santa Muerte, I humbly kneel before you and ask you to strengthen the love bond between Terry Anderson and myself. May we have a successful, happy, and intimate love relationship based on loyalty, fidelity, mutual trust, love, and respect. May we learn to overcome our differences and develop the tools to express our differences of opinion in a loving and respectful manner. Please, I beseech you, all-powerful saint, to keep our disagreements to a minimum so that our love will grow and strengthen over time. I pray to you, Pretty Girl, that Terry Anderson and I will enjoy never-ending love, passion, and companionship. I put my deep faith in you, Angel of Death, that my heart grows fonder over time for the man of my dreams, the man of my desires, the only man who can heal my fractured heart. Amen."

"Amen," Terry repeated.

Natalie opened her eyes and was surprised to see a lone tear snake down the handsome face of her fiancé as he opened his. She quickly wiped it away and began kissing him passionately, her fingers roaming freely to erogenous zones exclusively reserved for her hands only. Like a prisoner of love struggling to escape a rib cage prison, her heart began thumping wildly.

CHAPTER FIVE

On skinned and sore knees, a fifteen-year-old girl hobbled along the pothole-ridden street in Tepito, one of the roughest barrios in Mexico City. During her forward progress—a sacrificial gesture to win the favor of her guiding saint—her left knee pressed down on a jagged pebble and she winced as fresh blood squirted from a small gash and trickled onto the street. Lines of physical and emotional pain etched her furrowed brow. In her left hand, she clutched a stick with a bright red heart-shaped balloon fastened on the end. In her right hand, she clutched the skeleton figure of Saint Death, clad in a golden robe, a matching gold scythe firmly in its left hand. The skeleton's right palm was open, its index finger curled. "Come to me," it seemed to say.

The streets were crowded that stiflingly hot day, the atmosphere electric with devotional fervor, as throngs of devotees, many drinking alcohol or smoking marijuana, made their way to worship at the famous shrine of Enriqueta Romero, the cult's founding mother. Occasionally worshippers would stop alongside the girl. Some gave her candy, offerings to Saint Death; others blew tobacco or marijuana smoke into the face of the skeleton saint; still others doused the sacred statue with tequila. All this was meant to purify the spirit of Saint Death and activate her powers.

Juana Hernandez stopped for a moment and set the balloon down. She rubbed her bleeding left knee, steadfastly refusing to release the skeleton saint statue. Wincing, she thought briefly of proceeding the rest of way on foot, but quickly realized her guardian saint might take exception to this at a time when she needed her the most. *Only a block away. Keep going.*

On this evening, Juana had a very specific petition in mind for Saint Death. She lived in a ramshackle shack a few blocks away with her mother Marta and father Santiago. Two years ago, her uneducated mother had been fired from her waitress job. Two weeks ago, her father had been laid off from a construction job. All Juana's efforts to secure employment up to this point had failed dismally. And now with her father out of work, the family was starving.

Juana plucked a cherry-flavored lollipop from her shirt pocket and, as her stomach growled—she hadn't eaten in two days—quickly unwrapped the sweet, shoved it in her mouth, picked up the balloon, and plodded along amid a chorus of religious chants. She was about sixty feet away from the famous shrine to Saint Death, and the unending stomach pangs produced a feeling of nausea and dizziness. Maybe it was the rush of sugar on an empty stomach. Despite her best intentions, she closed her eyes and started her entreaty early, before arriving at the shrine. *Please, Holy Mother of all Saints. I'm hungry. Feed me, please. I beg you, please, feed my family, feed me. Please, Saint Death. I don't wanna die...*

"What's wrong?"

Juana brushed away a lock of her long black hair, opened her eyes, and saw an old man standing in front of her, his aged face creased with worry, gray eyes squinting down at her. She realized she had dropped her balloon and almost dropped Saint Death as she stopped to make her silent plea to the saint. Before she could answer, the man, who looked almost too old to still be alive, reached into a black cloth bag dangling from his slumped shoulder and produced a small package wrapped in tinfoil. He handed it to her. "It's a burrito. Eat, my child."

She removed the lollipop from her mouth, shoved it into her jean shirt pocket for later, and took the burrito. "Thank you, sir," she said in Spanish. She quickly unwrapped the burrito and began stuffing her face ravenously, aware that nausea and dizziness were retreating in the face of nourishment. In three bites, she'd wolfed it down, stifling a cough as she tried to thank the generous stranger a second time with a full mouth.

"Just eat," he said, producing another burrito and a bottle of water. He handed both to her and she took them eagerly, finishing off the second burrito in six bites and draining the bottled water in six gulps. He extended his hand when she was finished, took the empty water bottle, and stuffed it into his purse-like bag. Waving his arm, he motioned for her to proceed to the shrine. "Saint Death is ready for you now."

Before Juana could say anything more, he turned and disappeared into the wall of people.

As she neared the shrine, she saw worshippers holding their Saint Death statues high in the air. Some chanted: "Saint Death, we love you... Most Holy Death, we adore you... We see you... We feel you. You are right here."

Wincing from the painful protestations of bleeding and sore knees, Juana stood, weaved through the crowds, and arrived at the shrine of Saint Death. The glass-encased Skinny Lady wore a white wedding dress. Many gold necklaces adorned her neck—gifts for favors granted, gifts for favors wanted. As Juana watched the golden sun setting behind an oddly shaped skyscape of beaten-down buildings, an ineffable peace enveloped her, lifting her worry and sadness. "You answered my prayer, White Girl. Thank you. I love you. I adore you. I promise to worship you forever and spread word of your good deeds... "

Her monologue was broken by the static hiss of a microphone as the founding mother of the cult, Enriqueta Romero, also known as Doña Queta, stepped from the doorway of her humble abode and gestured to the crowd with both palms outstretched for quiet. A silence fell over the adherents.

Enriqueta cleared her throat, swiped a hand over a streak of gray in her black hair, and began. "Thank you all for coming. Let us begin the rosary to our beloved saint, so she may protect us, heal us, guide us in matters of the heart, and bring abundance, prosperity and much love into our lives."

The worshippers clapped and cheered. Then a quiet settled over the crowd and a middle-aged Mexican man emerged from Enriqueta's house. He hugged and kissed her on the cheek. She handed him the microphone and stepped back.

Juana kneeled down again, expecting her bloody, sore knees to protest vehemently as they met the pebbles and dirt on the warm, unwelcoming asphalt. But an inch before contact a kindly soul slid a black pillow under the girl's knees and she landed softly and securely.

"Here you go, sweetheart," he whispered, kneeling beside her with a kindly smile.

Juana recognized the old man instantly; it was the same man who had satiated her severely debilitating hunger pangs with burritos. She smiled, letting the peace and the communion with the old man and her protectress sweep her into an otherworldly dimension where the need for nourishment, health, and employment was non-existent.

The man with the mic cleared his throat and began speaking. "Brothers and sisters, we are going to make an offering at this time for our Most Holy Death, Our White Lady. In this moment, brothers and sisters, let's all raise our statues to heaven..."

Juana stuck the balloon stick into the waist of her jeans and raised her Saint Death statue along with the others.

The man continued. "Let's offer them to Lord God and to Most Holy Death. Repeat after me: Blessed Most Holy Death... "

Repeating the man's words, the worshipper's voices were unified and charged with energy.

He continued. "Angel of God, most pure death, presence of light and strength, allow me to receive your protective cloak, your balance of justice, and your powerful love for everyone present and for every statue that is here. Thank you, Most Holy Death."

He waited until his words had been repeated before continuing. "We are going to lower our statues, brothers and sisters, so that we may join hands in a chain of union and solidarity and a communion with Most Holy Death..."

Statues were lowered, hands joined.

"Remember the reason we hold hands is because each and every one of us is a link in the chain of strength that we make for Most Holy Death. We are going to ask for protection and help for each and every one of us here. Say your prayers now..."

Heads bowed. A silence, punctuated by low muttering prayers, followed.

Closing her eyes, Juana silently made her own entreaties. She became lost in a wonderful world of love, abundance, and prosperity.

The speaker went on. "Most Holy Death, oh Great Lady of the Night... "

Some worshippers repeated his words loudly, others mouthed them, and still others bowed their heads, closed their eyes, and silently made their own entreaties.

"...We ask and beg of you to give us strength for the hard days in our work. Strength to withstand all problems that may stand in our way. Amen."

"Amen," Juana said in unison with the congregants.

A chorus of applause followed.

Juana opened her eyes and looked around. The old man was gone.

She waited and watched the worshippers disperse. The black curtain of night was descending on the tough barrio and people didn't loiter. With over seventy-two blocks of Latin America's biggest black market, Tepito was home to drug dealers, pickpockets, smugglers, and murderers. But Juana, at this moment, had no fear of death. Saint Death had answered her prayers and she was under the protection of the magical miracle worker. When the remaining worshippers wandered off and only a few small barking dogs remained, Juana returned her gaze to the glass-enclosed skeleton statue in front of her. Its hollow eyes, illuminated by hundreds of glowing candles, seemed to invite one final entreaty.

Juana weaved her way carefully through the burning candles and arrived at the glass-encased Saint Death statue. She caressed and kissed the glass that held her Goddess. She planted the heart-shaped balloon into a nearby flowerpot, knelt down, and placed her small statue at her feet. She produced a gold candle, a symbol of wealth, abundance and prosperity. She lit it, gazing earnestly at the larger statue, then at her smaller one, and then closed her eyes and began to pray, filled with excitement at the certainty that her wishes would be granted. Finally an end to hunger. Finally an end to the friction that was tearing a wide chasm in the otherwise loving relationship of her parents, Santiago and Marta.

She began softly, her voice gaining passion, conviction, and intensity as she spoke. "Oh, Lord, Saint Death, I thank you again for answering my prayer for food. I now entreat you to help my mother, Marta Hernandez, and my father, Santiago Hernandez, find jobs. Please, my guiding angel, I pray to you to find good jobs for both my parents, so the fighting will stop, and the love and peace will once again return... "

CHAPTER SIX

Santiago studied his wife, who had hurt written all over her face. He wondered why he'd said it. It wasn't meant as an insult, really; it was just the way it had come out.

Marta had discovered a lonely can of beans in the cupboard about an hour ago. Returning home from another unsuccessful job hunt, Santiago, already out of sorts, had entered the shack to find her ravenously shoveling spoonfuls of cold beans into her mouth. In her haste and hunger, she had even dribbled some food particles down her chin and onto her white blouse. Surprised at his early return, she had clunked the can down on the kitchen table, the hollow tinny sound revealing it was indeed empty.

Santiago's face had flashed anger. "What, you couldn't even save me some... or how about saving some for Juana?"

Although Marta had meekly apologized ("I'm sorry, I was starving"), it hadn't contained Santiago's wrath. "'Sorry' doesn't put food on the table. 'Sorry' doesn't feed Juana. You ate them like a pig without considering us." With that he had stormed out of the makeshift abode, slamming the crookedly hung door so hard the rusted tin roof shook and clattered.

After a short cool-off period outside, he'd returned with the intention of apologizing. But seeing Marta now, avoiding his eyes, only irritated him more. The brown bean stains on her white blouse didn't help matters.

"I have something to say to you, and I want you to look me in the eyes," he said.

She brushed away a lock of thick black hair, craned her neck slightly, and then buried her face in her hands. Finally she raised her head, but avoided his eyes. "I said I'm sorry, Santiago. What do you want me to do now?"

"You can't even look at me when you speak to me." His tone barely concealed his anger.

Marta wiped her moist eyes and met his gaze. "I'm sorry. A can of beans can't feed our whole family anyway."

About to explode all over again, Santiago bit his tongue. She was right. She was hungry. They were all hungry. Irritation borne of starvation was starting to cause a rift in the family. On the long walk home, after being rejected at three construction sites, Santiago had almost doubled over on two occasions, hunger pangs violently snapping away at his stomach lining. For some reason, and he realized now it was flawed logic, he'd imagined coming home to a neatly laid table with three plates of steaming beef burritos, refried beans, avocado salad, cold beer, and a single white candle adorning the uneven, pock-marked kitchen table. *White candle. Where did that come from?*

Marta's pleading voice snapped his reverie. "Did you hear me?"

Now it was Santiago who turned away from his wife, a blanket of cold shame and guilt dousing hot anger. About to retreat to the cold comfort of the darkness outside, he suddenly spun around, bent down in front of Marta, gazed into her eyes, and kissed her on the cheek. Marta was normally selfless, quick to put her family's needs ahead of her own. This wasn't her normal behavior. It was a starvation-induced slip.

"I'm the one who should be sorry," he said. "We're hungry. I had a bad day. I couldn't find a job. I'm starving."

Marta put a hand on Santiago's head as he slumped over and stared at the dirt floor. Then she wiped her tears away and stood. "Sweetheart, I'm gonna check with our neighbors to see if they have some leftovers. I smelled beans and burritos cooking earlier."

Santiago looked up. A small grin creased his weathered face. He scratched his black head stubble. "You did? Funny, I was just thinking of refried beans and burritos."

Marta reached the door and turned around. "Did you see little Juana outside? She should be home by now."

"Where did she go?"

"Remember, she went to worship at the shrine of Saint Death."

"Right, I don't know why she bothers. It doesn't seem to be helping worth a shit."

Marta closed the door behind her. She turned left on the small street, passed two houses no bigger than storage sheds, and stopped at a tiny pink house. A small Chihuahua greeted her with a chorus of barks. It bit her ankle and she winced in pain. The dog darted off down the street in pursuit of a stray black cat that had just crossed its path.

As Marta approached the door, she noticed the kitchen light go out. It was only nine-sixteen, way too early for the Lopez family to turn in for the night. She stopped in front of the door, and was about to knock when she resignedly thought, *What's the use?* She knew the sign. Lights out meant they couldn't spare any food. It had happened before. They had spotted her, and turned out the lights, pretending to be asleep, too polite to say they just didn't have any extra grub. They had four mouths to feed and as it was they were living hand to mouth. Only yesterday, she had been so hungry she had knocked. Many times. Finally, it was eighty-six-year-old Emil Lopez who had hobbled to the door, opened it, looked at her with his sad eyes and gaunt face, and slowly shook his head. They couldn't expect to live off the generosity of the Lopez family, even though a few previous visits had yielded a pot of rice and a pot of refried beans.

Turning around without knocking, Marta was overcome with guilt. She put her hands to her face, making a futile effort to stop fresh tears. *Why did I eat the beans? I should have given them to Santiago. Or Juana. Or both.*

"Mommy, mommy, look what I got."

Marta spun around. Juana held a lit candle in her right hand and clutched the Saint Death statue in her arms. But there was something else. Something angelic about her daughter. Juana glowed bright yellow and the glow spread out around her head like a halo, contrasting starkly with the black of night. Marta rushed to Juana and gave her a warm hug, careful not to disturb the candle or the saint. Then she noticed the large plastic bag in Juana's left hand. The smell of spicy beef and melted cheese filled her nostrils and her stomach growled, in spite of the earlier bean snack. It had been her first meal in three days, and she knew her daughter had gone at least two days without food.

"What's in the bag?"

"Refried beans, beef and cheese burritos, avocado salad, and cold beer."

"Where did you get that, sweetheart?"

"Mommy, have you been crying?"

"It's okay now, sweetie."

"It is, Mom. It is. Saint Death answered my prayers. She gave me this food."

Studying the meticulously arranged kitchen table, exactly as he'd envisioned, Santiago couldn't believe his eyes. Everything was there, right down to the white candle. He finished his burrito in three bites and washed it down with a stream of cold Tecate beer. He turned to Juana. She still hadn't said where the food had come from, other than, "The Holy Saint has provided for us, Daddy."

Well, someone must have given it to her. He had difficulty believing a magical saint had swept down from the heavens and delivered a fresh, hot order of food into his daughter's waiting hands.

He took another swill of beer and wiped some refried beans from his chin. He would solve the food puzzle in due time. "What's with the white candle, sweetie?"

Juana smiled. "An old man gave it to me. In the worship of the Holy Saint," she pointed to her statue perched on a small table against the wall, "white symbolizes purity, protection, health, and gratitude. After we eat, let's pray in the name of white."

CHAPTER SEVEN

"It's a miracle," Anisa said. "I don't know any other way to explain it. One minute he's almost dying—I swear I saw his heart stop beating—the next minute he springs to life." She was, of course, speaking of her son Connor and his miraculous recovery shortly after praying to Saint Death. It was a balmy Wednesday afternoon and she was having lunch with her friend at the combination Tim Hortons coffee shop/Wendy's restaurant just down the street from Sobeys supermarket, where they both worked as cashiers. Since summer vacation had just begun, Connor was in daycare.

Helen Randon poked at her fries and finally met Anisa's gaze. "What happened exactly?"

Anisa brushed a lock of black hair away from her face, focused thoughtful black eyes on Helen, and told the story. When she neared the end, she said, "I couldn't believe it. Clapping thunder; then lightning blew a hole in my front lawn; then torrential rains, all happening as we prayed. But, during the prayer, when I looked up and saw that Connor's heart had stopped beating, I freaked out."

Helen dipped two fries in ketchup and put them in her mouth. She pulled a lock of her thick red hair behind her ear and scratched her freckled cheek. "Freaked out? What do you mean? What did you do?"

Anisa gazed around the coffee shop, noticing a few heads had turned in their direction. *Better keep my voice down. Lots of religion around here.* A few decibels above a whisper, she said, "I started screaming bloody murder and bolted from the house."

Helen noticed the interested parties and lowered her voice. "You're kidding!"

"What would you do? I panicked. I thought Connor was dead."

Helen abandoned her fries, watching Anisa intently through pale blue eyes. "Carry on. What happened after that? What did the doctor do?"

"Oh, he carried on praying calmly. I get outside and suddenly the rain stops, the bank of gray clouds disappears, lightning and thunder are gone, and the sun comes out, warming my face and stopping my panic attack. The next second I feel a tap on my shoulder and am about to start screaming all over again. But it's Doctor Ricardo. And he's smiling. And I look into his eyes and I just know. I just know that a miracle has happened. Doctor Ricardo escorts me back into the house, and there's Connor, sitting up in bed, fit as a fiddle, cheerful as ever, grinning from ear to ear. And you know what he says to me?"

Helen pushed the container of fries away, eyed her half-eaten cheeseburger for a second, then tossed it on top of the fries and shoved the plastic food tray aside. "No, what did he say?"

"He points to the statue of Saint Death and says, 'I love my new toy, Mommy. She saved my life.'"

"Oh my God. This is getting freaky."

"That was a few days ago, and since then I've been reading all I can about Saint Death. I'm too afraid to remove the statue from Connor's room. Doctor Ricardo was nice enough to gift it to us. He says it's activated now and must stay with us. He says he has plenty more."

"I thought you were a practicing Catholic."

"I was. I am. From what I understand, many devotees of Saint Death believe in God and are also practicing Catholics. The two aren't mutually exclusive."

"What's that mean?"

"One doesn't cancel out the other."

"Right. I wish I was smart like you."

"You *are* smart, Helen, just in a different way. You're artistic, aren't you?"

"I'm still painting, if that's what you mean. But I'm not good with words."

"Neither am I, really. I've just been doing a lot of reading on the religion of Saint Death, and I've memorized some intellectual-sounding words."

"Well, dumb it down a bit for me, okay? What did you learn?"

"Although the origins are a subject of debate among religious scholars, the worship of Saint Death is most likely an amalgamation between pre-Columbian Mesoamerican religion and Spanish culture.I memorized that."

"That's not dumbing it down."

"Sorry."

"When did it start?"

"Sometime in the late nineties or later. I'm not sure. But in 2001, Enriqueta Romero, a believer, decided to take a life-sized image of Santa Muerte outside of her home in Tepito, Mexico City, and build a shrine for it. It was visible from the street. She's considered the founding mother."

"It started getting popular after that?"

"Yeah. Exploding with popularity. Said to be the fastest growing religion—or cult, some people call it—in the world. Now it's estimated there are between ten and fifteen million followers worldwide, most of them in Mexico and Spanish-speaking barrios of the United States. But it's spreading to all walks of life."

"Really? Who would worship a saint of death?"

"Well, I've watched some documentaries where people say Santa Muerte has to do with relieving your fear of death so you can live your life to the fullest. She safely delivers followers to their destinations in the afterlife. Insures them of a good death, without suffering, which really everyone wants. But she's a multi-purpose miracle worker who also heals and protects and helps people in matters of the heart, wealth, even wisdom."

Helen had been listening skeptically but she was starting to become fascinated by Anisa's discovery. A practicing Catholic, she had prayed to many of the Catholic Church's canonized saints for wisdom or intelligence. But her prayers had fallen on deaf ears. "What does the Catholic Church think about it?"

Anisa's gaze swept around the coffee shop. Indeed, a few more heads had turned toward them. Listening ears. Watchful eyes. "Outside."

Sitting on a picnic table under the shade of an oak tree, in relative privacy, Anisa continued. "I know you're a God-fearing Catholic so I hope this doesn't upset you, or you think I'm some kind of a fanatical cult worshipper."

Hanging onto Anisa's every word, Helen had folded her hands on the picnic table, almost in prayer. "We're good friends, Anisa. Even if I don't share your religious beliefs, I'll still respect them. Saint Death saved Connor's life. Just tell me, will you. I won't say anything to anyone else, if that's what you're worried about."

Anisa paused for a long moment, crinkling her brow. "You swear? I would hate for this to get out around here. Doctor Ricardo made me swear to secrecy, and I already feel like I'm breaking my word. You know how much of a Bible belt it is here."

"I cross my heart, hope to die. I promise."

Anisa studied the parking lot. A dark blue early-model Camaro drove in and parked about thirty feet from them. Two teenagers climbed out, eyed them curiously for a second, then turned and headed for the restaurant/coffee shop. Anisa waited until they had entered and the door closed behind them before continuing.

"Okay, Helen, I'm gonna trust you. The Catholic Church has condemned the religion of Saint Death as satanic. Even blasphemous and evil."

"Why would they do that?"

Anisa wondered how much she should say. She didn't want to frighten or alienate her friend, although she had read that some Saint Death adherents were criminals, violent drug cartel members, who prayed for safe passage of drugs, revenge against rival Mexican drug cartels, even death to local authorities who were hunting them down. What about the people who killed or tortured others in the name of Saint Death? But this was wrong, and a perversion of the religion, much like Islamic extremists, many of them terrorists, had perverted the tenets of Islam to suit their Jihadist needs. After all, she wasn't here to proselytize or convert Helen. Or was she? Hadn't she promised Saint Death that she would spread the good word in return for saving Connor's life? One good deed deserves another, doesn't it? In her fervor in the aftermath of his miraculous recovery, perhaps she had. In any event, she decided in that instant to give Helen the watered-down version. *Let her do her own research if that's what she decides to do.* "In Christianity, Jesus defeats death by coming back to life. Santa Muerte is the worship of the saint of death. To the Catholic Church, this is fundamentally wrong."

Helen pondered this for a moment. "You mean mostly criminals worship Saint Death?"

"I don't know. For sure many criminals, but many other people from all walks of life. Many of them are marginalized in some way, people who have slipped through the cracks of life, have ended up on the poverty-stricken fringes of society and are struggling to get by. That's the thing with Saint Death. She doesn't discriminate. She's morally neutral and accepts everyone from all walks of life. But that doesn't mean all her worshippers are marginalized. Look at Doctor Ricardo, a respected physician here. Look at me."

Helen raised her eyebrows. "What, you don't think you're marginalized?"

Anisa was forced to look inward. Maybe Helen was right. Even though Anisa had graduated from the University of Prince Edward Island with an undergraduate degree in psychology, where had that gotten her? She worked as a cashier at Sobeys. Her choice of careers was wanting, partly due to the scarcity of jobs in her field on PEI. But she could have left, moved to Toronto or other big Canadian cities where more opportunities could be found. That had been the plan. That was, until she'd met Connor's father, one Jeff Worthington, a local fisherman. A one-night stand. Then came the unplanned pregnancy, the hastily planned marriage before Connor's birth, and, after two years as a bored housewife, the unplanned divorce. It wasn't that Jeff was a bad person, or a bad father. Anisa just never felt a love connection or a mental connection with him, partly because she considered herself an intellectual and Jeff, in his own words, was "just an average guy from an average family who wants an average life. No drama, just financial stability and happiness." He had no desire to meet new people, think outside the box, or ever leave Prince Edward Island; not even for a day-trip over the Confederation Bridge to neighboring New Brunswick.

So, after the divorce, Anisa could see few other options but to stay. Jeff and their son Connor, a mini mirror image of his dad, were molded from the same clay and had bonded like Crazy Glue. Maybe Jeff wasn't a match for Anisa, but she couldn't argue his role as a father figure in her son's life. She couldn't leave PEI and take Connor with her. Her son certainly wouldn't want that. He had a right to a relationship with his father. She couldn't abandon Connor and selfishly pursue her own career goals somewhere else; even though many times she was loathe to admit that thought had crossed her mind. When could she leave? At 35, it would be fifteen years before Connor turned twenty, an age of adulthood she hoped would create some independence in her son. But, starting a career at 50? Who does that? Even though she loved her son, a seed of resentment was beginning to take root in the pit of her stomach. She swallowed, hoping gastric acid would devour it, lest it fester and ruin her attempts at being a positive-minded maternal nurturer. It didn't entirely work. *All for Connor. I'm sacrificing my whole life and happiness for him.*

"Did I upset you?" Helen said. "I shouldn't have said you're marginalized."

"It's okay." But it wasn't okay. Somewhere along life's pothole-pocked highway the conversation had taken a dead-end turn and Anisa had for the moment lost interest in preaching about Saint Death and had become absorbed in self-pity. "You didn't say I was marginalized. You asked me if I was. Maybe the truth hurts, but I think I *am*. Look at me, a single mom with a degree in psychology working as a fucking cashier. Living in a small town with zero opportunities. And, don't get me wrong, I love my son. But because of Jeff and Connor, I'm trapped here."

Helen moved closer to Anisa and gently put a comforting arm around her shoulder. "I'm sorry I upset you. I didn't realize you felt that way. I'm here for you."

Anisa put her head into her friend's bosom and left it there for a long moment, both of them silent. Helen didn't move, even though they were getting more than a few glances from customers entering and exiting the parking lot.

Finally, Helen said, "What about me? I'm only a few years younger than you and I've never had a boyfriend, and I'm too stupid to go to university. I've slipped through the cracks. My mother said I have an inferiority complex. I had to look that up. My father calls it low self-esteem. That one I did know, because my grade 8 teacher told me the same thing. She also called me 'just plain stupid' one day. I've heard them all. Not the sharpest tool in the shed. Not the brightest lightbulb, not the brightest candle... "

"Wait!" Now it was Anisa's turn to be the nurturer. She lifted her head from her friend's ample bosom, looked her square in the eyes, and gently touched her shoulder. She felt a mixture of sadness for Helen and a weird sense of elation. *Why is it that hearing that someone else's misery is worse than your own—or at least on par with it—is uplifting? Misery loves company, that's why.* "I'm sorry about that. I never knew those things about you, never realized how much you struggle. But it's gonna be okay. When you said 'candle' it gave me an idea."

Helen wiped a tearful eye. "What?"

"I ordered another Saint Death statue online. And a bunch of candles used for worship."

"You want to give them to me?"

Anisa nodded. "See, you're not stupid like you think. I have a brown Saint Death statue. Also a brown votive candle. I'll give them to you, if you want."

In Helen's eyes, Anisa began to see a flicker of hope.

"Why brown?"

"So you're saying you'll take them."

"I don't know."

"In the worship of Saint Death, brown symbolizes enlightenment, discernment, and wisdom. Don't you want all those things?"

Helen took Anisa by the hand. "Let's go. We have to get back to work. I'll think about it, okay?"

As they took their respective places at side-by-side cash registers, tills 8 and 9, Anisa couldn't help but notice the renewed confidence and happiness in Helen's demeanor. She greeted each customer with a bright, joyful smile and comments like, "How are you this fabulous day?" and "I hope you have an awesome day." Anisa knew Helen's wheels were turning. With any luck—*no, divine intervention*—very soon Helen's wheels wouldn't only be turning, they'd be revving with a new-found intelligence and acumen.

Then Anisa shivered, the tiny hairs on the back of her neck springing to prickly attention. *But at what cost?*

She didn't think he would, but he did. Doctor Manuel Ricardo had activated Helen's Saint Death statue, blessing it with prayer, blowing cigar smoke over it and dousing it with Jose Cuervo Especial Gold tequila. Initially, just before leaving Anisa's house with the brown statue and brown votive candle—iconic symbols of her hope for wisdom and intelligence—Helen thought that she could just take them to her small one-bedroom apartment in downtown Montague and start praying. But Anisa had been quick to point out that wasn't the case. "Saint Death needs to be activated. I'm sure Doctor Ricardo can do that. But it's too late now. Tomorrow I'll contact him and see if he'll agree."

Driving home a few minutes later, Helen realized she couldn't wait until tomorrow. So she had driven past Doctor Ricardo's office, a few short blocks from her humble apartment and, as if by divine intervention, spotted the doctor locking up and leaving. She had stopped her car abruptly, gotten out, and approached the doctor. Initially he'd responded suspiciously. He hadn't been favorably impressed after Helen had told him Anisa had not only gifted a Saint Death statue to her, but had told her Doctor Ricardo could activate it. Finally he had relented, re-opened his office, led her into a small dark room adjoining his examination room, and consecrated the statue, insisting she swear to secrecy. "I need to have a word with that Anisa," he muttered.

Now, in the glowing comfort of her apartment bedroom, the symbolic candle-illuminated and tequila-doused Saint Death grinning down at her, Helen had all but forgotten about her promise to Anisa to keep her mouth shut. *She said Doctor Ricardo would have to activate Saint Death. She would've had to tell him it was for me, anyway. She wouldn't lie about that. She'll forgive me. I'll apologize tomorrow.* Helen smiled. She hadn't even started praying to the magical saint and already her powers of deduction were becoming sharper than before. More than that. She felt an odd and immediate connection with the holy miracle worker.

She poured two shots of tequila and set one on the bedside table in front of her holy savior. Bringing her shot glass to her mouth, she said, "Here's to you, Saint Death." She drained it, coughed, and set the glass down. "And here's to you being able to help me get smart."

She stood up, closed the Venetian blinds, returned to the small throw rug she had placed beneath the altar, and knelt down. She turned off the bedside lamp next to Saint Death, closed her eyes, and began praying. The candle flickered. An icy chill swept through the room, causing her to shiver and second-guess the whole idea. But it was too late now. For better or worse, she had decided to embark down this dark and mysterious path. This was her chance to become the ridiculer instead of the ridiculed.

"I pray to you, Holy Saint Death, give me brains so I might understand the nasty jokes about me and turn the tables on my tormentors..." But as she spoke, her mind began playing tricks on her. She no longer heard her entreaties for increased mental acumen. A darker side of her psyche plunged into a pit of despair, dragging up all the nasty expressions used to describe her lack of intellect. Insults she had either blocked from her memory or simply could no longer remember now hurled at her rapid-fire, a painful staccato burst of machine gun fire... *Not the sharpest tool in the shed... Not the brightest lightbulb... Not the brightest candle... A few bricks short of a full load... A few cards short of a full deck... When God was handing out brains, Helen thought He said trains and took a slow one... Dumber than a sack of hammers... The intelligence of a common house fly... A few clowns short of a circus... A few fries short of a Happy Meal... A few Cokes short of a six-pack... A few peas short of a casserole... The wheel's spinning, but the hamster's dead... One taco short of a combination plate... A few feathers short of a whole duck... The cheese slid off her cracker... Couldn't pour water out of a boot with instructions on the heel... She fell out of the stupid tree and hit every branch on the way down... An intellect rivaled only by garden tools... As smart as bait... Chimney's clogged... Forgot to pay her brain bill... Her sewing machine's out of thread... She's living proof that evolution CAN go in reverse... In the pinball game of life, her flippers are a little further apart than most... Not the sharpest knife in the drawer...*

But the bullet that tore a gaping hole was a recent comment from Ray Minowest, who she'd gone to high school with. Now he was a smart-ass thirty-something hippie-type. It had happened two days earlier while she was ringing up his purchases at the supermarket. Helen had totaled his purchases without realizing he had a box of Twinkies still on the conveyor belt. He said, "Jesus Christ, Helen. If you had brains you'd be dangerous." She could've sworn the box wasn't there before. *That fuck probably hid it behind his back and threw it down when I wasn't looking, just to fuck with me.* It wouldn't have been the first time. In high school, Ray was the instigator and, if not the inventor, at least the messenger of many of the aforementioned taunting expressions.

Still praying, Helen's face tightened. She clenched her hands together so firmly her knuckles turned first a jaundiced color and then a dark purple. *If I had brains I'd be dangerous. Not the sharpest knife in the drawer. We'll see about that, you little prick. We'll see about that...*

CHAPTER EIGHT

The black cloud drifted only slightly, allowing a thin spear of moonlight to illuminate a single drop of blood on the tip of the blade. Her eyes adjusting to the light, Anisa blinked twice, trying to see what was happening. Her eyes followed the drop of blood, along the scythe blade, down the long handle to a point at the end where two powerful hands gripped it. The spear of moonlight widened. The man was tall, lean, bald, and muscular. But for some weird reason no facial features were discernable. He stepped forward and raised the scythe high in the air. A dark figure splayed at his feet raised an arm in the air. A chorus of barking dogs erupted and then faded into the night.

"No... I'll get rid of them," the helpless victim said. "I promise."

"It's too late for that," the scythe-wielding man said. "I'm the Grim Reaper and I've come for you."

Frightened, Anisa opened her mouth to speak in an effort to help the victim. But no words would come. She realized she was sitting cross-legged, and tried to move. No use. She was frozen to the spot. Frozen in time and space.

The man raised the scythe higher, tightening his grip. "I promise you a quick death... that much I will do. But your life in hell will be full of torture and suffering the likes of which you couldn't imagine. I'm gonna fuck you up... gonna fuck you up."

Something in his tone, even in his words, sounded vaguely familiar to Anisa, but it was far, far away, and it disappeared.

The victim raised another hand, palm open. "No... no... please, I beg you... "

The scythe blade swiftly descended, slicing into the man's neck and decapitating him. A blood-spurting head rolled along the uneven asphalt of the parking lot, bumping into Anisa's knee and coming to rest between her legs. The dark eyes inside the blood-spewing head bored into hers. His mouth opened, twisted macabrely in pain and horror. His tongue lolled out and he vomited a stream of blood on her face. It was warm and tasted coppery.

"Aaaaaaaahhheeeee!"

She awoke sweat-soaked, shivering and terrified, her heart thumping rapidly in her chest. The bedroom door squeaked open and Connor peered in. "Mommy, are you okay?"

She forced a smile. "I'm fine, honey, just a bad dream. You better get ready. I'll be out in a minute to make your breakfast."

"Okay." Connor closed the door and she heard light thumping in the hallway as he ran into the kitchen.

It wasn't until she got Connor off to daycare that Anisa began analyzing her nightmare. Wearing a gray cotton tracksuit, her long hair tied back in a bun, she sat at her kitchen table, sipping coffee and trying to identify the voice of the murderer. Thursday being her day off, she didn't have to worry about work. *Thank God...or maybe thank Saint Death.* The nightmare had left her out of sorts and she realized the uneasy feeling that had pervaded her senses now had started during the conversation with Helen yesterday, when she was forced to look inward and face the wretchedness of her life. *Where do I know him from?* Her mind was inexplicably drawn to her childhood, before all the tragedy in her life had started.

Happier times. She was seven years old, playing in the remodeled basement of her parent's Montague home with her brother, one year her junior. He had a mock battle set up on the carpet; plastic tanks, soldiers, cannons, armored military vehicles, plastic planes. The battle had erupted and he held a plastic plane in hand and was zooming it over a line of soldiers. "Bang, bang, bang, bang, bang... you're dead. Wiped out, ha, ha."

About ten feet away, Anisa played with Ken and Barbie, walking them around a plastic toy garden outside of an ornate dollhouse—a miniature mansion, really. Barbie strolled on ahead, while Ken followed. Anisa gave voice to both of her lovers. Earlier they'd had a spat, and Ken, realizing it was his fault, was trying to make amends.

"I didn't mean to insult you, honey," Ken, through Anisa's melodious voice, said.

Barbie spun around. Even though she smiled, Anisa knew she was still mad. "Well, you did insult me. You shouldn't tell me you want to play with boys when we're supposed to be on a date."

"I meant, I want to play with my friend when the date is over... I mean tomorrow."

"Why didn't you just say that?"

"Sometimes I don't think."

"That's true. Sometimes you don't. You should be sensitive to my needs."

"I'm sorry, sweetie. Will you forgive me?"

Silently, Barbie spun around and continued walking. Ken went after her. "Please forgive me. I'm sorry."

She turned around. "Okay, Ken. I forgive you."

Ken rushed to Barbie and they locked in a passionate embrace. "Muah, muah, muah."

Her brother had stopped bombing the troops, crawled over to Anisa's little melodrama, and was watching with rapt attention as the lovers kissed and made up. "Muah? Is that the sound of a kiss?" he asked.

"Muah," she said, and kissed him on the cheek.

He wiped his cheek. "Yuck. You slobbered." But he grinned widely. "What are they gonna do now?"

"They're going inside the house for more kissing."

"Are they gonna screw?"

"You don't call it that, silly. It's called making love."

"I'm gonna fuck you up," her brother said and began tickling Anisa. She laughed hysterically, found a moment of opportunity, and tickled him back. He exploded into laughter and both of them rolled around the carpet in stitches.

A bird smashed into the kitchen window and shattered Anisa's reverie. She watched the small finch toss about on the grass for a few seconds, struggling to get its feet underneath. It finally found its balance, looked up at her, chirped twice, and flew up to a branch of the big old oak tree on her lawn.

Something was congealing in her mind and she paced about the room trying to cement it. *"I'm gonna fuck you up." That's what my brother said... and that's what the Grim Reaper in my nightmare said. Could it be?*

It had been almost twenty years since she'd spoken to her brother, Franklin Reiger. After the untimely passing of their father and two brothers, he'd disappeared, wracked by guilt and self-blame. No one knew where he was. Even when their mother Marina had died two years ago of a sudden heart attack, Franklin had not shown up for the funeral. He had left PEI at the tender age of sixteen and severed his ties with family and friends, although admittedly he'd had few of those to begin with.

Anisa wondered what had become of her brother. *Is he okay?* What had all that guilt and self-blame done to him? From her university studies, she knew self-blame was a common reaction to stressful events that could cause serious deleterious effects in terms of how a person adapts. One of the most toxic forms of emotional abuse, it had the potential to amplify her brother's personal inadequacies, paralyzing him before he could move forward. Associated with producing guilt, shame and depression, it could also lead to self-hate and low self-esteem in her learned estimation. Couldn't low self-esteem or self-hate manifest itself in outward hostility toward others? Anisa tried to put herself in her brother's mind. She remembered, after the deaths of their two brothers and father, how withdrawn Franklin had become. And not only withdrawn. Once a loving, caring, and gentle brother, he had snapped at her on more than one occasion when she had tried to pry him out of the privacy of his room. She had attempted to extricate him from the dark and wallowing depths of his despair and bring him into the bright light of a social situation, any social situation. She wanted desperately to bring the old Franklin back, restore the close and intimate bond they had shared prior to all the tragedy. But it had backfired.

"Get the fuck out of my room. I want peace and quiet, not to listen to your stupid bullshit. I don't hate myself. I hate you."

But Franklin's abuse hadn't lasted. Occasionally she would see that old tender and loving look in his eyes. It said, *"I'm sorry, sis. I love you. I just can't say it right now."* After the first few outbursts, he had stopped yelling at her and his replies grew softer and more polite. But there was something deeply troubling in the tone of his voice; a sort of grim resignation and a profound sadness—this was the new-and-not-so-improved version of Franklin and perhaps always would be.

"I'm sorry, sis, I don't want to go outside. Maybe tomorrow."

"I'm not feeling well enough to play Frisbee. Maybe tomorrow."

"I'm not going riding with you today. I don't feel good. I don't feel like myself anymore."

That was probably the last thing Franklin had said to her. The next day, he was gone. No note. A knapsack, some clothes, and his personal toiletries were missing from his bedroom. His bed had been neatly made and all his toys, which he'd long ago lost interest in, were as neatly arranged as they always had been. One of his strong points: he was very organized.

There was a small thing that Anisa noticed. His window blinds, normally closed, had been pulled open, bright sunshine streaming in and illuming an otherwise dark bedroom. Anisa often wondered if it had been a symbolic message from Franklin—"Now that I'm gone, bright sunshine will fill your life."

Anisa realized she was staring at the finch in the tree—which stared back at her—but not seeing it. The finch chirped. She closed her eyes, searching for a conclusion. *What had he become?* The nasty image of the Grim Reaper reappeared, sweeping her off to a dark place. *Could self-blame lead to sociopathic tendencies? He definitely became very withdrawn.*

The dark face of the Grim Reaper morphed into the fresh face of Franklin, still in his teens. *Could self-blame lead to psychotic tendencies? Could it turn him into a psychopath?*

Franklin grinned maniacally. With lightning speed and deadly accuracy, the scythe swept down and decapitated the pleading and helpless victim. Anisa shuddered, an icy chill convulsing her body. *Could it turn him into a cold-blooded killer?*

Anisa had tried for so many years to block out memories of Franklin. He obviously didn't want anything to do with her, so why should she with him? But the nightmare had changed everything. She didn't know how, but she knew. Franklin was perched on a dangerous precipice and desperately needed her help. He was her brother, after all, and something told her he was alive. The only living immediate family member she had left. It was time to break free from the constraints of her pitiful victim mentality and oftentimes self-serving agenda.

She raced into the living room, pushing aside a mug and a plate of leftovers on the coffee table and turning on her laptop—driven by a newfound energy and singular purpose. *Find Franklin. Save him.* She googled his full name and was about to press Enter when her cell phone rang. She answered.

Helen sobbed into the phone. "He's dead!"

Exactly thirty-six minutes later, Anisa parked her red Dodge Caravan in front of Helen's Main Street apartment. Getting out of the vehicle, she noticed Helen waving from her second-floor window, her moist face contorted with pain, confusion, and worry.

"I'll buzz you in," Helen said weakly.

Climbing the stairs two at a time, Anisa wondered what condition she would find her friend in. Helen had been hysterical on the phone, repeating over and over, "He's dead." Anisa didn't know who was dead or how they had died, but she had a feeling she was going to find out very soon. An eerie darkness enveloped her as she entered the apartment, and a gloomy thought crossed her mind. *By introducing her to Saint Death, did I bring this on? Am I responsible?*

Sitting on the couch in a mid-length pink nightgown, her hair in disarray, Helen pointed to the television. "It's on again. Look."

Silently, Anisa sat beside her friend and looked at the screen.

A middle-aged blonde reporter stood in front of a 1930s Victorian-style two-story home on a quiet tree-lined street. The morning sun shone brightly. Crime-scene tape bordered the property. A half a dozen police cars and larger investigative and forensic-type vans were parked in front. Police and investigators milled about the scene, some entering and leaving the house.

The reporter said, "The body of thirty-year-old Ray Minowest, a local construction worker, was discovered this morning at approximately four-thirty-six. Police rushed to 36 Fitzroy Street in Georgetown, Prince Edward Island, after a 911 call from a neighbor. The neighbor, Elma Sandringham, said she heard horrifying screams coming from the residence. When police arrived, they discovered a scene right out of a horror novel. Minowest's body lay in a blood-soaked bed and his decapitated head was perched on a nearby bureau, glaring eerily at investigators."

Anisa's nightmare, in all its grisly horror, flashed through her mind. *Decapitated? Wasn't Saint Death's scythe supposed to symbolize cutting away negative energy or influences? As a farm implement, didn't it also symbolize hope, prosperity, and abundance?* But Anisa couldn't deny it. The scythe was also a symbol of death—the razor-sharp implement the Grim Reapress used to harvest souls; a powerful representation of the moment everyone must inevitably face—meeting our maker.

The reporter continued. "Lead investigator Bryce Watson said a full investigation is underway and they have no suspects. According to Watson, the investigation is in its early stages and police are still trying to determine motive. They are conducting a full forensic examination of the crime scene as well as canvassing the neighborhood to see if Minowest had any known enemies... "

Anisa didn't hear the rest. Her mind was in turmoil. She turned to Helen, whose face had gone a jaundiced white. But at least she wasn't hysterical. "Did you know him?"

"Yeah. From high school. You could call him an enemy of mine."

Cutting away negative energy or influences... by killing them. "What?"

"He used to tease me for being stupid."

Anisa inched closer to Helen and put a hand on her knee. "I told you, you're not stupid."

"Not anymore I'm not."

"What does that mean?"

Helen explained how she had, with the help of Doctor Ricardo, activated her Saint Death figurine yesterday. She told Anisa of her entreaties to the Bony Lady. When she finished, she said, "I know what you're thinking. Why did I go to Doctor Ricardo by myself when you told me you'd introduce me? I'm sorry, Anisa. I just couldn't wait. I hope you'll forgive me."

"Was he mad at me?"

"I don't think so. But he said he wants to talk to you."

"Jesus. I wish you could have waited. I told you he swore me to secrecy."

"I'm sorry. I was desperate."

"It's too late now. Forget about it."

After a moment's silence, Helen rose. "I need a shot of rum. You want one?"

Anisa shook her head. "Don't you have to work?"

"I called in sick this morning. I was upset over Ray's murder."

"You want a drink at 10:36 in the morning?"

Helen nodded. "For what I'm about to tell you, yeah, I do."

What is she going to tell me? Did she kill Minowest? "Okay, you go ahead."

"Do you want anything?"

"Orange juice, if you have it."

"I do." Helen disappeared into the kitchen and returned a short time later with a full bottle of Bacardi rum, a glass with ice, and a glass of orange juice with ice for Anisa. She sat down, poured herself a stiff shot, and drained half of it in a single gulp without even making a face. Then she picked up the remote and killed the TV, which had gone into commercial mode.

Anisa sipped her orange juice. *May as well get right to it.* "Why were you so hysterical over Minowest's death? He was your enemy, but you didn't kill him." *Or did she?*

Helen's hands trembled slightly. She brought Anisa up to speed regarding her prayers to Saint Death and, more importantly, the changes that began taking place in her during those prayers. "All the nasty things he'd said blindsided me like a Mack truck. I think it started when he insulted me at work that one day. I don't know if I told you about that."

"I don't think so."

"He said, 'If you had brains you'd be dangerous.'"

Now she has brains. Was he right? "What an asshole."

"Yeah. Anyway, as I was praying to Saint Death, I felt this strange energy come over me and really dark and vengeful emotions. At the same time my mind was racing like a train and processing things superfast. Like I was getting smarter but also more hateful at the same time. I was praying but couldn't even hear myself, thinking the whole time how much I'd like to see Ray dead... " Helen paused, picked up her drink, and drained the remainder. "Here comes the kicker. I'm not too sure, because I started drifting, almost like fading in and out of consciousness... but I'm pretty sure I prayed for Ray's death."

"What? Is that all you prayed for?"

"I don't know."

"What do you mean, you don't know?"

"I told you, it was like I was drifting in and out of consciousness, like I was being dragged inexplicably down some dark and macabre path... "

"Inexplicably... macabre." I've never heard her use those words before. She's not the same. She's different. What's happening here?

Helen continued after the short pause. "You know what?"

"No, I don't, and maybe this is the wrong phrase, but I'm dying to find out."

"It wasn't only his death I prayed for. I think I actually prayed that I would kill him." At this revelation, Helen poured herself another full glass of rum. This time she took a small sip and set it down. She picked up the bottle again and held it out to Anisa. "Are you sure? It goes well with orange juice."

Anisa held up her glass. "What the hell... not too strong."

Helen poured about two ounces into the glass. Anisa stirred it with her finger, licked it, and took a sip.

"That's not the worst part," Helen said, some of the color returning to her face. "I blacked out and woke up this morning sprawled out on the floor, Saint Death's candle still burning brightly. She was grinning at me, with a look of mockery and pride."

"What are you telling me, Helen? Do you think you left the house during your blackout and actually committed murder?"

"I hate to think so, but it's possible. I lost about six hours of time."

Anisa glanced around the apartment, looking for any obvious signs. She remembered the rain pattering on her windows before she had fallen asleep last night. "Oh my God. Did you see any signs around here that you left? Muddy shoes, wet clothes, blood, a knife... anything at all?"

Helen's face went white and she covered her eyes with her hands. She began sobbing. "I was too afraid to look." She looked up at Anisa pleadingly. "I've never, ever thought about killing anyone in my entire life. What did you do to me? Why did you have to tell me about Saint Death? Can't you keep a secret? You said Doctor Ricardo made you swear to secrecy. Why did you break your promise to him?"

Anisa put her drink on the coffee table and put her arm around Helen. "I'm so sorry, Helen. I didn't mean for this to happen. I only wanted to help you."

Helen leaned back and wiped away tears. Anisa put a comforting hand on her shoulder.

The horrific image of the Grim Reaper in Anisa's nightmare the night before began morphing into something else—a demonically crazed Helen standing over a helpless Ray Minowest and delivering a fatal decapitating blow. She shuddered. *What have I done? I only wanted to help her...*

It was as if Helen had read her mind. She stopped crying and locked eyes with Anisa. "Maybe you did help me."

"What do you mean?"

There was a long pause before Helen spoke. "I never told anyone this before in my life. Buried it deep, blocked it out. But I think it's time. In high school, he raped me. Ray raped me!"

CHAPTER NINE

Gyrating to loud thumping bachata music a few days later in the disco of Lifestyles resort, pleasantly numbed by a steady stream of strawberry margaritas, Terry Anderson realized their prayers to the saint of death had been answered. Not a single argument had ensued. Their passion for one another had grown from a flickering candle to a blazing bushfire. Everything was perfect. As an added bonus, they hadn't seen the likes of Freaky Franky, who, in some weird way, Terry held responsible for the one tiff they'd had on their vacation. He looked at Natalie, bouncing beside him in a short black dress with a plunging neckline, and touched her arm. "Want another drink, honey?"

She smiled. "What?"

He made a gesture of sipping a drink and pointed to the bar.

She leaned in close, licking his cheek sensually. "Get some Cuba libres in plastic cups. We can drink and dance."

Why not? he thought. Other tourists were doing it. He nodded, turned, and began weaving his way through the packed dance floor to the bar. Once there, he placed the order, deciding to also switch to Cuba libres. He might pay for mixing alcohol tomorrow, but never mind that. The night was young and they were having a great time.

As he began making his way back, he froze—*Is someone attacking Natalie?*—and dropped both plastic cups, splattering the drinks on the floor. One drink splashed the sandaled foot of a woman dancing with her own drink in hand. She scowled at him. "Watch what you're doing, asshole."

"Hey, it was an accident."

But she didn't hear him. Her partner whisked her away and, locked in an embrace, they twirled toward the center of the dance floor.

Bumping shoulders with a few people on the way—"Watch yourself, buddy!"—Terry jostled through the crowd toward Natalie. Nearing her, he realized with horror that a man was dancing with her. But it wasn't consensual. He'd forcefully pulled her to the center of the dance floor and, once there, began tugging on her wrists, jolting her to and fro like a puppet on a string. She struggled to free herself. Other dancers had separated, forming a circle around the show, some of them cheering while others displayed apathy or mild annoyance.

Franklin. That's Freaky Franky. Terry clenched his fists and roughly pushed a few bystanders out of the way—*insensitive imbeciles*—and charged Franklin like a raging bull. But Franklin, almost as if he had eyes in the back of his head, released Natalie, spun around, and kicked Terry hard, flush on the jaw.

Like a sack of hammers, Terry dropped to the floor, smacking the back of his head violently. Multi-colored flashing disco lights faded and turned black in perfect harmony with the thumping music, which decreased to a soft hiss before disappearing entirely. Total silence and total blackness, enveloped him. He felt himself floating in the noiseless blackness, being swept away to an unknown destination. *Am I dying and being carried to heaven? Maybe you don't deserve heaven.*

His body moved swiftly at first, and then slowed and spun around to a sitting position. But he was in suspended animation, sitting on air. He tried to move his arms, then his legs, but they would not obey brain commands. He tried opening his mouth, but to no avail. Then his eyes, with the same result.

Raw fear and panic seized him. *I'm dead, oh my God, no. Please, please don't let me die. I have so many things to do. I'm too young.* Then his thoughts drifted to his life, and how he had lived it. Did his moral compass steadfastly align with magnetic north, or was it swinging wildly all over the map?

Hadn't most of his actions been motivated by fierce competitiveness? As a child, he'd always been competing with his older brother Brad and his eldest sister Sophie for the attention of his parents, Harry and Henrietta. They were both doctors who gave most of their lives to helping others. But they were so devoted to helping the sick, they were hardly ever there for their children. And during the short intervals that they were around, it was always a competition. Terry always lost the battle for his parents' affection to Sophie and Brad, who were now both doctors, holding jobs far more prestigious and financially rewarding than his position as an in-house financial advisor and mortgage specialist with Scotiabank. He had decided to get into the banking business to prove a point. Become a successful investment banker and blow his whole family away in terms of income and prestige. Show them all that he was really the star of the show.

Even when it came to relationships, in Terry's mind it was simple: do better than his brother and sister. Find a woman who was hot and emotionally stable. Hot and not too crazy, according to the Hot-Crazy Matrix video he'd seen on YouTube, and now subscribed to as if it were gospel. According to the video, all women were a little crazy and it was just a matter of degrees, or numbers. Brad's wife was maybe a six on the attractiveness scale, and perhaps also a six on the crazy axis. Sophie's husband was perhaps a seven on the hot scale but decidedly a six on the crazy scale. But Natalie blew them all away, a nine on the hot scale and a three on the crazy scale; a rare unicorn, well in the zone of wife material and a woman to be cherished and studied.

All the others before her? Well, over time they'd shifted into prohibitively crazy numbers, in some cases even prohibitively not-so-hot numbers. The result: they'd been disposed of like yesterday's stinky trash.

Taking stock of this, Terry, for the very first time, suddenly asked himself if perhaps maybe the Hot-Crazy Matrix was designed as comedy, a tongue-in-cheek mockery of women, and a sexist, condescending, and simplistic one at that. After all, the male version of the same matrix measured men overall as far less crazy and measured their attractiveness to woman based to a large extent on their financial success or lack thereof. *It's a little sexist.* But it was indeed his literal interpretation of it that in large part had led him not only to Natalie, but also to his career goals in the banking industry. Then there was another revelation. *You lied to her. You got passed up on the bank manager promotion to that ass-kissing motherfucker Cecil. How long is that lie gonna hold up? What will she say when she discovers that you're still a lowly in-house financial advisor? She'll dump of you like yesterday's trash, that's what she'll do. No, no, no...*

"Stop it and listen to me."

The tone was authoritative and commanding, snapping Terry out of his wallowing descent into self-pity. He slowly opened his eyes. Before him was the majestic figure of Saint Death, cloaked in a black robe, her bony skeleton face and skeleton hands glowing bright white. In her left hand she held a large black scythe, twinkling with a million bright lights. She was suspended above a puffy white cloud.

Oh no. Judgment day. Terry cleared his throat. "Am I dead?"

A bottle of tequila magically appeared in her right hand and she took a sip.

Saint Death grinned as she spoke, her eye sockets dimming slowly to black. "We'll get to that later. You have a sexist and superficial view of women, looking at us as mere objects that need to be acquired and exploited. Women are much more complicated than your dim-witted view suggests. We are in fact the superior sex, the nurturers of society; not nutcases, as you think. Is that what you think of Natalie?"

"I love Natalie."

The skeleton saint raised the scythe slightly, her grin tightening to a scowl. "Do you really? Is that why you lied to her? You said you got a promotion. You got no such thing. Do you think a relationship built on a foundation of lies can survive?"

A cold chill swept up Terry's back, stopping at the nape of his neck. Warm skin turned frosty. His jaw began throbbing with pain and the back of his head ached dully. "I'm sorry, Holy Saint. Please forgive me. I'll tell her the truth about my promotion, the truth about my belief in the matrix. I'll come clean. I'll change. I'll beg for her forgiveness. I... I beg for your forgiveness."

The grin returned. "Those who I choose to spare have to be shown worthy. They have to win my favor."

"What would you have me do, Holy Saint? I'll do anything if you spare my life; or, if I'm dead, you find it in your heart to resurrect me."

"Anything? You'll do anything?"

"Well, within reason."

"Are you suggesting I'd have you do something evil? I'm the miracle worker of well-being, health, love, and abundance."

"I know, I know. That's why Natalie and I started worshipping you. We saw firsthand your supernatural powers. Please, Saint Death, spare me. I beg you. Give me a chance to change, and I'll show you I'm worthy."

"You needed to come clean with Natalie. You needed to be honest with her. You needed to love her for her, not based on the superficial analysis that you've applied. If you would've realized love and respect in your life, all the abundance you've long sought—and had so much difficulty obtaining—would've rained down on you like a million diamonds."

Terry shuddered. *It's too late.* "You're speaking in the past tense. Does that mean it's too late?"

"Maybe it *is* too late."

Bowling balls of black thunder rolled overhead, deafening. In an instant, Saint Death vanished.

Terry felt warm tears streaming down his cheeks. "No, no, no! Come back! Please. I'm sorry. I don't wanna die. I'm too young to die. I'm sooorrrrrrry... "

"Wake up. Please, wake up!"

Pitch black turned from dark gray to light gray to yellow to white. Terry opened his eyes, feeling a throbbing pain in his jaw. His head ached dully. He saw two young women looking down at him concernedly, four blue eyes, two heads with long, flowing brown hair. They were identical. They both held ice packs to his jaw. He blinked three times and refocused. The two merged into one. *Natalie. That's Natalie.*

"Are you okay?"

A wave of dizziness swept over him and he waited for it to pass. "I'm alive."

He tried to get up and she gently pushed him back down. "Not now. You need some recovery time."

Gazing around the room, he finally recognized his hotel suite. Then the events that landed him in bed rushed into his disoriented mind like a raging river. *Freaky Franky, that fuck.* But those thoughts were overpowered by his magical experience with Saint Death, his epiphany. Something occurred to him about his new religion that had never dawned on him before. It was a deeper level of understanding. *Saint Death is all about death; controlling it, making sense of it, escaping it.* He had escaped its clutches. He had been given a second chance, a new lease on life. He had to make the best of it. Let Natalie explain what happened and, when he found the courage, he could make amends and level with Natalie, as the Holy Saint had demanded. "What happened?"

Natalie propped the ice pack under his chin, wiped the wetness from his eyes and face with a facecloth, and clasped her hands together. "Do you remember Franklin jerking me around like a puppet on the dance floor?"

"Yeah."

"You remember what happened after that?"

Terry scratched the goose egg on the back of his head. It smarted and he winced. "I tried to tackle him. I have no idea what happened after that."

"He kicked you flush on the chin, knocked you out cold, then you smashed the back of your head when you hit the dance floor."

"And after that?"

"He left right away. Released me and just walked calmly out the door. No one even tried to stop him."

"Did he say anything to you?"

A long pause. "I don't want you to go after him. He's dangerous."

"I'm not gonna go after him. But I'd like to know if he threatened you."

"I guess you could call it a threat."

"You 'guess'? What did he say?"

She crossed her legs and her light blue summer dress fluttered, exposing the dark V of her genitalia. It wasn't missed on Terry that she wasn't wearing panties. "It's pretty rude," she said.

"Please."

Before she spoke, Terry thought he saw a grin cross the curved lines of her lips, but it was only a flash and he couldn't be sure. It soon turned into a frown. "He said, 'I'm gonna fuck you to death. And you're gonna love every minute of it.'"

Terry clenched his fists. "Fucking sick pervert. Did you tell anyone?"

"Only you. After you hit the dance floor and Franklin left, three hotel security guards carried you to our room. I didn't say anything to them. I was too afraid. I was gonna call a doctor, even the hotel security guards offered to do it, but I didn't... I told them I'd wait first to see if you came to on your own. I'm sorry. Maybe we should have a doctor look at you now. I just don't trust doctors in third-world countries."

"It's okay. Let's leave it for now. What time is it?"

"Three-thirty-three am."

"How long have I been out?"

"About three hours and thirty-three minutes, actually. I got really worried when you started talking in your sleep, shouting fearfully, jerking convulsively, even crying. I've never seen you cry. Ever. What was all that about anyway? You have a nasty nightmare?"

A second chance. No, tomorrow, I'll tell her. I'm tired. And sore. But, as if by supernatural intervention, he felt the pain ebbing from his jaw and head and flowing through his shoulder. He raised his hand, pointed his index finger to the ceiling, and magically the pain gathered momentum and strength, coursing through his arm and out his index finger into the ceiling. He thought he even saw a brief white flash as it disappeared through the ceiling. He wondered for a moment if he could have used it as a weapon and indeed directed it at his enemies.

"What are you doing?"

Terry smiled. *A second chance. She's healing me.* "This sounds crazy, but I just shot all the pain through the ceiling."

"What?"

"You heard me, honey. Saint Death is curing me. This is a miracle." Even his head began to clear, the color returning to his cheeks. *She wants me to tell her now. Obey her.* "Do you want me to tell you now? It's late. Maybe you ought to get some rest."

"We're on vacation, honey. We can sleep all day tomorrow if we want. And I'm very interested in miracles."

"Okay. I think I had an epiphany."

"Really?"

He recapped the events with Saint Death, but stopped before explaining his sexist views of women and his missed promotion. *Nut-sack-licking Cecil.* This was gonna be harder than he'd thought.

Natalie's eyes said she believed him. They also said she knew he was holding something back. "Come on. What are your sins, according to Saint Death?"

Terry took Natalie's hand. She didn't resist. *One step at a time.* "I'm sorry. I lied to you, Natalie." *Nice work, diplomat.*

She jerked her hand free. "About what?"

"I have such a warped view of women—that they're all after money—that I thought you'd be endeared to me even more if I told you I got the bank manager promotion. Part of it was true. I was up for the promotion. I was on the short list for it, but I didn't get it. Nut-sack-licking Cecil got it."

Natalie slid a few inches away from Terry. "You think I'm after you for your money?"

"Maybe I thought that, honey, but I'm trying to change." *Better leave the matrix out of it for now. This isn't going well.* "I didn't want to lose you, Natalie. I was too afraid to lose you. You're the most perfect woman I've ever found, and I didn't want to screw it up."

Her face tightened. "If you didn't want to screw it up, you don't start off by lying. I'm a chartered accountant, a financial success in my own right. I don't *want* your money. I don't *need* your money. Of course I don't want to marry a financial loser, but that's just common sense. That doesn't mean I'm after your money."

"I'm sorry, honey. I promise I'll never lie to you again."

But Natalie's insecurities began trampling on the voice of reason. Hadn't her ex, Rex Fisher, said those same words to her the first time she caught him cheating? And what happened? He cheated again, and again, and again; and even then Natalie couldn't find the courage, self-respect, or self-esteem to dump his infidelity-prone loser ass. He had unceremoniously dumped her via text message. It came hurling back with the force and sting of a bullet to the heart: *I don't think this is working out anymore. It's true what they say about accountants. You're all boring. Lose my number, bitch.*

She slid to the foot of the bed. Her tone was coarse. "You say you have a 'warped view' of women? What does that mean, exactly?"

Terry was beginning to flush, his expression pained. "Can you calm down, please? I'm trying to come clean with you. It's what I need to do to salvage our relationship..."

She squinted. "'Salvage?' What the fuck does that mean? That implies the relationship is already fucked. Excuse me, I thought we had a good thing; but now I'm not so sure."

Terry realized he was digging his own grave. Ironic, since he'd just been resurrected. His choice of words was lacking, to say the least. "I didn't mean to use that word. I meant improve, you know, so we can be happy together."

"That implies we're not happy now." Natalie had heard enough. She was about to explode and say something really nasty, but she bit her tongue. *Handle it mature, girl. At least he's coming clean with you now. Trying to be honest.* But the unsavory character traits Terry had just revealed began to overshadow his attempts at honesty and reconciliation. *He's a fucking sexist, I think. He lied to me. 'Salvage?' What a stupid thing to say.*

She stood up quickly. "If I stay here any longer, I'm gonna tell you to go fuck yourself. And I don't wanna do that. So, I'm gonna get some fresh air and we can talk about this in the morning."

As she resolutely closed the door behind her, she heard Terry's voice, muffled but audible. "I'm sorry, honey. Please come back."

Terry was halfway to the door when he stopped. *Wait a minute. She has a right to be angry. Let her blow off some steam and calm down.* He went out on the balcony and sat down, listening to the gently lapping waves, watching the moon as a bank of clouds moved in and began obscuring it. *How fitting. A dark cloud hanging over our relationship.* But in spite of the dark and foreboding feeling, he stayed put. If he had learned one thing in his thirty-five years of existence, it was to leave a woman alone when she was angry. Especially if she didn't want to talk. If he caught up with her and tried to talk now, things could easily escalate from bad to worse to disastrous. Instead of focusing on his current predicament, he let his mind wander to other things. Thinking of Natalie now would just upset him more and propel him out the door in a fit of passion. Many unlawful acts were committed in the heat of passion. He didn't need that. He would give her an hour and if she hadn't returned by then, he would go looking for her, with any luck in a much calmer state than he was currently in. So he drifted back to the lost promotion, trying to make sense of it.

He was more qualified than Cecil Schmidt for the job, that much was true. Over the last three years, he had taken great pains to be tenacious and efficient in his work, even going so far as to socialize at various networking functions to attract mortgage and investment customers. And it had worked. He had brought more moneyed clients into the bank in the last three years than any of his predecessors. It was only in the last three months that his boss had started to take a shine to Cecil Schmuck. It was true, Cecil had one year of seniority, but his sales numbers were less than half of Terry's. But he was doing other things; bringing Ned Withers coffee and donuts, complimenting him on his tie; stealing some of Terry's clients and new bank policy ideas and claiming them as his own; acting as a surrogate secretary when Ned stepped out for a nip; even buying birthday presents for the boss's two children. *Let's just call it what it is. Licking Ned's nuts and French-kissing his butt.*

But there was more to it than that. Hadn't Cecil made a pass at the new blonde bombshell employee, Sally Yates? Hadn't he commented on the desirous quality and shape of her butt, a comment that in this day and age could be considered sexual assault? A pat on the ass and a remark like, "You've got a nice butt, baby," could land you in jail nowadays. Perhaps more so at the workplace. And Sally had told Terry: "Cecil's made some inappropriate remarks about my derriere. He even bumped into me one time at the photocopier. I'm not talking an accidental bump. At least it didn't seem accidental. Tell me, is it an accident when you bump into someone's ass with your crotch?"

Terry didn't think so, and it didn't take him long to come up with a solution. Saint Death had saved his life, spared him so he might strive to become a better person. What prevented him from going to the boss about Cecil's indiscretions in the past was the plain and simple fact he wasn't a rat. Enter the skeleton savior. He had to pray to her. He owed her gratitude because he was still breathing. And of course there was more. He wanted his relationship with Natalie back on track. He wanted to mete out justice to the scheming sexual assaulter Cecil Schmuck while there was still time. He knew Cecil had been given the promotion, that much had been conveyed to him prior to leaving for his vacation. But he also knew Cecil's new job title wouldn't take effect for another month. There was still time.

And there was still more. He wanted justice for Franklin for knocking him into Never-Never Land. And fucking with his fiancé.

A few minutes later he knelt down before the glowing statue of Saint Death. Two candles were lit beside the saint. Red, the symbol for love, to put him back on a romantic and blissful track with Natalie. And green, the votive candle representing justice and law, used to call upon the supernatural lawyer powers of the skeleton saint.

As Terry began praying, the words Franklin had said to Natalie lanced his heart like a determined scythe: *'I'm gonna fuck you to death. And you're gonna love every minute of it.'*

As if by some macabre and mysterious supernatural force, as if she were under some potent black magic spell, Natalie found herself being drawn to the apartment. Now, standing under the soft glow of a streetlight, she found herself looking up at the second-floor sliding glass door. Gazing at a flickering yellow light—maybe a series of lights, she couldn't be sure—she began crossing the street. *What are you doing?* But she couldn't will herself to stop, turn around, and return to Terry. She had been gone thirty-six minutes, walking along the beach and down the two-lane street that fronted the beach. Enough time to rehash recent events. It was the voice of reason that had defeated her insecurities for a change. Just because Terry had lied about his promotion, that didn't necessarily put him in the same league as Rex. She had never known Terry to be an adulterer. Maybe he was a bit sexist, but weren't all men, to some degree? Didn't they all judge women and discriminate against them based on sex? *Probably. No, not probably. Yes.* Certainly not always publicly, but definitely in their male hang-outs, locker rooms, man caves, or wherever the hell else they gathered exclusively with their male cronies. Maybe Terry's choice of words during his apology hadn't been the best, but men were infamous for putting their feet in their mouths when speaking to women. This certainly wasn't a revelation.

Calmer, she told herself to give Terry a chance, accept his apology and, if he was feeling better, even have some wild make-up sex before turning in for the night. After all, Saint Death had saved him, even magically healed him.

Right then, the omnipotent force seized her and turned her around. A voice in her head tried to justify it as revenge, but another louder voice said something else.

She stepped on the curb and walked up the parking lot to the stairs. At the foot of the stairs, three small dogs stirred, looked at her with wide-eyes, and scattered. She climbed the stairs and stealthily moved along the balcony to the sliding-glass door. The curtain was open a crack. She peered inside. It took a moment for her eyes to adjust to the suffused light inside. When they did, she could make out seven candles illuminating the face of a skeleton statue. *Oh my God. Saint Death. He worships her, too.* Her first instinct was to turn and run. She tried to move but the mysterious force had glued her feet to the floor. She pressed her head to the glass and looked inside.

She saw him kneeling in front of the statue, his faint grin lit demonically by the flickering candles.

He was praying. "Oh mighty saint, bring me Natalie, so I might consummate my lust for her, consummate my love for her..."

He knows my name. How does he know my name? She felt the furry mound between her legs moisten and brought her hand down, as if to stem the tide. A drop trickled down her leg and she wiped it with her hand. Then she brought her hand up to her nose, smelled it, grinned, and inserted her finger in her mouth, licking it clean with a loud slurping sound. *What are you doing? Get out of here.* But she was too far gone now. A soft moan escaped her lips.

Another potent preternatural force suddenly gripped her, willing her to run like hell. She struggled, warring with the conflicting forces of good and evil. She didn't realize she had spoken aloud until it was too late. "Goddammit, I'm under a spell. Saint Death, save me! Terry, save me!"

The sliding-glass door slid open and Franklin, shirtless and sweating, stepped out onto the balcony. He grinned and licked his lips. "Don't worry, baby. I'll save you."

Terry was going bat-shit crazy.

He had finished his prayers and platitudes of gratitude to Saint Death, the results of which had obliterated his head pain completely and electrified him with a new vigor and vitality. It was all he could do to count first the minutes and then the seconds on the remaining hour before bolting out the door in a worried frenzy to begin his search.

After combing the entire tiny beach community of Cofresi, he had come up empty-handed. He had run into a few drunken tourists on the way, staggering back to their rooms after a night of alcohol abuse, and all that had netted was mostly incoherent drunken ramblings. He had come within an inch of flying into a rage after one inebriated asshole had shouted, "I've seen her and she's a damn good fuck, you ask me." If it hadn't been for the asshole's buddy grabbing him by the arm and saying, "Pardon my friend. He's shit-faced and won't remember a thing tomorrow," Terry may well have smashed both of their faces to smithereens. Now, having just searched Ocean World, he wandered back to Lifestyles along the dimly lit street, stepping into the ditch occasionally to avoid getting struck by vehicles travelling at unsafe speeds.

Passing a dark vacant field, he heard a rustling sound and stopped. From his shirt pocket, he produced a small flashlight and shone it into the field. "Anyone there?"

He heard a soft moan.

Waving the flashlight, he stepped into the field. "Is anyone here?"

Silence.

"Fuck. What happened?"

Recognizing the voice, he rushed over to it. In his haste, he tripped over a rock and fell on his knees, his head careening forward and landing softly on wet, supple, carpeted flesh—Natalie's vagina. As a musty smell assaulted his nostrils, he winced, raising his head from her furry mound and taking stock of her condition. Her blue summer dress was pulled up to her waist and the area around her genitalia was red and slightly swollen. The plunging neckline of the dress had a small tear in it, exposing a perky left breast.

"Oh my God. Have you been raped?"

Natalie's hair was wet, strands of it matted to her face. She looked confused and disoriented. "I don't know. I don't remember."

CHAPTER TEN

Franklin lay in bed the following morning, plotting his next moves. The evening had gone well—better than planned, actually. He had fucked Natalie. And she had enjoyed it. It didn't matter to Franklin that the enjoyment was mixed with brief horrified flashes of recognition, flashes that on two occasions had catapulted her out of the bed and speeding to the door. But it was locked, and by the time she figured that out, the powerful love spell that he and Saint Death had orchestrated so well had her in its grip again, returning her forcefully to Franklin's love nest. He hadn't fucked her to death yet, but there was still time for that. Rome wasn't built in a day. Franklin knew it wouldn't be long before the magic spell would put Natalie on another helpless track toward his bedroom. And the next time he would be prepared to end her life, albeit with a satisfied smile on her face. Happy in life. Happy in death. Happily ever after.

He wasn't sure Alfredo could say the same thing. Oh, sure, Alfredo was dead all right. He'd started convulsing violently in the intensive care unit after a blood vessel in his head had ruptured. Must have been more than one, because when he opened his mouth to cry for help, all he produced was a fountain of blood. A fountain of death. The miracle-working saint of death had answered his prayers. Even the dogs were slowly dispersing, perhaps realizing that the hand that had occasionally fed them was now six feet underground, food for worms and rot.

Franklin rubbed his hands together with a satisfied grin. Next up, the beached whale caretaker Niamia Fernandez. After a quick jog on the beach and maybe a trip into town to scout out some new talent, he planned on returning home early to rehearse and write his next prayers. He wanted to be precise in the wording and not leave anything to chance. Niamia had turned what should have been a quiet building into a bustling super-mall with all her disruptive businesses. If he and Saint Death had anything to do with it, she would not die happily ever after, unlike the pleasure-filled expiration he planned for Natalie. No shit-eating grin on Niamia's face. He was going to devise a wish and a prayer that would bring forth horrible suffering to that inconsiderate and disrespectful bitch. *I'm gonna fuck you up.* As his mind delved into a well of creativity and he began to think of all the various methods of torture available, his phone rang.

He plucked it off the bedside table. *Fuck sakes. Turn it off when you're creating.* He saw the 902 area code and his brow furrowed: he recognized it as Prince Edward Island, his birthplace. At first he thought he would ignore it, but then he suddenly had a change of heart and answered in an irritated tone. "Who is it?"

A long pause. "Franklin? Is that you?"

"Who is this? How did you get my number?"

"You don't recognize my voice?"

Franklin was becoming more agitated. "No."

"Would you like to play dollhouse with me? With Ken and Barbie?"

Then it hit him like an avalanche, all those chilling childhood memories he had spent years trying to block out, in large part successfully. It was his sister, Anisa, the one he had so joyfully played with as a child. The tickling episode, the one to which she was referring to, flooded forth. *I'm gonna fuck you up.* Now, when he thought or spoke those words, he intended a punishment slightly more severe than tickling. At first he was confused about how to handle the situation. Should he feign ignorance, pretending to be someone else and dispose of the caller? Yes. His mind raced, trying to think of the words to use. And then she said it and his resolution melted like molten lava.

"I'm gonna fuck you up."

In spite of himself, he laughed, a deep throaty chuckle. "Anisa. How are you?"

"You know, getting by. I have a son now. I'm divorced. Single mom struggling to make ends meet. How about you?"

When Franklin had left PEI, he moved to Toronto, worked in construction, lived like a pauper in seedy boarding houses, and saved every cent he could. Many years later when he left Toronto for the DR, he had $150,000 saved up. After arriving, he'd arranged to have it transferred into a local bank that paid eight per cent interest. It generated $12,000 a year and that's what he lived off, never touching the principal. But he didn't want to tell Anisa the whole story, at least not yet. "I'm getting by. It's a lot cheaper here than there."

There was a long pause. Finally, Anisa asked, "Are you okay? I mean mentally."

"Why wouldn't I be, sis?"

"I don't want to bring up the past, Franky, but we endured some pretty traumatic experiences as kids. I think it set me back, to be honest. I just wondered if you're okay with everything."

He knew Anisa would see through his bullshit, so there was no point trying it. "I wouldn't be here if I was completely okay. I've tried to block it out and put it behind me."

"I know. You put all of us behind you."

After an uncomfortable pause, Franklin said, "How's Mom?"

"She's dead, Franky. Been dead for two years."

"I'm sorry. How?"

"Heart attack. You didn't know?"

"No. I severed all my connections when I left."

Her voice was breaking up. "I know. You cut me off. You were my baby brother and you cut me off."

"I'm sorry. I was in a lot of pain."

"I think you still are. And I want to help you."

"What do you mean?"

Anisa wondered if she'd said too much too fast. Maybe these bombshells would alienate him even further. But her chilling nightmare suggested an urgency to the situation, and she saw no point beating around the bush. "I want to come and see you."

"I thought you said you're a struggling single mom. Where are you gonna get the money? And who's gonna look after your son?"

"I can make arrangements for Connor. And I can find the money." He didn't need to know that that meant buying a plane ticket on her credit card and taking a cash advance for spending money. "Don't you wanna see me, Franky? We used to be so close. After twenty years, you still don't wanna see me?"

"Okay, okay. When do you wanna come?"

"Friday."

"The day after tomorrow?"

"That's right."

"You can come that soon?"

"I'll make it happen, Franky. Don't worry about me. It's you I'm worried about."

"Don't worry about me, sis. I'm getting—feeling—better. Everything's coming together for me."

I strongly doubt it. But she didn't say it. "Well, it would be great so see you. It's been so long."

They exchanged email addresses and Franklin described the Cofresi area. He told her to email her flight itinerary and he would pick her up at the airport. He fell short of offering to put her up in his two-bedroom apartment.

"I'll find you a nice suite as soon as I get your itinerary. Lifestyles is a great high-end resort right down the street."

"Okay. I have to go to work," Anisa said. "I'll call you tomorrow." She paused. There was a below-the-surface panic in her tone. "And Franky, promise me something."

"What's that?"

"Don't do anything stupid for the next forty-eight hours."

He hung up without responding.

With mixed emotions—dread and elation—Anisa stared at the flight itinerary on her laptop. Quivering, her finger hovered above the Enter button. *He didn't promise. You have no choice.* She pressed it and completed the purchase.

A few hours later, perfunctorily processing customer purchases at the supermarket, Anisa couldn't help noticing that Helen, operating the cash register next to her, was on fire. She processed customers efficiently and effortlessly, ringing items up with such speed a few customers were raising eyebrows in awe.

And Helen, as if thrilled by her newfound gift of efficient intelligence, greeted customers with an unusually cheerful demeanor. She smiled more broadly than usual, exchanging well-meaning and sincere social pleasantries. Where normally she would drop the "How are you?" and "Have a great day," remaining deadpan and bored, now she exuded a happiness and joy that brought smiles and even laughter to customers. She positively beamed with delight.

How could anyone be that happy? Anisa wondered, for she was slipping into a pit of paranoia and fear. The initial elation of finding her brother, speaking to him, and actually making plans to see him had worn off. Dread had elation on the ropes and Anisa struggled to find the punch combination that would turn the tables and knock out dread. *No wonder Helen's happy. Her arch-enemy is dead. Murdered. Who did it?* They had scoured Helen's apartment and were unable to find any obvious evidence that Helen had murdered Ray. But maybe she had concealed the evidence in her blackout.

After all, Helen had prayed for his death, and in her worship-induced frenzy, she'd wanted to kill him. And there was an unremembered period of time in which she indeed could have committed the murder. A blackout. Didn't people commit murder all the time in a real, imagined, or fabricated zombie-like state? The birth of the insanity plea. But Helen didn't come off as insane or as a liar. And Anisa doubted Saint Death had such a vengeful nature as to propel Helen to such a murderous act. But if Helen didn't do it, then who did?

The method of murder was one that made Anisa's blood run cold. Decapitated with a scythe. Saint Death's scythe? Helen was praying to the saint of death shortly before, during, or shortly after the death of Ray. Anisa remembered her nightmare of a scythe-wielding Grim Reaper mercilessly decapitating a helpless victim. Then, later, recognizing the murderer's voice: Her brother. Too many coincidences that felt far removed from coincidence. Anisa shivered. *What the hell's going on?*

She knew little of Franklin since his abrupt departure twenty years ago. Had he become a cold-blooded killer? Was he killing in the name of Saint Death? Was he perverting the religion to suit his own needs? *And here I am going to see him. What am I doing, walking into the lion's den? No, he's in trouble. He's your brother. You can save him.* But that didn't reassure her.

Maybe she didn't know as much about her newfound religion as she'd thought. Maybe she didn't know as much about Helen as she'd thought. Was the rape story just a red herring to mitigate the murder of Ray? She didn't know. The whirlwind of confusing thoughts creased the corners of her mouth downward.

Helen touched her arm gently. "Come on," she said cheerily. "The replacements are here. It's lunch time."

They crossed Main Street and found a quiet picnic table at Montague Waterfront Marina. The Montague River straddled the picturesque town and the marina was one of its main attractions, offering a bar, restaurant, monkey bars for kids, abundant greenery and scenery, and boats of all shapes and sizes.

Picking at a taco salad and sipping coffee, Anisa cut through the small talk and got to the point. She wanted another read on her friend to assuage her doubts, although she wasn't sure that was possible. Due to her sensitivity for Helen's precarious emotional state after learning of Ray's murder earlier, Anisa had not questioned her on the alleged rape. But now that Helen appeared to be flowering with happiness and joy, Anisa thought it would be a good time to get some answers. A thought crept into her mind: maybe she wanted to bring Helen down to her own level of misery. But she brushed that aside.

She didn't know how to say it gently, so just came right out with it. "You say Ray raped you?"

A frown creased Helen's joyful countenance. "Yes, he did."

Anisa studied Helen's face for a sign of deceit. She didn't find one. "We don't have to talk about it if you don't want to."

But it seemed like Helen wanted to get it off her chest. "I call it rape, but maybe sexual assault is a better term. I don't know if can be considered actual rape since he didn't penetrate me. And I didn't perform any sex acts on him. It happened in the eleventh grade. I stayed late one day at school, helping to decorate the gymnasium for the fall dance. Anyway, time ran away from me and I suddenly realized it was past eleven. I started home. I was going to take my usual route, but I thought my mom might be worried about me. So I took a shortcut through a wooded area."

Anisa noticed Helen was speaking with a swiftness of tongue previously unknown to her friend. "That's when it happened?"

"He must've been hiding behind a tree or something. He came at me from behind and tackled me to the ground, started tearing my dress off, real rough-like."

"You could identify Ray in the dark?"

"Not really. It was what he said to me as he was fondling my boobs."

"What did he say?"

Helen took a deep breath and exhaled slowly, but her matter-of-fact expression never changed, as if Ray's death had buried the emotional scars forever. "He said, 'You might not be the brightest lightbulb, but you've got the biggest set of headlights I've ever seen.' And he laughed. That sickening laugh of his."

Anisa was starting to believe the story. "How did you get away?"

Helen's eyes went dull, conveying an eerie unfeeling nothingness. "I tried to gouge his eyes. But he pushed my arms away. As he did, my hand found a rock, somewhere behind me. I thought it was God guiding me, but now I know better. It was Saint Death, come to my rescue. I picked up the rock and, with a strength I never knew I possessed, cracked him hard on the side of the head. It knocked him off. When I got up, I realized the rock was still in my hand. I could feel his warm blood on it. For a moment, a rage possessed me and I was gonna smash him over the head until I killed him. But I came to my senses and ran home. I climbed in my back window, showered and changed, and went out into the living room. My father was already in bed and my mother had fallen asleep on the couch in front of the television. I never told them. Never reported it. Never told anyone."

Although Anisa believed her friend, that belief did little to assuage her fears. *She's demonstrated she's capable of murder. But wouldn't it have been self-defense?* "Why not?"

"At first I didn't know. I was confused and hurt. I thought the story would get twisted and I would be found guilty. When I finally realized I should report it, another incident happened with Ray that definitely discouraged me."

"He threaten you?"

Helen nodded. "Came right up to me in the school cafeteria while I was having my lunch. Still had his head bandaged. Whispered in my ear."

"You remember what he said?"

"Word for word. I'll never forget it. I may be burying this thing, but when someone threatens to kill you, you never forget it. He said, 'You say a word, I'm gonna fuck you up... I'm gonna fuck you to death.'"

Anisa's face turned white and she tossed her plastic fork aside, giving up on the salad.

Helen had told the story as emotionlessly as if she were talking about an overdue utility bill. She put her hand on Anisa's knee. "Are you okay? You're as white as a sheet."

Anisa breathed deeply, trying to regain her composure, unsure about whether to tell Helen of her nightmare, the Grim Reaper's words—her brother's words—now resonating with a macabre irony that seemed much more than mere coincidence.

Helen's eyes focused intently on her friend. "You have something you wanna tell me?"

"I do," said a male voice from behind them.

Anisa started, lifting her hand to her face so quickly she clipped her plastic salad container, scattering the contents across the table and onto the grass.

Doctor Ricardo picked up the plastic container, retrieved the nearby fork, and placed them on the picnic table. "I'm sorry I startled you."

Helen offered a smile to the good doctor. "No problem. Good to see you."

Anisa's jaw dropped. She was more concerned about a reprimand than her wasted salad. She had lost her appetite anyway. "Doctor Ricardo. How are you?"

"Ladies," he said. "Good afternoon." He turned to Anisa. "You don't look so good. Are you all right?"

"I'm good," Anisa lied.

"How's Connor?"

"Better than ever. Thanks again."

"Do you mind if I sit for a moment?" He had already sat down across from them.

They shook their heads.

"Good to hear your boy is much better," he said, and then looked at Helen. "You're looking as bright as the beautiful sunshine. How is everything with you?"

"Never better," she said cheerfully. "I appreciate your help."

Doctor Ricardo clasped his hands together as if in prayer, and his eyes darkened. He ran a hand through his slicked-back black hair. "That's what I'd like to talk to you about. My help. You see, for the longest time, I've kept my religious beliefs to myself. Christianity is PEI's central religion. About ninety-three percent of our residents subscribe to some Christian denomination. It's practically split down the middle between Catholics and Protestants. PEI is one of the most religious provinces in Canada. I'm talking staunchly religious. A Bible belt, if you like." He stopped and his eyes passed quickly between both women, as if waiting for a comment.

"I used to be a Catholic," Helen said. "But not anymore."

Anisa knew he was going somewhere with this. She was sure it wouldn't be uplifting news. "Me too," she said quickly, wanting him to get to the point.

Doctor Ricardo continued. "Do you know I heard that in one small community here residents protested because school board officials introduced yoga into elementary school classrooms as part of the curriculum. The school board, rightly so, thought it would relax the students and bring them some inner peace, maybe help with concentration. But the protestors didn't agree. They claimed yoga was an affront to Christianity and some even said it was blasphemous and evil. I'm sure you know what the result was. It was banned from the elementary school in question. Can you believe it? Yoga, of all things."

"Here, I can believe it," Anisa said.

"If old-school Christians take such a radical stance against yoga, what do you think they'd do to me if they found out I worshipped Saint Death?" He didn't wait for an answer. "I've been running a successful practice here for many years. I'm a well-respected member of the community and I'd like to keep it that way." He looked at Anisa sternly. "When people make promises to me, I expect them to keep them."

"I only told Helen," Anisa said. "I'm sorry."

"I accept your apology," Doctor Ricardo said. "But Montague is a small town. Barely over two thousand people. The gossip grapevine here is more like a winery of whining.

Enough whining and I get blackballed from the community. I lose my practice. I love my job. I love making a real difference in people's lives. And I believe I have. Do you want me to get blackballed, lose my job, have my good reputation destroyed? All because I helped you?"

They shook their heads earnestly.

"I won't tell another soul," Anisa said, wondering what had leaked and where the leaks had come from. "I promise."

"I haven't told anyone," Helen said. "And I won't. Cross my heart and hope to die."

"Thank you," Doctor Ricardo said, suddenly looking much older. "Maybe I'm foolish to think people won't find out. Who am I trying to kid? This is Prince Edward Island. Most people know your business before you do. Probably know when your next bowel movement will be before you do... "

Helen laughed.

"Has something leaked out?" Anisa asked.

"I almost forgot," Doctor Ricardo said. "That's what started me thinking this way. Maybe I wouldn't have cared otherwise. After all, Saint Death saved Connor. Of that I'm convinced. And look at Helen here, now a confident and cheerful specimen of humanity as opposed to the frightened child with low self-esteem she once was. Why wouldn't I want to spread the good word? What should I care about my personal reputation, if I'm saving lives and bettering the lives of others? I'm a caregiver, after all. A healer. But then something occurred to me. What if people are perverting the religion of Saint Death to suit their own evil needs?"

Helen's face flushed slightly. Doctor Ricardo noticed. "I didn't immigrate to this country a long time ago to wreak death and destruction. I came here to help and heal."

He was flying into a tangent, and Anisa wanted to steer him back to his point. "Something leaked. What was it? Who was it?"

The doctor scratched his furrowed brow. "Right. I'm losing my train of thought. You ladies heard about the murder of Ray Minowest?"

They nodded and Doctor Ricardo gave them a long, interrogating look before continuing. "Murdered with a scythe. I'm sure you get the connection. Anyway, one of my patients told me the other day a reporter at *The Guardian* connected the scythe to Saint Death and is turning over stones here, trying to discover if there is an underground cult movement. Pardon my language, but he's a tenacious little shit, from what I hear."

"Holy shit," Anisa said. "This does have the potential to get out of hand."

Helen's face tightened. "Little bastard got what he deserves, you ask me."

"Did you know Ray?" Doctor Ricardo asked Helen.

"In high school. We were never friends. He wasn't a very nice boy and turned into an even worse man from what I hear."

"Did he ever do anything to harm you?"

"This is all confidential, right?"

"Of course."

"He tried to rape me in high school."

"Oh my God," Doctor Ricardo said. "You didn't kill him, did you?"

Helen shook her head uncertainly. "No. But I won't miss him."

Doctor Ricardo's face lost some of its color. "This goes back to what I said about perverting the good tenets of the religion of Saint Death... "

A middle-aged man with a white poodle on a leash walked past and they fell silent. He glanced at them perfunctorily, smiled, and tried to carry on, but the poodle had stopped, sniffing an old oak tree. The man waited patiently. The dog urinated on the tree, then squatted and took a shit. When the dog was finished, the man's face flushed, and he hurried along without looking at them, probably embarrassed because he did not have a plastic bag to scoop it up.

Doctor Ricardo looked at Helen. "I don't wanna know if you prayed for the death of Ray. The less I know, the better off we all are. It sounds like you had your reasons. And the rumors I've heard about his character certainly don't paint a picture of a morally upright, law-abiding citizen. But this is not how the worship goes, not from my understanding. If you wish for evil things, evil will befall you."

Anisa frowned.

A small, satisfied grin flashed across Helen's lips, but it was gone in an instant.

"I have to go to work now," Doctor Ricardo said. "One last promise, if you don't mind. I would like both of you to promise me you'll never worship Saint Death with evil intentions. Can you do that?"

CHAPTER ELEVEN

"I think we should report it."

"I don't think so," Natalie insisted.

It was two days after Natalie's attack. She and Terry reclined in a bed on a cliff outside the resort overlooking the beach.

They had been discussing the attack for the last twenty minutes, and Terry, although he had no proof, suspected Franklin was responsible. But if there had been any DNA evidence, it was long gone now. Immediately after the incident, Natalie had spent over an hour in the shower, scrubbing every inch of her body clean, before emerging scantily clad and apologizing to Terry for her angry and abrupt departure. His eyes had widened as he too apologized for his lies and his sexist views of women. And, in spite of his initial reluctance, the evening had ended with a bottle of champagne and a passionate lovemaking session. Although he had tried to insist she get some rest, those pleas hadn't lasted long. A stiff prick has no conscience.

Now, Terry bit his lip in frustration and looked at Natalie. "Don't you want to see the person responsible locked up?"

"Of course I do. But I don't know who did it. We have no hard evidence. I've read about what happens to rape victims down here. They can't get their cases to stick and usually they get even more victimized and traumatized by reporting them. And we're foreigners here. How do you think that would go over? Lawyers would milk us dry. And besides, I don't remember what happened. I honestly don't know who did this to me. Maybe I didn't even get raped. It's like my memory of it has been completely erased. Do you want me to lie to the police? Is that what you're telling me to do?"

"I guess not."

"Besides, didn't you pray to Saint Death for revenge? Why don't you let her deal with it? Look what she did to you. I've never seen a faster recovery from a double concussion. Even the bumps are gone. You're as good as new—better than new, if you ask me."

"It's nothing short of a miracle. And, yes, I did pray for justice. I suppose I wasn't prepared to report the assault on me. I guess we're both victims. You're right, honey, let's leave it in the hands of the skeleton saint. She'll mete out justice. She always does." Terry paused, leaned in closer to Natalie, and searched her deep blue eyes. "You sure you don't remember anything about the incident?"

Natalie shook her head quickly. "I remember walking around, processing our argument, and I reached the conclusion that I had acted immaturely. I was just about to return and apologize—I'd even planned some romance for us—when I was seized by this powerful force, like a black magic spell, that pulled me helplessly in another direction."

"What direction? You remember where you went?"

"Not really. I get some flashes of a dark apartment occasionally, but no landmarks to indicate where it might be." Then an image did pop into Natalie's head: the sweat-soaked face of Franklin grinning evilly, his black eyes boring into her soul as he thrust into her violently. And then she saw herself, mysteriously detached from her body, groaning in pain; but also moaning with pleasure. Bittersweet. She was horrified. *Oh my God. He fucked me. And I liked it. When Terry rescued me, I wanted more. Who does that? Screws a stranger and then soon after screws their fiancé? You're sick, girl. Something's wrong with you.*

Terry touched her arm. "Are you okay, honey? You lost your color. Are you remembering something?"

"I don't know." She did know, but didn't know how much to say. Then, it was as if the memory damn had burst and a painful childhood experience flooded into her mind. It was unrelated to Franklin. Or, maybe, in some strange way, it was. It involved her mother Melinda and her father Aaron. Even though she was only ten years old at the time, the traumatic scene materialized as vividly as if it had happened yesterday.

Her mother picked her up from choir practice and drove her home. It was December 20th, a bitterly cold and stormy day. They heard a pop upon entering the modest bungalow, the sound of a lightbulb shattering. Melinda screeched like a whimpering dog and dropped her bag of groceries. A carton of eggs broke and splattered on the hardwood floor. Melinda rushed to the bedroom. Without knocking, she swung open the door. Natalie was right behind her. Inside, Aaron stood shirtless, zipping up the fly of his jeans. Behind him, a young woman, holding half of her clothes in one hand and a wad of bills in the other, was climbing out the window. She had evidently knocked over a table lamp in her haste.

"It's not what you think, honey," Aaron said.

Melinda's face tightened, veins bulging in her neck. It was the first and last time Natalie had ever heard her mother swear. "Get out of this house now, you lying, cheating, fucking bastard. I never want to see you again."

That was the last time Natalie ever saw her father, and she'd never forgiven him. She never found out who the young woman was, although later Natalie realized she was probably just a transient prostitute. Natalie lost her male role model that day, and a part of her mother had also died. Melinda never dated after that, and never spoke of the incident, other than to tell Natalie repeatedly "men are all liars and are not to be trusted."

Maybe she had blocked it all out, but for the first time Natalie began to realize why she was the way she was. And she wasn't that happy about it. *No wonder you have trust issues with men. It's more than just Rex. It's your entire fucking upbringing.*

"Natalie, come back. If you don't wanna talk about it, you don't have to right now." Terry touched her shoulder gently.

She had a brief impulse to recoil but it passed and she hugged him tightly. "I'm sorry. I need some time to process this. Can we talk about it later?"

An hour later they found themselves on the Puerto Plata *malecon*. It was a bright and sunny afternoon, and they'd decided a day-trip away from the resort was what they needed. They had taken a taxi from the resort and gotten off at one end of the *malecon*, with the intention of walking clear to the other end and stopping at Route 66, a quiet little beachfront bar where they'd heard the food and ambiance were relaxing and pleasant. They strolled hand-in-hand along the beachfront boardwalk, commenting on the sights and sounds, trying to put the past in the past and concentrate on the here-and-now.

"I know about as little about your past as you do about mine," Natalie said. "But for now, maybe we should leave it there. I don't feel like dragging up a bunch of painful scars, do you?"

"No, not right now. My aim is to make you happy and be honest with you."

The word "honest" reverberated in Natalie's mind. Terry had asked about what she remembered and she had said she didn't know. But she *did* know, at least part of it, and she wanted to tell him, if not the whole truth then most of it—just not right now. An omission couldn't be considered a lie, could it? Everything was too fresh and painful, and she did need time to process it. She squeezed his hand. "Let's just have fun today and keep it light. No drama."

Out of nowhere, two motorcycles jumped the sidewalk curb and roared toward them.

Terry pulled Natalie toward the beach. "What the hell are they doing?"

It all happened so fast. A motorcycle skidded to a stop dangerously close to them, and a dark-skinned young man climbed off the back of the bike, approached Terry, and pointed a gun to his head, his other hand gesturing for Terry to empty his pockets.

The other bike stopped and another dark-skinned man climbed off the back, rushed up to Natalie and pointed a gun to her head, gesturing for her purse. They couldn't be older than eighteen. Natalie quickly handed her purse over to the man, who tossed it over to his driver accomplice on the motorcycle.

Motorcycles and cars passed without stopping. Pedestrians, while giving the robbery scene a wide berth, were deliberately oblivious.

In a harsh tone, the man said something to Terry in Spanish, which neither he nor Natalie understood. Terry was frozen to the spot, but refused to empty his pockets. The man moved closer, bringing the gun barrel a few inches from his head. Terry clenched his fists.

"What are you doing?" Natalie said. "Give him your wallet."

The man who had just stolen Natalie's purse stepped closer to her, forcefully pressing the gun barrel right between her eyes. It was hot to the touch and she winced. In a commanding tone, he said something in Spanish and eyeballed Terry menacingly.

"Terry, give him your fucking wallet," Natalie said, her tone tinged with fear. "Now!"

A flash of anger lit Terry's eyes for a moment, but it was replaced by concern for his fiancé's life. He reached into his pocket and flipped the robber his wallet. The robber tossed it to his driver accomplice, who deposited it into a small knapsack hanging from the handlebars. With lightning speed, the robbers climbed onto their respective motorcycles and sped away.

Waving his hands, Terry started shouting to passing vehicles, "We've been robbed. Help! We've been robbed."

Natalie touched the spot on her forehead where the gun barrel had been pressed. With her index finger, she circled the red imprint it had left. Then she fainted.

Terry rushed over and bent down, cradling her head in both hands. "Natalie!"

A young woman ran over and knelt down beside Natalie, who had landed at an odd angle, with her right leg and right arm trapped underneath her fallen body. The young woman reached for a leg, as if intending to straighten it into a more natural position, but then stopped, seemingly reconsidering. "What happened?" she asked.

Beads of sweat were popping on Terry's forehead. "We've been robbed. I think she fainted."

"Oh my God," the woman said, her dark eyes registering deep concern. "What can I do?"

Terry grabbed Natalie's left arm and pointed to a palm tree on the beach. "Could you help me get her into the shade?"

When they had Natalie propped up against a palm tree, Terry checked her neck for a pulse, which he confirmed she had. The woman produced a bottle of water and offered it to Terry. "Maybe this will help."

Terry took it and splashed water on Natalie's face and hair. They watched her eyes flutter for a moment, close, flutter again, and then open. "What happened?" she asked.

"You fainted," Terry said. "We've been robbed."

"I remember being robbed. I don't remember fainting."

A half hour later they sat under an umbrella at a plastic table in Route 66, facing the beach. It was the quiet part of the *malecon* with less vehicular traffic and fewer pedestrians. They had the bar to themselves and were sipping cold white wine, generously paid for the by the woman.

"I'm sorry," Natalie said after a sip of wine "I'm still a little dizzy. What did you say your name was again?"

"Anisa."

"Right. And you're staying at Lifestyles?"

"That's right. Got in two days ago."

"Well, we were supposed to leave in another week, but I don't think we can now."

"Why not?" Terry asked.

Natalie looked embarrassed. "My passport was in my purse."

"Oh shit," Anisa said. "Do you have a copy at the hotel?"

Natalie nodded. "I only had cash and the passport in the purse as far as valuables go. Maybe two hundred dollars. I have other ID and credit cards in the room safe."

"Well, if you have other ID and the photocopy of your passport, the Canadian Embassy should be able to get you a temporary passport pretty quick," Anisa said. "I don't know, but I would imagine."

"I hope so," Natalie said. "I gotta get back to work." She turned to Terry. "What about you? I'm sure you weren't stupid like me, carrying your passport around."

"You weren't stupid, honey. You couldn't know we'd get robbed. I had a credit card and a bank card and about three hundred bucks. I got another credit card and bank card at the room. But I'm gonna have to cancel those cards, and fast."

"Are you guys gonna report it to the police?' Anisa asked.

"I don't know," Natalie said. "Why don't we have another drink and discuss it? We'll pay you back when we get to the hotel. I'm still a little rattled and need some time to think."

"That's not a problem," Anisa said. She held up three fingers to the bartender. "Canadians help Canadians, right? That's what we do."

Three glasses of wine arrived at the table.

"I think we should report it," Terry said. "It might make things easier at the embassy if you have a police report."

"I don't think it matters," Natalie said. "I could just say I lost it. I'm Canadian. They'd still have to issue me a new one. And we're not gonna get anything back, that's for sure."

"I doubt they'd even catch the criminals," Anisa said, remembering Franklin's warnings. "Not from what I've been told, anyway."

"For now, let's forget about reporting it, then," Terry said. "We should get back to the hotel. I gotta cancel my cards and you've got your passport photocopy there. If there's still time, maybe we can get to the embassy this afternoon."

Anisa ordered the bill. There was something troubling her that was just starting to come into focus. It wasn't necessarily anything her brother Franklin had said over the last two days. It was more what he hadn't said. He had been vague when Anisa asked him what he did for a living, vague about what he did to amuse himself, and evasive late this morning when he'd dropped her off at the *malecon*. "I've got some unfinished business" was all he offered when she asked him what his plans were for the day. Sure, the reunion had been warm and hospitable enough; big hugs and big smiles; remembering some of the good times growing up (Anisa deliberately avoided mentioning the family deaths for fear of alienating Franklin); and two dinners together. But Anisa only had two weeks here, and Franklin was leaving her alone for blocks of time and refusing to allow her inside his apartment. "It's a mess. You can see it when I have a chance to clean it." What the hell was he hiding? So far, Anisa hadn't pressed the matter. But she decided she was going to find out, even if it meant sneaking around behind his back. Which reminded her. It was almost three pm, and Franklin had said he'd be finished by then and would pick her up if she wanted.

The waitress came with the bill and Anisa paid it.

Natalie stood. "Thanks again. We should get going. It hasn't been the best start to the day."

"I can call my brother," Anisa offered. "I wanna get going myself. He'll pick us up. We're in the same hotel anyway."

"It's okay," Natalie said. "We don't wanna wait. We'll take a taxi. Oh—what am I talking about? We don't have any money for a taxi."

For reasons she didn't understand at the time—maybe she thought they would think Franklin a weirdo—Anisa offered to go with them in a taxi.

Natalie agreed, under the condition that Anisa join them for dinner and drinks at the resort the next evening. "And I'll bring you some money for your trouble."

"I'm not worried about twenty or thirty dollars," Anisa said, even though she was paying for her vacation using a credit card cash advance.

The waitress called a taxi. It wasn't long before a white, air-conditioned mini-van picked them up in front of Route 66. On the way home, Natalie and Anisa exchanged contact information and chatted about their impressions of the DR.

"I liked it at first," Natalie said. "But because of the shit that's been happening to us, I wanna go home as soon as possible."

"You mean the robbery?"

"That's not the only thing." A long pause.

"You don't have to tell me if you don't want to."

Natalie looked at Terry, who had remained silent during the trip. "Should I?"

"Up to you, honey."

"Terry was assaulted on the dance floor at a disco in our hotel. Kicked square in the jaw and knocked out—all because he tried to save me from some asshole who forced me out onto the dance floor and wouldn't let go of me. Basically the guy was assaulting me on the dance floor, towing me around like a Raggedy Anne doll."

"That's terrible. Did you report it?"

Natalie shook her head. "No. Didn't think it would change anything, I guess. Maybe we're just scared of repercussions. I don't know."

"But you got a good look at the guy?"

"Oh yeah. We ran into the creep first at the beach. Got his name too?"

The taxi stopped in front of the hotel entrance. Anisa paid the driver and they got out.

"What's his name?" Anisa asked.

"Don't know his last name. First name is Franklin."

"I'll see you later." Spinning around quickly in an attempt to conceal her chalk-white face, Anisa hurried back to her room, locked herself inside, and took many long and deep breaths before she felt her heart rate beginning to slow.

CHAPTER TWELVE

Against her better judgment, Anisa walked along the beachfront road, on her way to visit her brother. After she'd calmed down she ordered room service, a chicken salad with sides of rice and beans, but only found the appetite to eat a third of it. She'd reached Franklin on the phone and he'd agreed to pick her up in two hours to go for a drink. However, she couldn't wait any longer. She had her reasons for wanting to surprise him. She'd escaped the hotel in stealth mode, not wanting to be seen by Terry and Natalie. Had they put the pieces together? She didn't know, but if they hadn't, surely it wouldn't be long. She tossed images of her nightmare in PEI around in her mind, trying to arrange the significance. Was it Franklin who was in danger, or was it his victims? Or both?

Approaching his apartment, she saw his black Bronco parked in the parking lot and weaved her way around it. At the foot of the stairs, she felt a tap on her shoulder and almost jumped out of her skin. She was strung pretty tightly right now. She spun around and a fat Dominican woman holding a dripping garden hose greeted her with a smile. The woman's teeth were crooked and decayed, her oversized white t-shirt wet and dirt-stained. Her black hair was tied down in a bun, but strands of it poked out in a sort of hair-halo, as if struggling for divine sovereignty. "You go visit Franklin?" she asked, her deep brown eyes probing.

Anisa tried a smile. "Yes. He's my brother."

"I see. You have same eyes."

"He's home, I presume."

"He home, but he no like visitors."

Anisa began climbing the stairs. "Well, I'll see about that." She stopped at the top of the stairs and glanced back at the woman, who stood watching her.

"Be careful," the woman said. She drew circles on the side of her head with her index finger. "He not always good. Sometime, he hate me."

Anisa approached the sliding-glass door and peered in through a crack in the improvised curtain. It was dark inside but for the soft glow of a candle. She stood there for a moment, but other than the candle's glow, couldn't discern any other details, or hear any sounds inside. Starting to feel like a deranged stalker, she knocked.

The door slid open. "What the f... sis, how are you?"

"Sorry, I was getting bored in the hotel."

"Give me a minute." He slid the door shut and she heard rummaging around inside for a minute and a living room light went on before he returned. He slid the door open and stepped out onto the balcony. He pointed to a wicker chair. "Would you like a seat?"

"Can I come inside?"

"Sure, I just picked a few things up in case you said that. Didn't want you to see a mess."

She went in and sat down on the couch, surveying the apartment while Franklin fixed drinks. Far from what she thought, it was meticulously arranged, although missing a woman's touch. Two black end tables and a black coffee table complimented a three-piece brown leather couch set. Oil paintings of beach scenery dotted the walls and the open-concept kitchen was neatly arranged, with not a single dirty dish. Kitchen table and chairs were black, modest, but comfortable-looking with brown leather-like cushions. One of the end tables had a lamp on it while the other was barren with only a few drops on it. Candle wax was Anisa's best guess.

"Cuba libre okay?"

"Fine. Not too strong."

He returned with the drinks and took an armchair beside the couch. "Don't worry, I don't pour them strong. I hardly drink. It's only because you're here that I'm indulging a bit. I never got a chance to ask you. How was your day?"

"Franky, I'm not here to mince words. I only have a couple weeks and I don't have time to go around pretending that everything is okay."

He sat back in his chair and sipped his drink. "What does that mean?"

Anisa sipped her drink and set it on the coffee table. *Tell it straight, but choose your words carefully.* She recounted running into two tourists who had just been robbed. "Their names are Terry and Natalie. And she says you assaulted her and her fiancé on the dance floor at the Lifestyles disco. Brother, what are you doing? Have you lost your mind? *That's not carefully.*

She watched his face muscles tense and then relax. It took a moment for him to respond. "Sis, I never said I was perfect. I was having a bad day and got really drunk."

"So, you're not denying it."

"No. I don't know what she told you but, I was just dancing with her. Yeah, maybe a little forcefully, but I thought she was into it. And that thing with Terry was self-defense. He attacked me on the dance floor. I was just defending myself."

"I was told a slightly different version of events. Basically, that you assaulted both of them."

"Who are you gonna believe, sis? Me or some strangers?"

"I don't know. You're like a stranger to me. Disappearing for long periods of time. And I just got here. I thought we'd spend more time together."

"We will. I promise. Do they know you're my sister?"

"I don't know."

"What does that mean?"

"When I asked them the name of the guy who assaulted them, they said it was you. But I didn't tell them we're related or that I even know you. But they may have been able to figure that out from the look on my face."

"It doesn't matter," Franklin said.

"What does that mean?"

Franklin frowned. "I mean, I don't care if they find out. I was wrong. I'll apologize to them. Is that what you want me to do? Tell me what to do? I don't know what to do. I don't want to be mean, but sometimes I do mean things. I want to be good, but sometimes I can't control myself. Tell me what to do. Please."

"I don't know if they want an apology. When they find out we're related, they may want nothing to do with either of us. I'm supposed to meet them tomorrow night for drinks. I could ask them."

"Maybe I could help them," Franklin said. "You said they were robbed by two *motoconchos*. I know of those guys. They've been terrorizing tourists for a while. They're known by the cops. Maybe I could get Natalie's passport back."

Anisa asked the question even though she knew the answer. "Isn't that better left to the cops?"

"We talked about that before. The cops are probably in cahoots with them. No. That makes no sense. I know who those fuckers are and I know just how to get her passport back. Maybe not the credit cards and cash, but the passport."

"That could be dangerous."

Franklin grinned. "Danger is my middle name, sis."

Anisa thought of trying to dissuade him from Mission Passport Recovery, but she couldn't. This was her brother trying to make amends for his sins. Even if it didn't win the favor of Natalie and Terry, how could she tell him not to try and make things right? He was trying to change. There were other things she wanted explanations for, but she felt like right now was not the time. She had made some kind of a breakthrough, and that was what she had come here for.

"Well, if you think you could get the passport back, I'm sure Natalie would appreciate it. And I think apologizing to them is a good idea. Whether they're willing to forgive you or not, that's not something you can control. But at least you can say you tried."

"It would make me feel a whole lot better," Franklin said. "Call me tomorrow night when you meet them. I hope to have it by then."

"Okay. Where are we going tonight?"

"I thought we'd go to Ocean World for a few drinks. Karaoke tonight. You much of a singer?"

"Too much of a chicken, I think."

"Oh, a few more drinks will give you some liquid confidence. You ready?"

They arrived at Ocean World's terrace bar early and found a private table overlooking the ocean. As they drank beer, a few customers floated in and sat down, many taking seats close to center stage near the karaoke microphone and multiple television screens.

Anisa had peeked into Franklin's bedroom prior to leaving and noticed a white towel that had been haphazardly draped over something, concealing everything but an outline of its shape. *Some sort of a statue. Of what?* Well, she wasn't in Montague anymore, and she was sure Doctor Ricardo's warning only applied there. She doubted her brother would be heading to Prince Edward Island anytime soon, if ever. A little gentle probing wouldn't hurt.

"Are you still a Christian?" she asked.

Franklin's black eyes became intent. "Not really."

"What do you mean? Either you are or you aren't."

"I'm not. What about you?"

"Not anymore. After my son got sick and was miraculously cured, I started practicing another religion."

Franklin had been glancing sideways at incoming customers. Now he looked directly at her. "Really? What's that, then?"

"Have you ever heard of Santa Muerte? Saint Death?"

"You're kidding me, sis. You mean we're practicing the same religion?"

"If you're saying you worship Saint Death, we certainly do."

"I do. For about five years now. I don't imagine that's a big hit in the Bible belt of Montague."

"I'm trying to keep it quiet. I don't want to be branded a heretic and tarred and feathered."

"Well, it's pretty old-school fundamentalism back there. What made you bring it up?"

"I saw a covered statue in your bedroom. I thought the outline looked like Saint Death."

"It *is* Saint Death. I hid her because she's not always well-received by non-believers. I didn't want you to think your brother was a devil-worshipper or something real crazy."

"Well, you don't have to worry about that now. You can bring her out in the open."

"I'm sure she'd like that."

A woman got up, took the mic, and began singing "Love Is In The Air" by John Paul Young.

"What changed for you, Franky? What made you start believing in Saint Death?"

He finished his beer, waved over a waiter, and ordered two more. He waited for the waiter to place the drinks on the table before continuing. "As a kid, it didn't help me to pray to God, Jesus, or even any of the canonized saints in the Catholic religion. They didn't answer my prayers."

"I know." Anisa couldn't be sure in the suffused light, but she thought she saw his eyes glaze over for a second or two.

"You *know* what happened, sis. Everyone around me started dying. Dad, our two brothers. I used to pray to Jesus to keep our family safe long before Dad died. God didn't listen, so I began reading up on other types of religions. I stumbled across Saint Death and have been hooked ever since."

"Why did you run away, Franky?"

"I began to think I was jinxed by the devil. Everyone around me was dying. I thought if I stayed, you'd be next, Mom would be next, or maybe I'd be next."

"I'm still here."

"You're the only one left. I'm sorry Mom's dead. I'm sorry I never kept in touch, but I was convinced if I did contact you guys, someone would die. I thought for a long time that I was cursed, until Saint Death showed me otherwise."

"Tell me, Franky, what kinds of things do you ask Saint Death for?"

There was a long pause before he answered, and Anisa knew. It terrified her.

"I've prayed for you," he said. "That you live a long and prosperous life. That you fulfill your goals. That you find love and happiness."

Anisa knew there was more. If he had prayed for someone's death, and they had indeed died, did she really want the details right now? Maybe a warning would suffice. "I appreciate that. I just want to tell you, I have a doctor friend in Montague, the man who introduced me to the religion. He's studied Saint Death extensively and comes from the part of Mexico where it's said to have originated. He warned me. If you pray to Saint Death for evil things, evil will befall you. I hope you're not doing that."

"I wish I could say I haven't. But I can't."

Franklin's matter-of-fact answer surprised Anisa. "Well, stop it. Please."

"I'll try, sis. I'll try."

"Don't try, do it."

"Okay."

Anisa thought his quick answer was more of an attempt to placate her rather than an affirmation of good intentions. It was probably time to change the subject anyway. "Who's that woman I saw around your building? She a caretaker?"

"The fat, ugly one? Rotten teeth?"

"Well, she has rotten teeth and she is overweight. But beauty is in the eye of the beholder so I'm not gonna call her ugly."

"That's Niamia. She *is* a caretaker. Bat-shit crazy."

"Well, she doesn't seem to think too highly of you." *Why did you mention that, you idiot?*

Franklin's posture stiffened. "Why? Did that bitch say something about me?"

Surely a white lie wouldn't hurt. Or an omission. "Not really. She just said you don't like uninvited guests."

"How did she know you *weren't* invited? Nosy bitch. You're my sister, for fuck sakes."

"Calm down, please. She isn't worth getting bent out of shape about."

Franklin squinted. "Well, she pisses me off. She's constantly renting out my private parking stall... has all these stupid businesses going that cause non-stop disruptions around the building."

"Not tonight, Franky. Can we enjoy ourselves? Please?"

And for the next two hours they managed to do that. Franklin continued to nurse his beer, while Anisa switched to Cuba libres. She was beginning to consume them with a voracious appetite and the liquid confidence had indeed brought her up to the microphone for two songs. She sang a pretty good rendition of "Bad Moon Rising" by Creedence Clearwater Revival. It didn't seem to bother her that the lead vocalist was male, and it didn't bother the audience much neither. They clapped and hollered while she sang and even gave her a standing ovation when she finished.

Reaching for her drink, she sat down next to Franklin. "What do you think, bro?"

He had just finished clapping. "Excellent. How does a woman manage to sound like John Fogarty?"

"I don't know. I must be a little drunk."

"Is it your fifth Cuba libre?"

"I think so. But who's counting? Don't you want another drink?"

"No. I hate to spoil your good time, but I've got to go."

"You got a hot date?"

"I don't have a girlfriend."

"Maybe you should get one. Lots of beautiful women around here."

"Maybe I will."

The alcohol had loosened Anisa's lips. "You should. And I should get a boyfriend. I get real lonely sometimes. Don't you?"

"Occasionally." Franklin had other things on his mind right now. Earlier, he'd prayed to Saint Death for the death of Niamia, but now his sister's words had thrown him into an inner turmoil—a tug of war between malicious and beneficent forces. Should he leave the request out there and let the chips fall where they may, or try and reverse the petition to Saint Death? The issue was causing an inner confusion, a paroxysm of emotion. He waged an inner war with it for a moment before steering his thoughts onto a hopeful track, a track that offered some chance at redemption. The stolen passport. He had a pretty good idea where Carlos and Victor were right now, and he was certain they had it. It was just a question of retrieving it and then saving face with Natalie. Maybe he could truly win her affection instead of relying on preternatural forces. But time was of the essence. "Can I pay the bill now?"

Anisa reached for her drink, misjudged its distance, and tipped it slightly. Franklin's hand crossed the table with lightning speed and righted the glass before it could spill.

"You're fast, bro," she said.

"I like to stay in shape."

"I can see that."

Franklin paid the bill and helped his sister to the Bronco. Weaving to and fro, she thanked him and said how much she loved the Dominican Republic, and how good it felt to be reunited with him, and how good it felt to escape her mundane existence in Montague. He tried to say yes at the appropriate times, but the darkness had taken hold, and to keep it at bay, he had to focus on the immediate task at hand.

As they approached his apartment, his jaw dropped. Three cop pickup trucks and an ambulance were parked out front. The ambulance blocked half the street and he slowed to a crawl.

"Oh my God," Anisa said. "What happened?"

"I don't know."

But it didn't take long before they *did* know. As they were passing, a stretcher, guided by two men in white, rolled out on the road, stopping at the back doors to the ambulance. Franklin's first instinct was to floor it and high-tail it out of there. But a morbid curiosity made him stop and roll down the window. He recognized the blood-soaked face of Niamia instantly. Her brown eyes stared directly at him and her mouth hung open in a frightening grimace of pain. A large gash on her forehead oozed blood. Joy and sadness waged a war inside Franklin's head.

"Is she dead?" he asked an ambulance attendant.

The man swung open the ambulance doors and glanced at Franklin, business-like. "Quite. Fell down the stairs."

Fighting an urge to speed away, Franklin slowly rolled up the window and inched forward. A cop shot him a suspicious glance.

"Did you do that?" Anisa demanded as the Bronco pulled into the Lifestyles parking lot.

"No. We were in the bar. How could I?"

She seemed to have sobered up quickly. "You know damn well what I mean, brother."

"Listen," he said, his voice rising with agitation. "You're drunk. I don't want to talk about this now. Sleep it off. We'll talk in the morning."

But Anisa wouldn't let it go, the booze now fueling her anger. "What did she ever do to you? Sure, she's running some disruptive businesses, but that doesn't mean she should die, does it? Is she a criminal? Did she ever do anything to physically harm you? Tell me, Franky, who died and made you God? You think you can do this shit and it ain't gonna come back and bite you in the ass?"

He was a decibel short of shouting. "I told you we'll talk about it when you're sober. Now get out of the fucking vehicle. Right now." He jammed it into Park, stepped out quickly, rushed around to the passenger side, and opened her door. "Out, I said."

Remaining seated, she opened her mouth to speak, her anger beginning to rise with his—the beginnings of a nasty brother-sister battle. Franklin reached a hand in, about to remove her from the vehicle by force.

Before he could touch her, a hotel security guard rushed up behind Franklin. "Is there any trouble?" he asked. "Does someone need some help?"

Franklin spun around. "She's a guest here. And she's drunk. Help her to her suite, if you don't mind."

Anisa stepped out of the vehicle. "Don't lay a hand on me, any of you. I know where my room is and I'm perfectly capable of finding it by myself."

Looking confused, the security guard retreated a few steps.

Anisa walked purposefully toward the hotel entrance, the security guard following at a safe distance. She spun around after she heard the Bronco door close. Franklin sat in the driver seat with the window rolled down, watching her.

"I'm warning you," she said. "You fucking murderer. You fuck with Saint Death and Saint Death will fuck with you." She turned around and stomped off, clenched fists swaying at her sides.

Franklin's head was swirling with a maelstrom of emotion as he pulled away from Lifestyles. There was anger, sadness, and confusion boiling up inside him and he had to pull over to the side of the road and take stock of the conflicting emotions before he could continue. He sat silently for five minutes before he could even begin to process his thoughts.

Normally, he would have been elated after Saint Death had answered his prayers. But Anisa's warning rang hollowly in his head. *If I fuck with the Holy Saint, she's gonna fuck with me. But*

I'm not fucking with her; I love her. She's answering my prayers. No, you're perverting the tenets of the religion and payback will come. Swift and vicious. It's just a matter of time. Fuck, things are not going to plan.

The last thing he wanted to do was get in an argument with his long-lost sister, the only remaining member of his immediate family. He fished through his pocket and pulled out his cell phone to call Anisa and apologize. But halfway through punching in her number, he changed his mind and stuffed the phone back in his pocket. *She's drunk. And angry. Bad timing.* His thoughts drifted back to Natalie and the sensational lustful encounter he'd had with her. *She was under a spell. Saint Death's spell. That wasn't an evil prayer. We're meant to be together. I just have to change the strategy. Not forceful. Gentle. That's it.*

With a resolve bordering on desperation, he put the Bronco in Drive, shoulder-checked, and pulled out onto the highway. The night was dark, the traffic sparse. He turned right into an entry-way to San Marcos, an impoverished barrio, drove about eight blocks along a dusty and bumpy road and made a left, slowing as he ascended a steep hill leading into cloud-covered mountains. At the end of the undulating, pot-hole laden road, he pulled the truck to the left, parked, and turned off the ignition and lights. He looked over at the wooden shack with a corrugated tin roof and noticed with a small smile that a single incandescent lightbulb dangled in a window. Silently he climbed out of the vehicle, leaving the driver door ajar. Stepping around debris, he extracted his switchblade from his pants pocket, pressed open the blade and closed it again, tucking it into his upper shirt pocket. Just in case.

He knew Victor and Carlos all right, but maybe not in the way Anisa might have suspected. They were hired goons he used to threaten wayward hookers who had threatened to report him to the police for his occasional rough treatment of them. No, he never beat them up, but he had forcefully removed a few from his apartment when they got too comfortable. To him it was just a business transaction, but to them it often turned into an opportunity to falsely accuse him of a crime (rape, robbery, assault) in an attempt to extort money. He never asked Victor or Carlos what they did to deter the girls, and he didn't care. Maybe they beat them, but that was none of his business. He knew the two Dominicans robbed tourists on the side and he'd heard rumors they'd even killed a few. But, up to this point in his life, Franklin hadn't given a shit about that either.

He knocked on the door. Nothing. He pressed his ear to the door and could hear a faint hissing. White noise. He rapped again, louder.

A response, in Spanish: "Who is it?"

"It's Franky. Open up."

The door squeaked open. A skinny, shirtless man holding a bottle of rum stared at Franklin.

Recognizing the gently swaying man as Carlos, Franklin stepped inside, closing the door behind him. Outside a dog yelped, its whine fading into the night.

"You got another hooker problem?" Carlos asked.

Franklin surveyed the dump. Victor was passed out on a beaten couch, an empty rum bottle in his hand, closed eyes facing a hissing TV screen that danced with colored fuzz. "No, not a hooker. Another problem."

"You want a drink?" Carlos asked, retreating to a plastic chair beside the couch.

"No. I want a passport."

"What?"

"Don't play stupid with me. I'm in no mood for it. I know you steal passports and sell them to forgers. You picked the wrong victim. I want that passport back."

Carlos set the rum bottle down and leaped from his chair. He produced a handgun from behind his back and pointed it at Franklin's head. "You calling me stupid?"

"Listen. I don't want any trouble. Why do you want to ruin a good relationship? We work together. We're friends. Friends don't shoot one another. I'll pay you for the passport. The name is Natalie. You and Victor robbed her this afternoon on the *malecon*."

Carlos waved the gun to an empty plastic chair. "Sit down. Now."

It took all Franklin's reserves to keep himself from charging the man and bowling him over. He'd quickly sized up Carlos's state of inebriation, realizing in an instant he could probably overpower him and have the gun, or his switchblade, pointed at his neck. But his talk with Anisa earlier had infused him with a level of restraint. He calmly sat down. Victor stirred, burped loudly, and sank into a nasally snore.

His eyes sweeping over the littered coffee table in front of the snorer, Franklin saw the scattered passports—maybe six in total. "How much do the forgers pay for them?"

"One thousand pesos."

"I'll give you two."

"Make it three and you got a deal."

"You have it?"

"I think so."

"Check, please."

Carlos stood up and, still training the gun at Franklin, went through the passports on the coffee table. He flipped one to Franklin. "It says Natalie."

Franklin opened it, looked at the photo, and grinned. He reached into his pocket and Carlos cocked the hammer, moving closer. "No tricks."

"Please, I'm getting money."

"Okay. Get the money. This won't get reported. No cops. I'm not going to jail." Carlos stepped closer and leveled the gun barrel right between Franklin's eyes, maybe an inch away from making skin contact. "If I go to jail, you'll go to hell."

Franklin felt hot anger rise up his throat. He bit his tongue so hard to contain it, he drew blood. He opened his mouth, grinning blood-soaked teeth. "Put that gun down. We're friends here."

Franklin handed Carlos three thousand pesos. Carlos took the money, stuffed it in his back pocket, and backed away, lowering the handgun. He sat on the plastic chair. "You're right. We're friends." He picked up his rum bottle, took a long swig, and offered it to Franklin with a toothy grin. "You sure you don't want a drink?"

Franklin stood and tucked the passport in his shirt pocket, feeling the cold, comforting steel of the switchblade. "Next time, partner. And trust me, there will be a next time."

CHAPTER THIRTEEN

Anisa woke up with a pounding head and nervous anxiety, the kind of anxiety fueled by an alcohol-induced blackout. Most people remember the terrible anxiety the morning after a drinking binge: trying to put the pieces of the night-before puzzle together and as each one snaps into place, you begin to realize with a dread certainty that you said or did some things that are going to require an apology. Shame and regret drive the recollection effort further.

For Anisa, the pieces snapped slowly into place. An eye-opening conversation that demonstrated a sensitive and caring side to her brother Franklin. His remorse about doing bad things and the indication of a willingness to change. An enjoyable time at Ocean World terrace bar. *Damn, did I sing "Bad Moon Rising"? What was I thinking?*

Then she remembered seeing the dead woman Niamia, and the downward spiral thereafter. She remembered getting dropped off at the hotel, but struggled with the content of the conversation she'd had with her brother, although she vaguely remembered railing on him. *What did I say?* Then it hit her like a ball peen hammer upside the head. *"You fuck with Saint Death and Saint Death will fuck with you." But wait a minute, what's so bad about that? That's a true, albeit direct warning.*

As she climbed into the shower, something else hit her. Something she'd said before the warning. *"You fucking murderer." I called him a murderer? But he didn't physically kill Niamia. He was with me. Shit, I need to apologize.* She stepped out of the shower, changed into red shorts and a white cotton V-neck short-sleeved blouse, and combed out her long black hair. She picked up the remote and flicked on the TV, not seeing the news but instead thinking of today's plan: call Franklin and apologize, spend some time on the beach, and then later meet up with Natalie and Terry. Then she remembered. Franklin had offered to try and retrieve Natalie's passport. Is that what he'd done last night? Why hadn't she tried to talk him out of such a dangerous assignment?

She opened the mini-refrigerator and cracked open a bottle of cold water. She took two long gulps and then located two Extra-Strength Tylenol pills and washed them back with more water. She knew this was going to be a day filled with more drama, and she needed all the strength and equilibrium she could muster.

A half hour later, the thumping in her head had abated to a dull roar. She was just about to call Franklin and then go down for breakfast when there was a knock on the door.

She was surprised to see Terry.

"Oh, hi," she said.

"I need to talk to you," he said. He looked both ways down the hall as if he were being followed, and then stepped inside the room quickly. "Close the door."

She did. "What's wrong?"

"Sit down, please."

She sat on the bed and he sat in a nearby armchair. "Did you hear?"

"Hear what? Where's Natalie?"

"She's been a bit overwhelmed lately. She's in our room. She wants some time alone right now."

"Is she okay?"

"She'll be fine. The news this morning freaked her out."

"What news? What are you talking about?"

"The cops returned my wallet this morning. No cash, but my credit card and bank card were there."

"Wow, that's great news. What about Natalie's passport?"

"We don't have that yet. But there's something else."

Anisa's nervous anxiety upon waking returned full throttle. "What?"

"The cop I talked to spoke a little English. He said my cards were found in the home of two Dominicans wanted for robbing tourists. Both of them were murdered."

A terrible image of Franklin towering above decapitated victims wielding a bloody scythe popped into Anisa's mind. "How?"

Terry looked at the TV. "Oh my God, there it is."

Anisa looked at the screen. Two bloody victims lay on their backs on a blood-pooled dirt floor of a shanty shack. Their decapitated heads had been collected and placed neatly in the folded arms of each victim. Literally, they had their heads in their hands. She gasped, recognizing one of the faces from the *malecon*. "Oh... my... God... no."

Terry grimaced and covered his eyes with a hand. "You recognize them too. I know I do. They're the ones with the guns, not the driver accomplices." Terry opened the mini-fridge and grabbed a beer. "Do you mind?"

"Go ahead." Her stomach growled and she was tempted to sample a hair of the dog who'd ravaged her last night. *No, food first*. But she'd lost her appetite. "Grab me a water, please."

"Who do you think did it?"

"How would I know?" Anisa had her suspicions, but she wasn't about to make them public.

Terry sat on the bed beside her. She smelled the pleasant rosemary or caraway of his cologne, mixed with a hint of grapefruit. He pulled out fifty dollars and handed it to her. "For your help yesterday. Thank you."

Anisa waved a hand at him. "I don't want your money."

He stuffed it in her hand. "Take it. You were very helpful and calmed down Natalie quite a bit."

Anisa set it on the bed. "Thanks."

"There's something I want to ask you."

Anisa had a sense where this was going and she felt her neck muscles tense. "Ask away."

"Yesterday when we got back to the hotel, Natalie said something that made you go white. She told you the name of the guy who assaulted us. Do you remember?"

May as well come out with it. They're gonna find out anyway. "Franklin is my brother."

Terry sighed deeply. "After we got to our room, we discussed your reaction and came to that conclusion. We didn't know what to do at first. Natalie suggested completely disassociating ourselves from you, but I didn't think that was fair. You're nothing like him. I can tell. I wanted to give you a chance, that's why I'm here."

A cold chill crept up Anisa'a spine. "I was freaked out for sure. I didn't know what to say at the time. But I planned on telling you tonight after dinner."

"Well, you're not your brother, and I can understand your reaction. Natalie might be willing to see you again, but I doubt very much she wants to see your brother. I'm not sure I want to see him either—after he cold-cocked me the other night."

"Well, I don't blame you." Anisa's brow knotted in confusion as she tried to figure out how much to tell Terry. He seemed like a nice guy, but how would he react to news of the death of Niamia, her suspicions about the murderer of the *malecon* robbers, and her brother's obvious misuse of the religion of Saint Death? For all she knew, Franklin could be concocting nasty prayers to use against Terry and Natalie right now. She really needed to speak to him, and Terry's presence was only increasing her sense of urgency. Certainly mention of Mission Passport Retrieval would point accusing fingers at Franklin. But Anisa didn't even know if Franklin had Natalie's passport. Besides, in light of all the unexplained suspicious deaths lately, she certainly needed an ally. Did blood run thicker than water?

Terry touched her arm gently. The sensation was warm and pleasurable. "Are you okay?"

It gave her confidence to continue. "I was with Franklin last night at Ocean World. I told him I met you guys on the *malecon* and about the robbery. I also confronted him about what he did to you and Natalie."

"I haven't told you all my suspicions."

"In a minute, please."

"Sorry, go ahead."

"He was very remorseful about what happened. He wants to apologize." She said it in spite of her reservations. "He offered to try and get Natalie's passport back, as sort of a goodwill gesture or a peace offering."

"When did he say that?"

"Last night."

"Oh shit. You don't think he killed the robbers, do you?"

"Honestly, it crossed my mind."

"Do you think he has her passport?"

"I don't know. I haven't spoken to him today. I need to."

"Well, fuck it. If he has it, I'll take it. I don't know if Natalie wants to see him, but I'll meet him and get the passport. If he wants to apologize to me for what he did, that's fine. And I'll pass his apology on to Natalie if that's what he chooses to do. I googled a news story in English about those robbers. They were both suspected of murdering at least three tourists. Fuckers could have killed us. Now that I think about it, if Franklin did kill them, maybe they deserved to die."

After they'd exchanged phone numbers, Anisa said, "I'm gonna call Franklin soon. If he has the passport, maybe we can meet in the main dining room at seven tonight. If Natalie doesn't want to come, that's her choice."

"I have a better idea," Terry said. "No offense, but I'm not sure I want to have dinner with your brother. Why don't we meet tonight at eight at Juan's Calmado, just up the road? Cheap beer and a nice ocean view. We'll make the plan regardless of whether he has the passport or not."

"What about Natalie? Don't you have to confirm it with her?"

"I suppose you're right. Tell you what. After you talk to your brother, why don't you meet us on the beach for a drink, early afternoon? By yourself. If Natalie doesn't want to see your brother and she doesn't want me to, I should respect that. I wasn't thinking. But, if he has her passport, we will want to get it back. We haven't had a chance to go to the embassy yet."

Anisa agreed and Terry went to the door.

"Wait," Anisa said. "What did you say about your other suspicions about my brother?"

"Maybe later," Terry said. "Natalie swore me to secrecy. See you later."

After breakfast, Anisa felt a little better. Still tired, confused, and a little frightened, but better. Franklin picked up on the first ring.

"I'm sorry about last night," she said. "I had way too much to drink."

His tone sounded sad and remorseful. "I'm sorry too, sis. I lost my temper. I shouldn't have done that."

"Forgotten?"

"Forgotten."

"Behind us?"

"Behind us."

"Good. Did you get the passport?"

"Cost me three thousand pesos, but yeah, I did."

A palpable fear caused the bacon, eggs, hash browns, and juice to churn in Anisa's stomach and rise up her esophagus. She tasted an acidy lump, and with some effort swallowed it down. "Did you see the news?"

"No, I just got in from my swim in the ocean. Did three miles today."

"The robbers are dead, Franky. Decapitated. Tell me you had nothing to do with it."

After a pause, he said, "I don't think we should be having this conversation on the phone, sis, but no, I didn't kill them."

"Are you sure?"

"When I left them, they were both alive. One was passed out drunk, the other was close to being passed out drunk. I swear to Saint Death."

While Anisa had her doubts, she knew he was right. She needed to see his face when she asked such a question to try and determine if guilt was written all over it. "Why don't we meet for a coffee at the Mexican restaurant next to your place?" After Niamia's untimely death, Anisa no longer wanted to set foot in Franklin's apartment.

"Is one hour okay? I need to shower."

"See you then."

She hung up and called Terry. He picked up on the first ring. She skipped the social niceties. "He has Natalie's passport and says he had nothing to do with the murders." She wasn't yet prepared to mention Niamia and her certainty that Franklin had prayed for it. Never mind the murder of Ray Minowest, either perpetrated by Helen or a result of her prayers to the skeleton saint.

"That's good. I'm at the beach having a drink with Natalie... He's got your passport, honey... She's cool if you want to join us for a drink later on."

"Is she feeling better?"

"Yeah. And we'll meet you at Juan's tonight at eight."

"I'll text you later about the drink on the beach. We're definitely on for eight tonight at Juan's though."

"Okay."

CHAPTER FOURTEEN

Franklin looked lost and disoriented, but he did not look like a murderer. He and Anisa were sipping café lattes on the patio of Los Charros y Los Pinches Chaparros, a Mexican Restaurant right next door to Franklin's apartment building. Anisa had begun the meeting by apologizing again for her behavior the night before, and Franklin had repeated his own apology.

Anisa searched his eyes, looking for a tell, some kind of indication that he was guilty. She couldn't find anything. Either he was a master of deception, or just plain innocent. But that was a first impression; she hadn't begun to question him about his relationship with the thugs, how he'd managed to find them, and what kind of trouble may have occurred during the passport extraction. There was no time like the present.

"So you just paid three thousand pesos, got the passport, and left?"

His eyes dimmed. His face was a mask of disapproval. "You don't believe me?"

"I didn't say that."

"I went to their house. One of them pulled a gun on me. But I got him calmed down and bought the passport and left. I went straight home to bed after that."

But Anisa saw some confusion in her brother's eyes. The same confusion she'd seen in Helen's eyes after learning about the murder of Ray Minowest. Had Franklin blacked out and murdered the robbers? Was he struggling to paint a comprehensive picture from a sketchy memory? "You remember everything clearly?"

"I wasn't drunk, sis. Maybe you don't recall, but I only had two beers last night. Didn't even drink half of that Cuba libre before we left."

"How do you know those guys?"

"They've actually helped me before. I hope you don't judge me too harshly, but I had a hooker stalker who was relentless. Don't worry, she was legal age and everything. She got pissed off at me and threatened to trump up some fake charges and go running to the police—an extortion attempt. It happens all the time down here. I didn't know what to do so I hired Carlos and Victor to dissuade her from that and to keep her away from me. I don't know what they did, but it worked."

She didn't like where this was going. "Maybe they killed her?"

"No, I ran into her at the supermarket the other day. She made brief eye contact but that was it. Didn't bother me at all."

"What about the cops, Franky? If you went to their house to get the passport, maybe someone saw you."

"I don't think so. It was dark and late. I didn't see anyone around."

"Do you have any idea who did it?"

"No. But did you know they were wanted in connection with the murder of three tourists?"

"I did know." She blurted it out without thinking. "Terry told me."

"Terry?"

"Yeah, the guy you cold-cocked. Remember?" Anisa didn't know why she was being so confrontational. Perhaps it bothered her more now that she had gotten to know Terry a little better and she liked him. His words echoed in her mind. *"I haven't told you all my suspicions."*

"Oh, right. Did you tell them I have Natalie's passport?"

Funny that he would remember Natalie's name and not Terry's. What did he do to her? Later, let's see how they interact together. That'll speak volumes. "Yes, and they've agreed to meet us at Juan's tonight at eight if that's okay with you. You can apologize then if you want and give her passport back."

Franklin's face lit up. "That's great, sis. Thanks for arranging that. I *do* want to apologize. Juan's is perfect."

Anisa still felt the residual fatigue from her bender last night and decided it was time for a nap. The missing details were troubling, but other domestic concerns began pressing into her mind. She needed to check in on Connor and give Helen a call. She wanted to know if everything had settled down after the drama just prior to her departure. A call to Doctor Ricardo wouldn't hurt. He seemed to have a priest's insight into the worship of Saint Death. It might be a good idea to get some more advice from the man. Then, if there was still time, maybe a relaxing drink and dinner with Terry and Natalie prior to the meeting at Juan's later tonight.

She stood. "I need a nap, but I'll see you later."

"Wait," Franklin said, touching her wrist. "Give me a few more minutes. I wanted to explain something to you. This country is nothing like Canada, where you can usually rely on the police to solve your problems. The cops here don't make fuck-all, and most of them are corrupt. Sometimes you have to solve things other ways. That's why I took it upon myself to get Natalie's passport. That's why I hired Carlos and Victor to deal with the crazy stalker hooker. Chances are she had the cops in on her scam, and they would have gotten a percentage of the money she planned on extorting from me."

"I've read a few things about the cops here. But I certainly don't have your insight."

A white police pickup stopped on the road in front of the restaurant and two Dominican cops got out.

Franklin frowned. "Fuck. Speak of the devil."

One of them pointed a gun at Franklin while the other produced a pair of handcuffs.

The gun-pointer said, "Put your hands up and don't move."

Franklin raised his hands. "I didn't do anything."

Some passing tourists stopped to enjoy the spectacle.

The cop handcuffed Franklin's hands behind his back. "We want to question you."

"For what?"

"Murder."

Anisa stood up and clenched her fists. "Leave him alone. He's my brother. He didn't do anything."

The gun-pointer holstered his gun, grinned at her, and undressed her with his eyes.

"They don't speak or understand English," Franklin said as they stuffed him in the back seat of the pickup. "Don't worry. I'll be out soon. I'll see you at Juan's later."

Anisa paid the bill and hurried back to the hotel, ignoring the tourists and locals watching her as if she were a serial killer who'd just gotten away with murder.

CHAPTER FIFTEEN

Helen wacked the meat cleaver down hard and sliced a big piece of fat from the sirloin steak. She picked up the rubbery substance and chucked it into a nearby wastebasket. With two more precise cuts she had the steak as lean and mean as she knew the customers wanted it. She put it in a Styrofoam tray, rolled it twice with sticky cellophane, stamped a price on it, and placed it in a wheel-equipped tray.

In less than a week after pledging her undying devotion to the Bony Lady, she had already been promoted to meat manager. It wasn't her fault the previous meat manager had developed a nasty hacking cough that had rapidly progressed to bronchitis and was finally diagnosed as lung cancer. Stage four—there was no stage five. Only death. Apparently two previous doctors had misdiagnosed Sam Ellsworth's condition. Now, with only months to live, he was receiving palliative hospice care and treatment for the pain associated with his rapidly advancing cancer. *He can check out any time he likes,* Helen thought, trying hard to contain a grin. *But he can never leave.*

She trimmed and packaged another sirloin and looked at the tray. It was full so she wheeled it over to a refrigerated glass display case, bent down, and started arranging the meats.

"Nice fucking breasts."

She thought she recognized the voice. She straightened up, her eyes following the bulky outline of his body, stopping at his dark eyes. With a slight grimace, she realized they were fixated on her ample breasts. He wore a shit-eating grin and an overgrown afro.

"What did you say?" she asked.

He met her steel gaze. "Do you have any nice chicken breasts?"

The recollection of who he was and what he'd done came to her instantly. Randall Safferty, a high school classmate. Back then, students had nicknamed him Sapphire, as if to mockingly suggest he was a diamond in the rough, or a gemstone in the rough. But he was neither of these things. He was a piece of shit sexual predator and a horny one at that. His other apt nickname was Randy-As-Hell. That he was, and since none of the girls back in high school would date his fat ass, he took to copping a feel whenever the opportunity presented itself, whenever he thought it wouldn't be noticed and could be explained as merely an accident.

Helen remembered. Grade 9. The last day of school. Final bell. Students rushing from class, excited to leave their studies behind and enjoy summer holidays. The hallway was packed. She saw Randy approach, a mischievous glint in his eyes, that same shit-eating grin on his face. She'd tried to duck behind two students, but it was too late. He'd rushed at her, dropping his books and pretending to trip over them, and as he fell he cupped and squeezed her large breasts with both hands. He'd offered a token apology, which Helen knew was bullshit. Before gathering up his books, he'd added, "Nice fucking breasts."

Fucking piece of shit.

She didn't know if he recognized her. She hadn't seen him in maybe ten years. She pointed to another display case. "All the fresh chicken is over there. Third cooler over."

He finally removed his eyes from her breasts. "Okay, thanks. Do I know you?"

"Randy-As-Hell. Sapphire. A diamond in the rough." Helen laughed.

His shit-eating grin was wiped clean off his acne-scarred face. "I... I prefer Randall. And Safferty is my last name. Where do I know you from?"

"High school, Randy. Don't you remember me? The geeky kid everyone picked on."

He paused, eyeing her up and down.

You stop at my boobs again, I'm gonna leap over this counter and throttle your fat loser ass.

His eyes stopped at her eyes. A flicker of recognition crossed his face. It was mixed with fear. "I was picked on too, you know. I do remember you now. I think we had a math class together."

"Science, Randy. Science. Greg Tibbs. The nose-picker teacher. Remember?"

"It was a long time ago, but I think you're right."

"I *know* I'm right, Randy. Tell me, has much changed since high school? I mean, have you been able to land a date yet? I know back then, no girl in her right mind would go out with your sorry ass."

Anger flashed across his flushing face but was rapidly replaced by embarrassment. Maybe some dim awareness warned him that if he engaged in a verbal sparring match with the new-and-improved Helen, he would be beaten to a pulp.

"I gotta go." He spun around and shuffled away, not even bothering to stop at the chicken breast display case.

At home later that evening, Helen lit two black votive candles and placed them in front of the darkly shrouded skeleton saint. She drained a two-ounce shot glass of tequila and offered a drink to her holy savior. She knelt down, closed her eyes, and began to think of an appropriate prayer. She knew the force would come and guide her, and she waited patiently for its powerful intervention. She wasn't worried about ramifications or repercussions. The police had not a single lead in the murder of Ray Minowest. Not a single print was found at the site. Detectives had been unable to trace the origin or owner of the mysterious scythe found at the murder scene. It was like it had appeared magically out of thin air. A calmness and clarity settled over her. Her body began tingling with a kind of carnal energy. Words began to form in her mind, a poetry of justice.

The phone rang, snapping her out of the trance-like state. "Shit, I thought I turned that off."

She picked it up and looked at the incoming call. It wasn't someone she wanted to talk to right now, but some inner voice of reason or morality propelled her to press Talk.

Doctor Ricardo skipped the formalities. "I know what you're doing. And I want you to stop it right now."

"You want me to stop drinking? Don't worry, I won't overindulge."

"Don't play games with me, Helen. You promised me. I warned you what would happen if you started this."

"Started what?"

"Randall Safferty ring a bell? I overheard your conversation in the supermarket today. I saw your eyes, Helen. I saw the malicious intent."

"Well, he's a fucking sexual assaulter."

"He's trying to change. Let him try and change."

"I'll let Saint Death change him."

"You'll kill him. Just like you killed Ray Minowest."

"I didn't kill Ray." But she wasn't sure if that was true. She had been able to dig up very few fragments of the blackout, none of which necessarily pointed to her innocence.

"Please, stop it. More people are talking."

"Let them talk."

"Let me in."

"What?"

"I'm downstairs. Buzz me in."

Helen went to the window, drew up the curtain, and looked down at the street. A dark figure directly below her was illuminated by a street light. He had a phone tucked to his ear. He looked up. "Let me in."

That same voice of moral correctness that had prompted her to answer the phone encouraged her to press the buzzer.

She opened the door and he sat down on the couch beside her, his gaze flickering nervously to the votive candles, still lit, and the glowing black eye sockets of Saint Death. "Can I talk some sense into you?"

She poured herself another shot of tequila and poured one for Doctor Ricardo. He didn't hesitate to accept the drink.

Helen's demeanor softened. "I'm sorry. I get so angry sometimes at the people who abused me."

"Revenge is not what you think. It's not sweet. Mahatma Gandhi said, 'An eye for an eye makes the whole world blind.'"

"Maybe that's what's driving me. The notion that revenge will be sweet. I seem to be getting more hateful lately. This hate creeps up on me and becomes all-consuming."

"That's because you're buying into it," Doctor Ricardo said. "And also because you're perverting the good tenets of Saint Death. I told you, the religion is not to be used to wish evil on your enemies. That will only fill you with hate. It will become an insatiable appetite for revenge. Each bad deed might give you a brief sense of enjoyment, maybe even a high, but you'll want more. You'll become addicted. You'll become like a hopeless junkie willing to do anything for that fix. And you know what happens to most junkies."

"Indeed," Helen said calmly.

"I see you've changed," he continued. "You're smarter. You've already been promoted. Why don't you use that new intelligence for good instead of bad? Why don't you use it to help people, instead of hurt them?"

"What do you propose I do?"

"Well, for starters, next time you see Randall, why don't you tell him you forgive him and see what kind of reaction that draws?"

Helen stiffened. "You don't know what he did. He grabbed my boobs in high school. That's sexual assault. And do you know what he said to me in the supermarket? 'Nice fucking breasts.' Little pervert."

"There's something to be said for killing your enemies with kindness, if you'll pardon the expression. If you do run into him again, treat him with civility and kindness and see how he responds. If you can't forgive him, which ultimately I still believe is better for your mental health, then you could at least try and put the incident behind you. If you can't forgive, maybe you can forget. All I'm saying is if you embark along a dark path of hatred and revenge, it'll fast become a self-destructive dead end..."

Helen's phone rang, cutting off Doctor Ricardo's lecture on moral uprightness. She looked at the number and then at Doctor Ricardo. "It's Anisa."

"Answer it if you want," he said. "I'd like to know how she is."

Helen answered. "Anisa, how are you?"

"Are you alone?"

"No, Doctor Ricardo's here."

"Put me on speaker phone. I wanted to talk to him too."

After the social pleasantries had been dispensed with, Anisa got to the point. Or points. "I talked to my son today. He's doing very well. Thanks again Doctor Ricardo for saving his life."

"My pleasure."

"Listen, some strange things have been happening around here. As it turns out, my brother is also a devotee of Saint Death. But I fear he's using it for the wrong reasons: to get revenge on his enemies. Two people who Franky knew and retrieved a stolen passport from are now dead. Decapitated, the same as Ray. A little while ago, two cops took him away for questioning." There was a note of panic in Anisa's voice. "Now he isn't answering his phone."

Doctor Ricardo gave Helen an "I-told-you-so" look. She blushed.

"Have you guys heard anything more about Ray?" Anisa asked. "Did they catch the killer?"

"No," Doctor Ricardo said. "Doesn't look like there are a lot of clues. They can't even trace the origin of the scythe."

"Oh shit," Anisa said. "What about you, Helen? Do you remember anything else from that night?"

"No."

"Do you think you killed him?"

"No."

"But you prayed for his death?"

"I told you I did."

"I hope you're not praying for any more deaths."

During the ensuing silence, Doctor Ricardo gave Helen another one of those looks.

"Helen?"

"I'm here."

"Are you up to no good?"

"Not yet."

"Don't, please."

"Okay." It didn't sound convincing.

"Doctor Ricardo, what should I do?" Anisa said.

"What do you mean?"

"About my brother."

"I presume you already told him if he plays with fire, he's gonna get burned."

"I did."

"And you say he's in jail?"

"I think so."

"Pray to Saint Death for his safe return. Ask the Holy Saint to help him correct his ways."

"Okay." Anisa explained she had to meet some friends for a drink, wished both of them well, and promised to check in in a few days.

After she'd hung up, Doctor Ricardo looked at Helen rather smugly. "Now, if that isn't evidence enough for you, I don't know what is."

Helen seemed resigned. "All right. I'll tone it down."

"Don't tone it down, stop it."

"Okay."

"You promise?"

"Okay."

Doctor Ricardo was about to stand up, but changed his mind. "I know you're not that good at keeping promises, but if I tell you my story, will you keep it secret?"

"You don't have to tell me anything." But she wanted to know. "Does it involve Saint Death?"

"Yes."

"Is it the story of how you came to worship the Bony Lady?"

"Yes."

"Go ahead and tell it. I won't tell a soul. I promise."

"You sure?"

"Yeah, I'm dead certain."

His eyes rolled around in his head, as if searching for the right words. Then he looked at Helen squarely and began. "It happened many years ago. I lived on the fringes of society in Tepito, Mexico. My impoverished upbringing led me to pickpocketing. That escalated to a low-level position with a drug cartel. I ran kilos of cocaine from one point to another drop-off point, where eventually they were destined for the

United States. My boss worshipped Saint Death. One day I was pulling up to the boss's house when I heard gunshots inside. I saw two masked men—rival cartel members, I presumed—flee the house as I was speeding away. Knowing they had a baby girl inside, I drove around the block and returned."

Doctor Ricardo had Helen's undivided attention. "What happened next?"

"When I got inside the house, my boss and his wife were riddled with bullets. Dead as doornails. Their little newborn baby girl was wrapped in a blanket underneath a shrine to Saint Death. Still alive. Quiet as a mouse. I think that's the only reason they spared her. Because of their fear of Saint Death. Anyway, I panicked, took the child and the Saint Death statue, and fled."

"What did you do with the baby?"

"I'm getting to that. I interpreted the baby being alive underneath the statue of Saint Death as a sign. A message to me that if I worshipped Saint Death I would be spared as well. It was also a message to leave the cartel. I returned the cocaine to the storage facility, told one of the underlings about what happened, and disappeared."

"That's when you came to Canada?"

"Yeah, via the States. But not before placing the baby with some friends. I couldn't take her with me. It was too complicated."

"Did you pray for the death of the killers?"

"No. But I saw what happened to my boss. Two nights before he and his wife were murdered, I saw him praying to Saint Death for the death of a rival boss."

"Did the rival boss die?"

Doctor Ricardo shuddered. "Yes."

"How?'

"Decapitated."

"Oh my God."

"You see... I saw firsthand what can happen if you use Saint Death for evil or vengeful intent."

"Why didn't you turn the baby over to the cartel's family?"

"That just didn't seem right," Doctor Ricardo said matter-of-factly. "I wanted a better life for her."

"How do you know it was better?"

"I know the family. They aren't criminals."

"Have you ever been in touch with them? Or the baby?"

"No. She'd be fifteen now. Usually the only way you can leave the cartel is in a body bag. I didn't want to jeopardize the safety of my friends or the girl by communicating with her foster parents. I left everything behind and started a new life."

"What about your immediate family?"

"I don't know who they are. I was an orphan, an abandoned child, much like the girl I put up for adoption, I suppose. And my foster parents have been dead for a long time. A terrible car crash."

"I'm sorry," Helen said. She had absently loosened a button on her blouse, revealing a sizable amount of cleavage. She saw the good doctor's eyes find the fleshy V and then quickly dart over to the window overlooking Main Street. She caught him and he knew he was caught.

"You're more than just a pretty face," she said. "You have balls. That's quite a story."

"That's only a small part of it. Everyone has a story," Doctor Ricardo said, trying to recover his composure. "I told you that in the hope that you'll see the error of your ways."

Helen stood. "How about a rum and Coke, doc? Tequila's a little strong for me after a few."

He stood. "Thanks. I really should be going. I have to use my head tomorrow morning. Big patient load."

Use my head... big load. Helen wondered if the doctor was cognizant of the sexual innuendo. Combined with the booze, it was certainly having an influence on her. "Come on... one drink won't hurt. It's not even nine."

But he was already at the door. As he opened it, Helen heard a loud crash. Shards of glass from the living room window exploded into the room and a brick thudded across the floor, skidding to a stop on the small throw rug.

Doctor Ricardo rushed to the demolished window and looked out. Helen followed.

On the sidewalk below, two baseball-capped men dressed in black waved fists at them. It was hard to make them out in the darkness.

"Fucking devil-worshippers... Go rot in hell," one said.

"Satan-worshippers burn in hell," said the other.

This was followed by a burst of cackling laughter.

Helen pitched her shot glass out the window and it exploded on the sidewalk. But they had already turned and were sprinting off into the night.

Helen shook her fist out the window. "Better run, you fucking cowards."

Doctor Ricardo grabbed her wrist. "Please, let me help you clean up this mess."

Helen went into the kitchen and emerged with a broom and dustpan.

Doctor Ricardo picked up the brick. His brow crinkled. He turned to her. "There's a message scrawled on it."

"What's it say?"

He looked fearful. "I don't think you wanna know."

"It's my house, doctor, I have a right."

"It says, 'Death to Saint Death cult worshippers.'"

After they cleaned up the glass and taped the window with plastic, it didn't take a lot of convincing for Helen to accept Doctor Ricardo's invitation to spend the night at his home in the country. For now—for their own reasons—they had agreed not to report the incident to police.

Winding down a dark country road in Doctor Ricardo's Audi, glancing up ahead at a glowing full moon, Helen's adrenaline-fueled bravado earlier began to fade. It was replaced by a palpable fear that ignited in the pit of her stomach and fanned out, burning every fiber of her being.

Doctor Ricardo seemed to sense it. "Don't worry. Everything's gonna be okay."

But, at least to Helen, his reassurances sounded hollow and without conviction.

CHAPTER SIXTEEN

It was only a quarter past eight, and already Anisa was beginning to worry. She'd arrived promptly at eight, found a table and chairs off to the side of the stereo speakers (the volume, for a change, was respectably low) and ordered a bottle of rum, a bucket of ice, a bottle of Sprite, and a bottle of Coke. Terry and Natalie showed up at five after eight and they were already well into their first drinks. The night was calm, with a gentle breeze blowing off the ocean. From where they sat outside, they could see the waves lapping on shore and hear the soft hissing of the sea. Occasionally a motorcycle or large bus drove by, transporting tourists to and from Ocean World. The noise would drown out their conversation. There was another table of Dominicans beside them—two men and two women, also drinking rum. An elderly, sullen-looking foreigner sat alone at another table, making love to his Cuba libre.

Anisa searched the faces of Terry and Natalie, but they gave away no fear. Natalie even had a small smile pursing her lips and her eyes were a little glazed. If Terry was hammered, he hid it well. His face was calm, his eyes clear and alert. Anisa had respectfully declined the drinks on the beach and the planned dinner at the resort earlier, opting for a nap instead. By the looks of it, Natalie had indulged, maybe overindulged.

"Are you sure you guys are up for this?" Anisa couldn't think of anything else to say.

"I need my passport," Natalie said. "As I said, we have less than a week left."

"Right."

"You say he's got it, right?"

Anisa nodded and reached for her drink. She hadn't said anything about the cops hauling Franklin off to jail, but perhaps it was time. Keeping secrets like that could cost lives.

"Is he usually on time?" Terry asked.

"I don't know what he usually is. I haven't seen him in twenty years." Anisa realized she hadn't provided any backstory on Franklin, and she was starting to think some might serve to draw some sympathy for, or at least a better understanding of, her brother.

"What's his story, then?" Natalie asked.

"My story is I'm sorry." Three heads turned and saw Franklin standing behind them. He was freshly shaven, his black crew-cut gelled. He wore a black V-neck short-sleeved shirt, new pressed blue jeans and stylish leather Italian-made sandals. Clearly dressed to impress.

Taking a seat, he reiterated his profuse apologies to Terry and Natalie for his earlier transgressions and offered another group apology for being late, although he fell short of offering a reason for his tardiness. As all eyes at the table studied Franklin, Anisa tried to break the tension by pointing to the bottle. Franklin nodded and she poured him a Cuba libre.

"Not too strong, sis." He took a small sip, then reached into his back pocket and produced a passport. Holding it up, he looked at Natalie. "I'm sure after what I did to you and your fiancé, you don't think too highly of me. And you have every reason to think I'm a piece of shit. It was nasty, and I don't know what came over me. If you knew anything about my past, I've suffered many losses. I'm talking tragic deaths of family members. I'm not trying to justify my behavior, because it can't be justified. I just want you to know I'm trying to be a better person."

He put the passport on the table in front of Natalie. She picked it up and a warm smile blossomed on her pretty face. It illuminated the entire beachfront.

Franklin continued. "I just hope you'll view that passport as a symbol of my efforts to change. Maybe it's also a peace offering, which, with any luck, will go some way to you guys finding it in your hearts to forgive me... "

"Thank you," Natalie said. She picked up a napkin and dabbed at a tear in her eye.

"You're welcome. I just want you to know I'm not a bad person at the core. I'm not saying I'm a great person, or even a good one. But it's something I'm striving for."

"Good people sometimes do bad things," Terry said. "It's at the core of human nature. I hope it wasn't too much trouble getting the passport."

"Not really," Franklin said. "I paid for it. That's all. And I won't take any money from either of you, so don't go offering it."

Franklin gave Anisa a look. She knew what it meant. He wanted to know if she'd told them about the cops hauling Franklin off and questioning him in connection with the double homicide. She shook her head discreetly and he smiled, hoping Natalie and Terry hadn't noticed.

As the drinks flowed, the tension began to evaporate. To Anisa, it seemed like a True Confessions gathering. Each took turns telling stories of their past, recounting events that had shaped their lives and personalities. Terry talked of his competitive nature, how he was always trying to one-up his siblings, and even touched on his sexist views of women and how an epiphany had helped him change his ways, or at least put him on a path of wanting to improve. Natalie openly discussed her insecurities about men, and how it had all stemmed from her father's infidelity with a hooker and his subsequent abandonment of her and her mother. Franklin talked about the deaths of his father, two brothers, and most recently, the death of his mother during his absence. He explained how he felt jinxed and subsequently fled to the DR in an effort to save his remaining family. The story left Natalie and Anisa with wet eyes. For her part, Anisa told the others that, although she loved her only son Connor, she often felt burdened by his presence and then felt guilty for feeling burdened, the vicious cycle causing periods of depression and anxiety resulting in an inability to further her psychology-related goals. She explained how she often felt trapped because of her responsibility to Connor and the need to provide him with a father figure, her ex, who would never leave PEI.

She sipped her Cuba libre and noticed a haze developing around Terry, Natalie and Franklin. Again, she had lost count of how many drinks she'd consumed. "But I don't want you guys to get the wrong impression. I love my son; more now since he almost died and Saint Death saved him." *What did I just say?*

"What did you just say?" Terry asked her.

"Nothing."

"Did I hear you say Saint Death?"

Anisa poured another drink, trying to buy time.

"Because it's okay if you did." Terry looked at Natalie, who was looking at Franklin, who was looking back at Natalie. "Do you mind if I tell them, honey?"

"Go ahead."

"I got it," Franklin said. "That epiphany you mentioned earlier. That was Saint Death. Am I right?"

"Damn right," Terry said, looking at Anisa. "You can tell me. Was it Saint Death who saved Connor?"

Anisa slowly nodded.

"I don't believe it," Terry said, turning to Franklin. "I suppose you're gonna tell me you worship the skeleton saint as well."

"Damn right," Franklin said.

"Natalie and I both worship Saint Death. So our common ground is Saint Death," Terry said, holding up his drink. "A toast to the Holy Saint."

A chorus of "cheers" followed as they touched Styrofoam cups.

Anisa detailed the story of Connor's recovery and explained how that miracle had made her a believer. She turned to Terry. "I wanna hear about your epiphany in the context of Saint Death. But first I'd like to know what made you believe in the Bony Lady."

"Seems like True Confessions to me around here," Terry said. "This sounds terrible—even a little juvenile—but I did it to spite my family. They're die-hard Catholics and I wanted to shock them and prove to them that my religion was better than theirs."

"How's that working for you?' Franklin asked.

Terry swallowed half of his drink. "They barely speak to me now. But I want to change that. As I got into the religion I realized two things. One, I had gotten into it for the wrong reasons; and two, that it actually works. Positive changes began to occur in my life. I met Natalie, for one. I realized I was a fucking materialist, and a sexist one at that. And the last one, the epiphany, really drilled it home that Saint Death is real. That was just the other night. Right in Lifestyles hotel." He looked at Franklin. "When you knocked me out, security guards brought me to my room. While I was unconscious, I met Saint Death. Basically, she threatened to kill me if I didn't change. Not only did she give me a second chance, I regained consciousness with no residual effects from a double concussion. I'd call that a miracle."

Franklin frowned. "Again, my apologies."

Terry patted Franklin's arm. "Hey, no problem. And I just realized something. Maybe it was a blessing in disguise. Maybe you knocked some fucking sense into me."

"What about you?" Franklin asked Natalie. "Do you have a Saint Death miracle to relay to us?"

Natalie looked at Franklin a long time before she answered. "I can say that when Terry and I pray to Saint Death together, usually to strengthen our relationship, it sure makes a hell of a difference. Oops. Maybe that's the wrong word. It makes a heaven of a difference to our intimacy."

Anisa thought she saw a look between Natalie and Franklin that spoke of some secret intimacy, but she quickly wrote it off on the rum. *Alcohol impairs your judgment. Simple.* She let it pass.

"What made you start worshipping Saint Death?" Franklin asked Natalie.

"It's nothing dramatic like you guys. I'm a follower, not a leader. So, when Terry suggested it to me, I thought, why not? I'm a new devotee. Three months."

While Franklin went inside the *calmado* for more drinks, the lone aged gringo—who Anisa noticed had long ago replaced his Styrofoam cup with a full bottle of rum that he'd begun swilling liberally—stood up, grabbed his chair, and swayed over to the three. Before they could say anything, he plunked his chair next to Franklin's, pushing it back slightly, and sat down. He grinned stupidly at the others. His yellow t-shirt was drink-stained, his eyes bloodshot and wild, his teeth crooked; strands of his gray hair branched out crookedly like struggling tree limbs.

Anisa grimaced. She thought his hair vaguely resembled Albert Einstein's but doubted the man possessed Einstein's intelligence. His next words proved it.

"I'm sure you don't mind if I sit here. Sometimes I hate these fucking Dominicans." He took two swigs from the bottle. "Everyone's crazy around here."

Frowning, Franklin returned with a fresh supply of rum and soft drinks and squeezed into his chair, outside the circle.

The drunkard stared at Franklin. "I've seen you around here. Don't you think everyone's crazy?"

Franklin moved his chair back a bit. "No, I don't."

"You probably think I'm crazy, then."

"I didn't say that."

"Maybe you didn't, but I know you thought it. Keep it up and I'll have you fucking killed."

"You're too drunk to have anyone killed," Franklin said evenly.

Terry put down his drink and balled his fists. "Hey, why don't you get the fuck out of here? We didn't invite you to sit down. You sit down and start insulting us."

The man slammed his bottle on the table. The drinks shook, teetered, but miraculously did not spill. He laughed. "I'm sorry. I guess we got off to a bad start." He held out a hand to Anisa. "My name's Riley. And I get riled easily."

More out of fear than anything else, Anisa shook Riley's hand. It felt cold and clammy. She released it quickly, watching Terry and Franklin tense as she did.

Riley extended a hand to Natalie. "I just wanna be friends."

She shook it quickly and wiped her hand on her short blue skirt.

Riley watched her. "Nice legs."

Terry stood. "That's fucking enough!"

Swaying to his feet, Riley looked at him with unbridled hatred. "You want to fucking die? I know people here. I can have you killed instantly."

Franklin stood, a mask of calm and composure. He stepped closer to Riley and looked straight into his eyes. "I don't believe your company is appreciated here. I'm only gonna say this once. Please leave. Now."

Scooping his bottle off the table, Riley turned around and left. He plunked himself down beside the table of four Dominicans. Everyone watched silently as the Dominicans welcomed his company. Riley turned to one of the males, a large muscular man with a shaved head, threw three thousand pesos on the table, and pointed to Franklin. The man scooped up the money quickly and glared at Franklin, sizing him up.

Franklin grinned at the man. The man did not return the affection.

Conversation ensued around Riley's table. A waiter appeared and Riley ordered a round of drinks.

"I think it's time we left," Anisa said. "This is not gonna have a happy ending."

Terry clenched his fists. "I agree. If I stick around I'm gonna smack someone."

"You can go if you want," Franklin said. "But I'm gonna hang around. Just for a minute. Down here, you can't back down from threats. If you do, it might be the last time you do."

His bravado fueled a resolve in Natalie, Anisa, and Terry. They stayed.

Terry, trying halfway successfully to affect a calm demeanor, poured himself a stiff drink and drained half of it. Anisa noticed that the previous alertness in his eyes had been replaced by a drink-induced haze.

After five minutes of tense conversation, the Dominican muscle-bound giant rose from his table and sauntered casually over to the others. He looked Franklin square in the eye. He spoke perfect English. "I think I know you."

"Possible," Franklin said. "Been around here some time."

Terry squeezed his Styrofoam cup a little too tightly and it disintegrated in his hand, spilling his drink. Anisa and Natalie grabbed napkins and began wiping it up. The Dominican barely noticed.

Franklin's eyes never left the Dominican's. He extended a hand to Franklin. "Francisco. Pleasure to meet you."

Franklin hesitated only for a second, then took the man's hand and squeezed tightly, his eyes never leaving Francisco's black squinty eyes. "I'm Franklin."

It took a long time for Francisco to release Franklin's hand. When he did, he said, "Almost the same. Our names."

"Yeah."

"I'm pretty sure I know you. You're from Austria."

"No," Franklin said. "I'm Canadian."

Francisco sized up the others. The adjacent table was all eyes and ears. Then Francisco's eyes met Franklin's again. "I don't think so. You're Austrian."

Terry stood up suddenly and extended a hand. "He's Canadian. And I'm Terry." Francisco shook Terry's hand, jovially and gently this time, and with a mocking grin. When he released it, Francisco studied the ladies. His eyes lingered over their exposed body parts. He opened his mouth to speak, but Franklin was first off the plate.

"Anisa, my sister, and Natalie, Terry's fiancé."

A tense silence ensued as Francisco continued to shift his eyes back and forth between Natalie and Anisa.

Terry clenched his left fist.

Franklin clenched his right fist.

Anisa bit her tongue so hard she broke the skin.

Natalie felt an acidy rum-and-Coke flavored puke ball rise up her throat.

"Your drink, Francisco," Riley shouted. "You don't want it, I'll drink it. Get your ass over here."

Francisco grinned sardonically at his new friends. "You all have a pleasant evening now." He spun around quickly and returned to the adjacent table.

Anisa wiped her bloody lip with a napkin and exhaled a long, nervous sigh. After the adrenaline had worn off and she began crashing down to reality, she realized that an all-out bloody brawl had been narrowly averted. Then something else occurred to her. The threat was far from over. It was probably just the beginning. The beginning of another nightmare, maybe another murder. She stood up. "Now, Franky, I *do* think it's time to go."

CHAPTER SEVENTEEN

Helen started when she heard a *thunk* outside. She approached the front door, peered out the window, and noticed a newspaper had just been delivered. She went outside and picked it up. Her eyes widened as she read the front-page headline: *DEVIL WORSHIP ESCALATING IN PEI*. She hurried inside, sat down at the kitchen table, and read the news story.

A satanic cult that has been active in Mexico for over a half century is gaining ground here. The recent murder of Ray Minowest, decapitated with a scythe, is the kind of classic ritualistic and sacrificial killing performed by devotees of the cult of Santa Muerte or Saint Death, according to Catholic Pastor Paul Bishop.

"It's obvious," Bishop said. "Most of the statues used in the idolatrous worship of Saint Death carry scythes. It's well known that there is violent and deviant behavior associated with the cult worship... I want to formally condemn it as dangerous, blasphemous, and satanic."

Bishop said an unnamed source had recently revealed that at least a dozen people in Montague are worshipping "the personification of death. Make no mistake about it, this cult will only bring death and misery to its devotees. I urge you, if you've embarked down this dark and ill-fated path, to see the error of your ways and embrace Jesus Christ as your Lord and Savior."

Since he learned of the cult about five years ago, Bishop considers himself somewhat of an expert on the subject. "The fact that Minowest was killed with a scythe is a powerful symbol that the killing was done in the name of and as a human sacrifice to Saint Death. The perpetrator undoubtedly wanted to win favor from the immoral saint."

Police still have no solid leads and no suspects in the murder of Minowest.

"And believe me," Bishop warned. "Where there is one, there will be more."

According to Bishop, in Mexico and the United States, the worship of Santa Muerte is often associated with violence, the illegal drug trade, and murder. Saint Death is a popular deity in prisons among inmates, and many cells contain shrines to her. Although the majority of believers are poor people and not necessarily criminals, the upsurge in violent and ritualistic deaths related to Saint Death has associated her with crime and more pointedly, at least according to Bishop, with ritualistic and sacrificial murder.

Independent research has linked a number of murders in Mexico and the United States with Santa Muerte worshippers.

Mexico Killings:

Tepito, Mexico City, 2004. Authorities arrested a local car thief who later died in prison. The powerful criminal killed virgins and babies once a year, sacrificing them to Santa Muerte to win her favor and supernatural protection.

Nuevo Laredo, 2008. Gulf Cartel enforcers captured Sinaloa Cartel members and executed them at public Santa Muerte shrines. It is believed perpetrators killed them as offerings to Santa Muerte.

Ciudad Júarez, 2008. Authorities discovered numerous decapitated, stacked bodies believed to be linked to Santa Muerte worshippers.

Ciudad Júarez, December, 2008-January, 2010. A number of people were murdered and links suggested Santa Muerte ritual killings. At one crime scene, authorities found remnants of an altar and the words "take care of us, skinny." In one murder, a victim was burned behind a house containing an altar and a small Santa Muerte statue. Allegedly wanting "something big," gang members performed multiple human sacrifices.

Camargo and Miguel Aleman, April, 2019. Cartel members tortured and decapitated rival cartel victims, placing their heads on the roof of a desecrated chapel. The perpetrators comprised members of the Los Zetas Cartel, known Santa Muerte worshippers. Many of the gang members have Santa Muerte tattoos on their upper arm or chest.

Cancun, June, 2010. Six tortured victims were found in a cave outside the resort city, three with their hearts cut out and with the letter "Z" carved into their abdomens. It is believed the killers belonged to the Los Zetas Cartel, and the victims belonged to a rival group.

Sonora, March, 2012. Police arrested eight people for allegedly sacrificing a woman and two ten-year-old boys to Santa Muerte. The woman was attacked with an axe and the children were beheaded in rituals. Serial killer Silvia Meraz was the alleged orchestrator and she is currently serving life in prison.

United States killings:

South Texas, 2005 and 2006. Gabriel Cardona Ramirez, Los Zetas Cartel assassin, committed multiple homicides. In a phone conversation intercepted by DEA agents, Cardona bragged about slashing two teenagers with a broken bottle, gathering their blood in a cup, and toasting Saint Death.

Chandler, Arizona, October 10, 2010. A cartel kill team stabbed and beheaded thirty-eight-year old Martin Alejandro Cota "Jando" Monroy in his apartment for allegedly stealing drugs. Police found evidence of Santa Muerte worship at the crime scene, including votive candles and a statue of the skeleton saint.

Chicago, Illinois, April, 2011. Police investigating a dozen murders—some victims' throats were slit—identified multiple suspects as Santa Muerte followers. Shrines were found in the homes of the alleged perpetrators, and two had tattoos depicting the skeleton saint.

Sullivan City, Texas, September, 2011. A man was found stabbed and burned to death in what was left of his trailer. Nearby, authorities discovered a Santa Muerte shrine with burning candles. Although police are associating the shrine with the victim, they are still investigating possible motive.

According to Bishop, the cult is spreading around the globe like "wildfire," and while he wouldn't name names of local worshippers, he made a plea to Islanders to be vigilant. "I implore local residents to come forward with the names of anyone you suspect is playing with the devil of death."

The article even listed Bishop's home phone number, as well as his cell number.

Doctor Ricardo, who last night had insisted Helen call him by his first name, Manuel, walked into the living room, adjusting his tie.

Helen handed him *The Guardian*. "Take a look at this. What a load of crap."

She waited patiently until he finished reading it. His face was tight. "They don't say anything good about Saint Death. It's a slanted article that only tells one side of the story. Besides, some of those murders only have suspected links to Saint Death. Nothing concrete in many of them, and a lot of conjecture. The thing that worries me most is that Paul Bishop. He's a nut-job."

"I know," Helen said gravely. "He's pure fundamentalist. No gray area. His way or the highway."

Manuel sat in an armchair facing Helen. "He wants people to inform on Saint Death worshippers. It doesn't say what he plans on doing with them."

"That's what worries me."

Manuel put the paper down. "This is all negativity. The story doesn't say anything at all about the positive elements of the skeleton saint. About the miracles, about all the health benefits, love or wealth."

"Why would it? You're in a Bible belt, remember? And besides, people love dirty laundry. They wouldn't list the benefits of the religion because of a fear of attracting more converts. The biased message of this article is clear—stay clear of Saint Death or you'll be blackballed in the community. Hell, maybe they'll even stone us or tar-and-feather us."

"I don't think so," Manuel said. But he didn't sound convinced. "As I said, you're gonna have people from all religions perverting it to suit their evil agenda. That doesn't mean it's evil any more than Christianity or Islam is evil."

"We've been through this, Doctor Ricardo. I mean, Manuel. What do we do now?"

"I presume you have to work today?"

"Yes. I was hoping to get a ride with you."

"I was going give you one, but I don't think we should go in today. I've got a bad feeling."

"What do you propose we do?"

"Why don't we take a drive into town and just try and get a sense of how we're received."

"Someone put a brick through my window last night, remember? I don't think we're gonna get the red carpet treatment."

"Probably not. But I'm beginning to worry about what might happen to us if we go to work. You know, mob mentality is difficult to contain. Defies logic or reason."

"Why don't we go and pay a visit to Paul Bishop?" Helen asked.

"I'm not so sure about that, either."

"Why not? The eye of the tiger. Find out what he plans on doing with the heretics. See if he knows about us. I'll be able to tell by looking at him. I'll get a vibe, and I think it'll be right on."

Fifteen minutes later, they headed into Montague in Manuel's navy-blue Audi. He had arranged for a Doctor Reynolds to take his patient load for the day, and Helen had simply called in sick. She worried that someone from work might spot her driving around Montague and rat her out to her boss. After all, there were employees at Sobeys supermarket who were still pissed off at her rapid advancement. But, in the end, she reasoned that her life and mental health were far more important than being the new meat manager. Besides, she was with the town doctor. If she were to be seen in public, surely Manuel would vouch for her and even create a fake doctor's note, if need be. She decided to take her chances.

"Where to first?" she asked.

"Let's go for coffee."

"Okay." She tried to put her mind at ease as they drove north along Commercial Road into town. She had to admit, staying at Manuel's private and serene country home on 30 acres overlooking the Atlantic Ocean had gone some way to calming her down. She'd erroneously expected some action (she wasn't sure why she'd been so horny lately; she was positively on fire with desire) but the good doctor had been a paragon of virtue and, after a mug of hot chocolate and fifteen minutes of TV news, had shown her politely into a guest bedroom with an adjoining bathroom, saying, "Make yourself at home." Of course, Helen wasn't willing to acknowledge another possible reason for this increased sexual energy coursing through her. She hadn't been laid in seven years. It leant a new meaning to the term "seven-year-itch," which she conveniently ignored.

Put it out of your mind. It's a beautiful day, the sun is shining, and you have a day off with a handsome doctor. After her conversion to the worship of the Holy Saint, she felt much more confident now; more adept at reading men's emotions and perhaps influencing them to fulfill her desires. *If he's like most men, in time he'll lose his virtue. They all do.*

The crunching of metal snapped her head back, slamming it hard into the head rest. Dazed, she glanced back and saw a black pickup with tinted windows revving up for another ram.

"Fuck," Manuel said, accelerating. "Someone's trying to kill us."

It was one of the few times she'd ever heard Manuel swear, and she liked it. "Lose the fucking assholes."

He put some distance between them and the pickup, and veered sharp right at the last second onto Peters Road. The pickup skidded on the pavement, not anticipating the sudden move, and gave Manuel time—time to put a little more distance between them.

Helen rubbed a small lump on the back of her head. "I bet it's those losers who threw the brick through the window."

"I don't know," Manuel said. "But we gotta lose 'em."

"That we do."

"Hang on. I'm gonna see what this thing can do." He sped up and Helen watched the odometer—120kmh, 130, 140, 150, 160...

She looked back and saw the pickup shrinking in the distance. "We're losing them."

Manuel had both hands tightly gripping the steering wheel. As the intersection approached, he hit the brakes and the Audi Quattro fishtailed, the rear end sliding out on asphalt, parallel with Benjies Road. He floored it at the perfect time and the tires whistled and screeched before the vehicle plunged ahead.

"That's some driving," Helen said. "Maybe I should call you Bond... James Bond." She said it with emphasis and a pretty good British accent.

They cracked up laughing.

Helen glanced back. "Here they come, Bond. And they're gaining on us."

"How far away?"

"I don't know. Couple—three blocks maybe."

Manuel looked back. "Shit."

"Watch out," Helen screamed.

It was all he could do to slam on the brakes. The Audi skidded and fishtailed all the way up to the SUV that was backing out of a driveway. They stopped maybe two inches before T-boning it. The driver's hands were frozen to the wheel, her face tight and white, her mouth popped open in a wide O of horror.

She was blocking the small two-lane road. The only way around her was ditch-surfing.

"Get out of the way," Manuel yelled. "Quick."

For a second she was speechless and motionless. Then her eyes widened. She slammed the SUV into reverse and backed the vehicle up into the driveway, tires screeching.

Manuel accelerated.

Helen screamed.

A loud metallic crunch snapped both their heads back and sent the Audi careening into the ditch.

The pickup stopped and two masked men got out.

Manuel kept the pedal to the medal and tires spun dirt, greenery, and gravel as the Audi bounced forward.

Dazed, Helen gasped for breath, the adrenaline surge sending her heart rate into overdrive. Instinctively, she lowered the passenger window and released her seatbelt.

They heard voices as the men approached.

"Should we kill them?"

"Why not? Fucking heretics."

A shot rang out, blasting through the driver side window and windshield and spraying shards of glass on the occupants. Another shot rang out and Helen heard the sound of a vehicle window shattering nearby. *Shooting the witness. My fucking God!*

Another gunshot whistled past the Audi as Manuel slammed it into reverse, accelerated, then slammed it into first gear. Tires dug into the soft ground, rocketing dirt, gravel, and greenery into the faces of the would-be assassins.

"Fucking bastard," one said.

"Shoot the fucker."

"I can't see."

"I don't care. Fire your fucking gun."

"Get down," Manuel said, also ducking.

The Audi found traction, spun out of the ditch, and hit pavement. Two more bullets blasted through the rear windshield. One bullet tore through the dashboard gas gauge, right where Manuel's head had been.

The other imbedded itself in the dashboard above the passenger side glovebox, where Helen's head had been.

They drove in stunned silence. Manuel turned left on Point Pleasant Road. Finally, he said, "Are you okay?"

Helen exhaled deeply, examining the bullet hole where her head had once been. She waited until she caught her breath. "My neck is killing me. And I got a little goose egg on my head. But otherwise, yeah, hunky-dory."

"Can you turn your head?"

"Not really. It hurts."

Without slowing down, Manuel glanced back quickly. There wasn't a vehicle in sight. "Probably whiplash. Let's go to a public beach—Panmure Island beach—where I can examine you. There'll be lots of people there. We should be safe."

"I don't know about that. I think they shot at that lady in the SUV. I heard another windshield shatter."

After a minute, Manuel said, "Do you have a better idea?"

She responded with a resigned "no."

It wasn't until they'd pulled into the busy parking lot of Panmure Island beach that Helen spoke again. "You have a cut in your head," she said.

He parked alongside a giant white motorhome with a blue whale painted on its side. A small boy wearing a red bathing suit opened the door of the motorhome and stepped out. A large blue beach towel was slung over his shoulders.

With widening eyes, he looked at Manuel, then turned and sprinted to the beach. "Mommy, Mommy—that man's bleeding."

Manuel touched his forehead above his right eyebrow and noticed for the first time that a tiny spear of glass was imbedded in it. He drew his hand away; it was wet with blood. Some of it had formed a tiny red river along his eyebrow and down the side of his face. There was a steady drip on his white starched shirt collar.

"You're bleeding," Helen said.

He reached into the back seat and retrieved his medical bag. He opened it and pulled out a pair of surgical tweezers. He handed them to Helen. "Are you afraid of blood?"

"No."

"Then you're the doctor now." He gently touched the glass spear. "Pull that out please. But gently."

Wincing with the protestations of her sore neck, she inched closer and put a hand on his chin, steadying his head. She brought the tweezers closer. "Do I need to sterilize these or something?"

"No. They're clean."

"You smell nice."

"Helen, just take out the glass, please."

"Sorry. It was just a compliment." She brought the tweezers closer and gripped the thin edge of glass. She tugged.

Manuel grunted. "Slow."

"Okay." She eased it out. "Got it."

She examined it. "Wow. It's almost an inch long. You're lucky it went in sideways, or it might have penetrated your brain."

The removal of the spear caused the blood flow to increase. As Helen dropped the piece of glass on the glass-covered dashboard, Manuel disinfected the wound, bandaged his head, and cleaned up some of the blood. "It's your turn. I want to examine you."

"I wish you would. We have to stop meeting like this, doc."

They laughed. Soon they were giggling like teenagers.

"Oww... it hurts when I laugh," Helen said.

"Quit cracking jokes, then. Can you move? I'd prefer to examine you outside. We're covered in glass."

"I don't want a shard of glass up my ass," she said, and laughed again. "Oww."

"I warned you."

They got a few odd looks while Manuel examined Helen on a nearby picnic table. Helen didn't notice. He diagnosed her with whiplash, noting the small bump on the back of her head probably wasn't grave enough to warrant serious concern. He gave her two painkillers, ordered some ice cubes in a plastic bag, and had her press them to the back of her neck.

A waitress at the Sandbar & Grill was kind enough to loan them a vacuum cleaner to vacuum the shards of glass in the interior of the car. Manuel got most of the glass off the dashboard, seats, and floor, and returned the vacuum cleaner to the waitress. Then he joined Helen on the outside patio, where she sipped a coffee. It was a calm, beautiful sunny day and the view out to sea was spectacular.

"I got you a coffee," Helen said. "I don't know how you take it so I put the condiments here."

"Thanks. Some of your symptoms may be worse tomorrow. Sometimes, with whiplash, the pain is worse after twenty-four hours. You may have headaches, lower back pain, and dizziness. The ice should help. How are you feeling?"

"I'm a little better. I can feel the painkillers kicking in."

"Good." After a short pause, he said, "You didn't tell anyone about Saint Death, did you?"

"No."

"You sure?"

"Yes. But they obviously figured it out."

"Yeah. Do you think Anisa would have said anything?"

"No. She's pretty solid."

He sighed. "I guess it doesn't matter anyway. People know. It's all my fault."

Helen set the ice cube bag on the table. "How could it be your fault? You were only trying to help. Look what you did for Connor. You saved his life. Look what you did for me."

He spoke barely above a whisper. "By introducing you to Saint Death, I've put you in danger. It looks like I've put Anisa in danger also. And what have I done to you, Helen? Sure, you're smarter than before, but you've also got a streak of hatred in you. You want revenge on anyone who has ever insulted or assaulted you."

"Well, doc, you've begun to teach me the error of my ways."

He studied a young family of four sitting two tables away. When he was satisfied they weren't eavesdropping, he went on. "Have I? What's gonna happen when I'm not around? You gonna pray for more deaths?"

"I hope not."

"Were you like that before?"

Helen frowned, her eyes glistening. "No. I was a timid, polite little pushover. Afraid to speak out. Walking around thinking everybody was better than me, smarter than me. No self-esteem. Getting stomped on like a helpless little ant. Frankly, Manuel, if I can learn to control my mean streak, you've given me a new lease on life. I like this Helen much better. I shouldn't be blaming you, which I'm not. You shouldn't be blaming yourself, which you are. I should be thanking you. Besides, that mean streak probably has nothing to do with Saint Death. After so many years of repressed hatred, wouldn't you think it natural that, now that I have the capacity to recognize it, it would have a tendency to manifest itself in a destructive fashion? Too much repression leads to an explosion, am I right?"

"I suppose you are."

"I don't think we have the luxury of dwelling on my problems right now. We have bigger fish to fry."

"That's also true."

Helen examined the parking lot and glanced briefly at two of the occupied tables. "We don't have a lynch mob after us here."

"It doesn't look like it."

"Do you think we should go to the police?"

"Oh shit. I almost forgot. That woman in the SUV. We should probably make an anonymous call to the police in case they killed her. Or maybe she's injured and needs medical attention."

"Oh my God. We must have been in shock. I almost forgot her too. I like your idea about an anonymous call."

"My thoughts are, if the cops are in on it, we're... "

"Fucked?"

"You could say that."

"I just did."

They laughed. But it was contained, lacking the giddy and uninhibited quality of the earlier outbursts. The gravity of their situation was beginning to sink in.

Manuel said, "Let's go see Pastor Paul Bishop."

CHAPTER EIGHTEEN

Under the black curtain of night he moved through the thick jungle silently. Using a machete, he expertly slashed away foliage in his path. He arrived at the building and shone the flashlight beam up the wall, spotting some footholds and handholds—serious safety concerns and architectural errors to some, but Godsends to others. With the tiny flashlight beam, he found the window. No bars. Perfect. He quickly switched it off and tucked it in his pocket. He clamped his teeth down on the blade of the machete and began climbing. He had been told the window wasn't even locked and would easily slide open. *This is gonna be easy,* Francisco thought. *Like slicing a coconut open.*

She actually likes me, Franklin thought, and the realization brought forth a turbulent swirl of conflicting emotions. Negative black thoughts intermingled with positive white thoughts and a fierce internal battle erupted. His earlier thoughts and actions regarding Natalie flooded forth like a tidal wave. He *had* grabbed her violently at the disco and dragged her, against her will, onto the dance floor. He'd also said some nasty things: *"I'm gonna fuck you to death. And you're gonna love every minute of it."* And those were only the spoken words. In the vicious grip of a spiral descent into a black abyss of hate-filled despair, he'd thought of various methods he could employ that would inflict pain upon her and shower him with pleasure. *But what about the lovemaking? Wasn't that mutually satisfying? Yes. But she was under Saint Death's spell. That's different. It sure as hell wasn't your good looks, charm, or magnetic personality.*

No, that wasn't quite right. Maybe it had been the spell earlier, but not anymore. Earlier tonight at the *calmado*, Franklin was sure Natalie wasn't under any spell. And she had paid special attention to him. One could even call it a flirtatious attention. Those deep blue eyes that seemed to be attracted to him. Her smile. Laughing at his jokes. Asking him questions. Interested in him and his life. That wasn't a spell. That was the beginning of a love affair.

Reclining on his couch, he focused on the Saint Death statue and the flickering black votive candle in front of it. What to do? He'd planned a vengeful prayer earlier to make quick work of Natalie's fiancé Terry, but now his heart wasn't in it. He was beginning to like the guy. Sure, Saint Death had rid him of Niamia and Alfredo, but that was different. They'd lived in the apartment building and had caused nothing but disruptions in Franklin's life. But now, ruminating about it, he even had a pang of regret. He could have just moved to another building if he found them so disruptive. And, he had to admit, the regret was mixed with a hint of fear. Drunk or not, Anisa had warned him in no uncertain terms: pervert the good tenets of the religion of Saint Death and bad things will happen to you.

He was sure the deaths of Carlos and Victor were different. Those scumbags had it coming. They were robbers, con artists, and murderers. But that begged the question. Was he any different? *Of course I am. I've never killed anyone with my bare hands, or with a scythe for that matter.* Had he prayed for their deaths? He honestly couldn't remember. Had he actually committed the murders? Again, a blank white page. And even if he had murdered them, there would be no legal consequences. Of that, he was sure. The cops had been easy. Twenty thousand pesos and no more questions asked. He was a free man. A police escort even accompanied him home. Service with a smile.

He went to the fridge for a glass of water and returned to the couch. He considered blowing out Saint Death's black candle, but decided against it. More thought was required in terms of what to do with Natalie. A voice inside his head spoke: *"Forget about her. She's engaged to be married."*

He clenched his fist and slammed it into the coffee table. "Shit, fucking shit. Why can't I get what I want?" But as the anger slowly dissipated, Franklin felt a subtle change taking place inside him. A long-buried rational, good side of him began to emerge. *If it's meant to be, it will be. Leave Natalie and me to divine intervention. It's always worked before.* He felt the white positive emotions enveloping the black negative emotions and he suddenly realized that he was capable of change. Natalie had shown him love; Terry had demonstrated love in a more platonic form; and Anisa had shown him a level of love and concern unrealized in his life for perhaps twenty years. She'd found him and dropped everything out of a deep concern for his wellbeing, rushing to his aid. He dreaded to think of what might have happened had she not arrived. Perhaps Terry and Natalie would both be dead. He pushed the thought away, but dark thoughts started to gain the upper hand. *You can take the beast out of the wild, but you can never take the wild out of the beast.*

He pounded his fist on the coffee table again so hard the glass of water tipped over, rolled onto the floor, and shattered, spreading a trail of glass and water onto ceramic tile. He was determined to win the mental battle. "Yes you *can* take the wild out of the beast. I'm capable of change and I'll fucking prove it."

He retrieved a dustpan and broom from the kitchen closet, swept up the water and glass, and deposited the remains into a wastebasket. He blew out the black votive candle, the symbol for protection and harm and tucked it away deep in his kitchen closet. He replaced it with a red candle, symbolic of love and passion. A new petition to the skeleton saint began to form rapidly in his mind. He would pray that Anisa, Terry, and Natalie find love and passion in their lives. He would be very specific regarding Natalie. If it was meant to be that she and Franklin should be together, then so be it. If not, let the chips fall where they may. After apologizing to the Bony Lady for his earlier vengeful prayers, he would implore her to use her supernatural powers to heal his self-pitying sickness and help him become a better and more caring person.

He poured Saint Death a shot of tequila, lit the red candle, knelt down, and began praying. When he'd finished the prayer, he thanked Saint Death for her divine benevolence, and drained a shot of tequila. "Amen."

As he rose from his knees, he heard a door click open and glanced at the bathroom. But the dark machete-wielding man was already upon him. The man rushed into the living room, raised the weapon high in the air, and it descended swiftly. It was all Franklin could do to duck his head and spin, purely on instinct. He could barely make out the man in the suffused light of the flickering candle. The attacker was aiming for the jugular, but instead the machete sliced into Franklin's right shoulder.

He felt hot pain and brought his left hand to the wound, feeling the blood pulsating and spurting out. In an instant he knew who it was. Of course. In reliving the love-struck emotions with Natalie—and in planning his new-and-improved resurrection—he'd overlooked the most important threat to his happiness: Francisco and that crazy fuck Riley.

Franklin saw the glint of the blood-soaked blade retreat and rise, then rapidly change direction and come swinging toward him in a horizontal arc aimed at his throat. Instead of ducking, he stepped back a little too quickly and somersaulted over his couch, landing on the floor on his back. He brought his blood-drenched right hand down to his waist and unbuckled the sheath containing his combat knife. But as he tried to extract it, he felt sharp, bone-snapping pain in his wrist as Francisco's knee crunched down hard on it.

With his other hand, Franklin grabbed Francisco by the throat and squeezed tightly, digging his nails into flesh. He heard a wheezing-gurgling sound not unlike a percolating coffee maker and felt hot pain as Francisco mercilessly slashed at his left arm. One, two, three, four large gashes—blood splattered into his eyes, nose, ears, and mouth—and Franklin's grip loosened. His arm dropped to his side. Francisco immediately pinned it with his other knee and raised the machete up high as he gasped for breath.

Franklin bucked but to no avail. Francisco was too big, too strong; easily twice his size. The machete descended swiftly and Franklin moved his head. The blade clanged into ceramic tile and almost slipped free, but Francisco quickly found purchase and raised it again. A spear of incoming moonlight found the blade and it glinted and glittered like a shooting star.

For Franklin, things began to go in slow motion. Helpless, he watched the blade descend. Out of the corner of his eye, he saw Saint Death's hollow, glittering eyes, her grin mocking him. Anisa's warning popped into his head. *"I'm warning you, you fucking murderer. You fuck with Saint Death and Saint Death will fuck with you."*

"Why?" Franklin said. "Why kill me?"

The blade stopped. "Three thousand pesos. That's all your life is worth, gringo."

"I'll pay you double. I'll give you ten thousand pesos." Franklin thought grimly about the irony of his situation; how he'd bought Natalie's freedom for three thousand pesos while Riley wanted to end his freedom for three thousand pesos.

"Riley will give me as much as I ask for," Francisco said. "Why do I need your money?"

The blade hovered above his throat and then he felt a hard dent as it began to press down. Instead of swinging it, evidently Francisco had decided to decapitate him with slow carving pressure. Certainly the ape had the strength to pull it off, Franklin thought, although he'd read that it takes quite a lot of strength and stamina to actually decapitate someone using a machete.

He felt his neck slice open and warm blood dribbled down his neck.

Francisco was enjoying himself. "You know how much that bitch Natalie is worth?" He didn't give Franklin time to answer.

"Two thousand pesos. Same for your lousy sister and that Terry fuck-wad."

A seething red adrenaline-fueled rage shot through Franklin and he kicked up his legs, bucked and rolled, and he was free. Reaching for the combat knife, he scrambled to his feet. But the right wrist was limp, broken, so he quickly unsheathed it with his bloody left hand. Waving the blade, he stepped back.

Francisco got up and even in the darkness Franklin could see him grinning. He stepped slowly toward Franklin, the machete held firmly in front of him like someone might hold a samurai sword. "Oh, I got you, redneck. You want a fair fight." He moved closer. "Okay, you got one."

It wasn't missed on Franklin that the fight was hardly fair. He had a broken right wrist, a large gash on his right shoulder, multiple lacerations on his left arm, and a cut and bleeding throat. A wave of dizziness swept over him and he fought to keep it under control. *Losing a lot of blood. Don't have much time...* He went on the offensive, lurching forward and plunging the blade deep into Francisco's chest. But at the same time, Francisco swung the machete and sliced a large opening in Franklin's abdomen. Franklin groaned in pain and fell into the wall, clutching the gaping wound, feeling his large and small intestines spill into his hand. As he melted to the floor, Franklin felt the ebb and flow of consciousness and he wondered grimly if his combat knife had found its mark—Francisco's heart.

But Francisco seemed unfazed. He slid the knife out, wiped the blood on his chest, and tucked it into his belt. He knelt down in front of the weak and dying Franklin, raised the machete, and plunged it deep into Franklin's chest. He withdrew it as Franklin gasped, groaned, and gurgled. Then Francisco licked some blood off the blade and, grinning from ear to ear, gripped it tightly in both hands. He raised it above his head again. So lost was Francisco in the euphoria of the kill, he became deaf to extraneous sounds.

The balcony door slid open quietly and a woman rushed toward Francisco. She clobbered him hard over the head with a garden shovel. As he tilted sideways and groaned, he flung the machete at his attacker. It lodged deep in her stomach.

In a haze of stars, Francisco spun around, slid the machete out of the woman's stomach, and went for the throat. But she dodged and weaved, bringing the shovel down a second, third, and fourth time, until the blunt force trauma finally felled Francisco.

He lay on his back, groaning, blood gushing from multiple cuts and contusions. As she moved closer, he found some superhuman strength and flung the machete again. It stuck in her chest and she groaned and staggered. She dropped the shovel and clutched the machete with both hands. Wincing, she slid it free. She dropped it and brought both hands to the wound, trying to plug the gushing geyser. She weaved, staggered, and fell down, landing on Franklin's chest.

As her heartbeat slowed, she listened for his heartbeat. But his chest was silent. She reached out with dying strength and touched his cheek. "Franklin?"

He slowly opened his eyes and smiled. "Natalie. I knew you'd come."

He closed his eyes.

Her labored breathing became still. She closed her eyes.

Defying all odds, Francisco got to his feet, took two stagger-steps, slipped in a pool of blood, and fell head-first into the glass coffee table, shattering it. He groaned and became silent.

The moon disappeared behind a bank of clouds. The lone red votive candle—a symbol for passion and love—flickered and went out.

Pitch blackness and an eerie silence enveloped Franklin's apartment.

CHAPTER NINETEEN

On a balmy, starlit summer evening, Helen and Doctor Ricardo stood outside the door of Pastor Paul Bishop's house on a quiet residential street in Montague. His modest bungalow fronted Montague River on Riverside Drive. The plan had been to arrive much earlier, but at the last minute they decided to stop for coffee at Montague's Tim Hortons to gauge the town vibe. There, it soon became obvious that hateful eyes were watching them a little longer than politeness and cultural norms would allow. As they were leaving, Helen was sure she heard a young punk say "devil-worshippers," and another old fart mutter, "Leave town if you know what's good for you."

Then Helen began suffering a whiplash-induced headache and Manuel revised the plan. He dropped her at her apartment for a nap, took his car into the glass shop after removing the embedded bullets, and rented a 2015 black Chevy Silverado. He must have run some other errands, but Helen didn't bother to ask. He'd picked her up at seven-thirty. She felt much more refreshed and less headachy after a three-hour deep sleep. She'd cooked spaghetti, and two hours later, here they were "knock, knock, knocking on heaven's door."

Three raps from Manuel produced nothing.

"But he must be home," Helen said. "His white BMW is parked in the driveway."

Manuel stepped onto the lawn and peered through the living room window. "There's a dim light at the back. Let's try again."

Helen knocked three times. Silence.

"Let's go around to the back," Manuel said.

"You think so?"

"Yeah."

Moving quietly on the expansive back deck overlooking a picturesque river view, Manuel approached the back door and peered through the small window. He could see nothing.

"Over here," Helen whispered. "It's a bedroom, I think. There's a light on."

Like two peeping Toms, they put their hands on the windowsill and looked through the window. The sheer window covering, along with a small bedside lamp, gave them a silhouette view of two bodies. The hand of a young boy was in motion and an old fat man lay on the bed, moaning. To say the scene was deeply disturbing would probably be an understatement.

"I can't watch this," Helen said, stepping away.

Manuel turned around and studied the shining glass-like river view. "What a sick man," Manuel said. "Neither can I."

"Something you could cure?"

He balled his fists. "I could think of one effective treatment."

A muted moan echoed from the room. It was followed by the sound of shoes walking on a hardwood floor.

"Let's get out of here," Manuel said. "We'll try the front door again."

They were stepping onto the front porch when the front door opened. A young boy—Helen recognized him as fifteen-year-old Peter Matheson—stepped onto the porch, looked at them guiltily, and hurried away.

Pastor Paul stood in the doorway, his white comb-over flying in all directions and exposing a large glistening bald spot on the top of his head. His white shirt had been improperly buttoned and hung awkwardly on his bulky seventy-four-year-old frame, the left side a few inches longer than the right. He flushed. "Doctor Ricardo. Helen. To what do I owe the pleasure of your visit?"

"Late night Bible study?" Manuel said.

Pastor Paul brushed it off. "Oh that. Peter's been having some problems with his parents lately and I've been counselling him."

"I'll bet you have."

"He's a good lad, just a little misguided." His eyes narrowed and his flippant tone changed. "You caught me at a bad time, so if you'll tell me why you're here, maybe I can be of some help."

"You've been speaking to a reporter by the name of Roger Granger?" Manuel said.

Pastor Paul eyed them suspiciously. "Indeed I have. He did an excellent piece on that terrible cult that's spreading like wildfire here."

"You mean Saint Death," Helen said.

"Yes."

"What makes you think it's so terrible?"

"Why? Are you a believer?"

"I didn't say that."

Manuel jumped in. "Look, I'm not gonna name names, but I may know some people who do subscribe to the religion of Saint Death. I found that news story disturbing. You want all this reported to you? What do you plan on doing with these people when you find them? I mean, after all, you refer to Saint Death as 'the devil of death.'"

It took Pastor Paul some time to respond. When he did, he appeared to choose his words carefully. "Certainly if I discover any ritualistic killing—human sacrifice—associated with Saint Death, I'll obviously report it to the police." He studied his uninvited visitors with skepticism. "As I hope you and any other law-abiding citizen would."

"Of course," Manuel said.

Helen nodded and looked at her toes.

Pastor Paul went on. "My only aim is to counsel non-criminal cult worshippers. I want to bring them back to the veneration of the Lord and Savior Jesus Christ. I want to show them how the worship of Saint Death is blasphemous and evil. Not to mention immoral."

The words hurled from Helen's mouth like a venomous snake before she could stop them. "And what do you call diddling young boys, Pastor Paul? Is that moral?"

His jaw dropped. "I did no such thing. I don't know what you're talking about... "

It was too late for her to stop herself. "I saw you, Pastor Paul. *We* saw you. But, wait a minute, maybe you're right. It wasn't you diddling Peter. It was Peter diddling you. Peter diddling Paul. Maybe you'd already finished diddling him."

Manuel grabbed Helen's wrist. "Helen, that's enough."

With a jerking motion, she snapped his grip loose. "Like hell it's enough. I'm just getting started. How dare you criticize Saint Death worshippers when you're nothing but a sick pedophile and a religious hypocrite? Let me tell you something, Mister Man of the Cloth. I haven't had a great fucking day at all today. Someone tried to run us off the road. Then they shot at us. Now I have a sore neck and my headache is returning. And that's not all. I had to listen to people call me a devil-worshipper under their breath and tell me to leave town if I know what's good for me—"

Manuel willingly gave her the floor, or the front porch as it were. He now stood on the lawn a few feet away.

She definitely had Pastor Paul's attention now. "Get off this property now!" he shouted.

But she stepped closer to him, her face tightening. A vein was popping and pulsating on her forehead. "I'm not finished yet. I almost forgot. Last night some thugs, probably your congregants, threw a brick through my window. On it was a message. 'Death to Saint Death cult worshippers.' They could've killed me. I have a feeling you're behind this. I'm warning you, Pastor Paul. If anyone else tries to kill me or Doctor Ricardo, your pedophilia is gonna be known far and wide. You're the one who'll be tarred and feathered and blackballed. Blackballed, I like that. It would be a fitting end to a pedophile."

"I told you to leave."

"One more thing," she said, backing off the porch. "Drop your Saint Death crusade. Whatever happened to religious freedom? If I read anything else in the newspapers about your witch-hunt..."

He began closing the door. "If you don't leave now, I'm calling the police."

"Go ahead and call them. I'd really like to clear the air around here because it's thick with religious hypocrisy and unlawful sexual behavior. Drop your witch-hunt, Pastor Paul. And call off your goons. Or else."

The door slammed so hard the echo reverberated throughout the neighborhood.

It was a few minutes after they left that Helen finally calmed down. The thought occurred to her that Manuel probably would have handled the situation with more tact. And while they certainly had caught him red-handed on pedophilia, she had presumed he was also guilty of threats, murder attempts, and inciting a witch-hunt. She had acted as judge, jury, and executioner. Her temper, which for the last twenty years lay buried in a shallow grave, had finally reared its ugly head and lashed out like a deadly serpent.

She looked at Manuel, driving calmly and carefully through Montague. "Sorry about that."

He gave her a small smile. "It's okay. I wish I had the balls to put it to him that way. And in the end, he wasn't denying anything, was he?"

"I guess not. My temper got the better of me though. I don't like that."

"Just take some deep breaths and calm down. It's done. Other than presuming him guilty of some things, you told it like it was. Rather colorfully, I might add. And I have no sympathy for people who abuse young boys."

"Same for me. I think that's what got me, but it was also the stress build-up of all the shit that's been happening."

"I understand." He turned right on Commercial Road and proceeded south, leaving Montague, The Beautiful, as the welcome sign proudly proclaimed.

"What do you think is gonna happen now?" Helen said.

"I don't know. But I'm not gonna take any chances." He pointed to the glove box. "Open it, please."

She did. "A gun?"

"It's a 57 Magnum. Do you know how to shoot?"

"Yes. My father was into guns."

"Good. Take it out and keep it handy. Careful, it's loaded."

She tested its grip and weight, and then tucked it into the crotch of her jeans. "Where did you get it?"

"Let's just say a little bird gave it to me."

"Okay. What's the plan now?"

"Considering your whiplash, you could now legitimately take a week off work. You know I'll write the note and the prescriptions. Given the tense atmosphere around here, I don't think it would hurt for you to lay low for a while. And anyway, you do need some time to recover. I wanna make sure those headaches go away. How are you feeling now?"

"Right as rain."

"Good. How about a glass of fine Scotch next to a blazing fire?"

"Sounds absolutely peachy, doc. You think of all the best remedies. I could sure use a drink right now."

CHAPTER TWENTY

It had been many years since Anisa looked forward to the changing of the seasons. She could barely remember the last time she had seen Mother Nature's markers as a chance for new beginnings. The first winter snowfall, blanketing everything a cleansing and purifying white; the first green buds of spring, signifying growth and change; the first hot day of summer, lounging on a towel in her bikini at the beach, enjoying a chilled wine cooler; the vibrant reds, yellows, and oranges of fall. Now everything seemed to be just the unexciting passing of time toward an inevitable and disparaging end.

This September Friday, the first day of fall, was no exception. She felt only emptiness, despair, and sadness. A bright red maple leaf twirled down from a tree and landed in her hand as she walked. Turning into Saint Mary's Cemetery, she examined the leaf. It was almost perfect but for a dime-sized, rough-hewn hole in its center, probably the work of a hungry insect or maybe the beginning of some disease-causing infestation. *A hole in the heart,* she thought. *But I suppose that's as it should be. In fall, everything dies.* She dropped the leaf and watched it swirl to the ground. Just before it landed, a chilly gust of wind blew in, scooped it up, and swept it high in the gray cloud-covered sky. She watched it until it disappeared. Then she shivered, buttoned up the top two buttons of her red sweater, and carried on.

She found the tombstone. She knelt down and placed a bundle of roses—five red and one pink—on the yellowing grass in front of it. It was a modest tombstone made of orange-red granite, the top of which was shaped like a heart. Below the name and dates, the epitaph inscribed on it was simple and hopeful: *May your patron saint carry you safely and peacefully into the afterlife.*

It had been three months since Franklin's death, and this was the first day Anisa had been able to find the courage and strength to visit the gravesite, alongside all the others. Franklin's ashes, according to his wishes, had been buried in the family plot, next to his father Cole, mother Melinda, and brothers Nelson and Caleb.

Anisa closed her eyes, clasped her hands together, and said a short prayer. "Dear brother Franklin—in death, I pray that you find the peace, joy, and love that eluded you most of your life. I love you. Amen." As she stood up and glanced at the neat row of tombstones that represented her entire family, she suddenly wavered, overcome with grief at the grim realization that she was the sole surviving member. She steadied herself by clutching the heart of Franklin's tombstone, buckled over, and let the tears flow—slow and silent at first, but soon her sorrow was punctuated by loud, wracking sobs. She cried herself dry, mopped her face with Kleenex, and began the short walk home.

It occurred to her that she had been crying for more than just the loss of Franklin, who had shown so much promise in his last days. She wept for her two brothers and her mother and father. She wept for Natalie. She wept for Terry's loss. She wept for her circumstances, her sadness, and her inability to change her wretchedness. She wept with the hope her tears would wash away her haunting memories of the brutal murders in the DR.

By the time police had arrived at the murder scene the next morning, Franklin's apartment was a death pool of blood. Three dead bodies with multiple contusions and lacerations floated in a macabre red river—a scene right out of a slasher horror movie. The best police could tell, Franklin had fought bravely before his death. Natalie, too, had fought like a warrior, with detectives surmising that it was likely her blows with the shovel that had fatally felled the hired assassin. Bravely fighting to save Franklin's life, she'd killed Francisco. Only problem, it was too little too late. Anisa never really understood how Natalie had known Franklin was in trouble or how she ended up in his apartment on that ill-fated evening. After some brief conversations with Terry—they'd commiserated over more than one bottle of wine—they'd both decided to drop the matter. The truth was waiting for them somewhere after all, but perhaps finding it would only slice deep cuts into hearts that were already suffering from multiple gashes. They might have had their suspicions, but in the end they'd kept them to themselves.

The murders were never traced back to that drunken fuck Riley. Terry arranged for Natalie's body to be flown to Toronto and Anisa had Franklin's remains transported to PEI. After that, she hadn't heard from Terry. After Franklin's funeral, she'd thought about calling him, maybe even flying to Toronto to attend Natalie's funeral. But then she'd spotted Natalie's obituary in the paper and realized Franklin and Natalie had been buried on exactly the same day—exactly three weeks after their deaths. *Terry has my number,* she'd thought, perhaps a little selfishly. *He can call me.*

Walking briskly, Anisa turned left on Main Street. She tasted coppery blood, realized she'd been chewing on her lower lip, and stopped. Stopped walking. Stopping chewing. Visiting Franklin's tombstone had not only created a maelstrom of depressing emotions, it was also causing her to rehash events that she was trying hard to forget. An image of five red roses and one pink rose appeared in her mind and she thought, *Slow down. Smell the roses.* She didn't slow down. She didn't smell any roses. It was fall, after all and everything was dead or dying. But she did attempt to steer her mind in a more positive direction, if for nothing else than for her son, Connor.

His father would be dropping him off at her house in two hours. Since she'd arrived home from the DR, she'd been zombie-like, mechanically going through the mundane chores of daily life with little or no enthusiasm for her son, or anyone else for that matter. Not even work. Even her sympathetic boss, sensing her grief, had last week offered her a medical leave of absence.

It was time to try and cheer up. She'd had her cry. *Suck it up, girl, and get moving with your life. Let's count the positives.*

There were some positives. Helen and Manuel were getting along like a house on fire. Hell, they were even talking about moving in together. Sure, after Anisa had been brought up to speed on the disturbing events that had happened during her absence, she'd been horrified. After all, there was still the unsolved murder of Ray Minowest (not to mention the unsolved murders of Carlos and Victor, the Dominican Republic robbers). Then there was the attempted murder of Helen and Manuel. Unsolved, even though an eyewitness had been shot in the head and was now comatose in the hospital, fighting for her life. Then of course, the awareness by the townsfolk of the rise in the worship of Saint Death and subsequent threats, led by Pastor Paul Bishop, to "cleanse the town of this evil scourge."

Lately, though, it was as if a hot water tap had been abruptly turned off. Nothing in the papers, Pastor Paul Bishop had fallen silent, and no more derogatory comments from community residents. Even in her grieving semi-aware haze, Anisa noticed a subtle change, like a strange mist had invaded Montague, silencing and frightening the entire population and shutting down the witch-hunt. If anything, most people just silently ignored her now. Some even took great pains to avoid eye contact. *Better that than when they open their stupid mouths,* she thought as she passed the Montague Church of Christ, now halfway home.

Thanks to her late brother Franklin, her financial situation had greatly improved. He'd left her $150,000, his life savings. Twenty thousand of it had gone to funeral costs and the cost of transporting his remains to PEI. But she still had enough to one day make a change for the better, maybe even pursue her career aspirations. That is, if she could ever get herself out of the funk she was in.

Money, my life, my health, a few friends, my son. Time will fix the rest. Happiness, love, goals. It always does. At least that's what she told herself. She wanted to arrive home with positive thoughts, lest Connor begin asking her questions again. He was too young to fully understand death and had never met Franklin, but he could certainly sense her mood, which brought forth a battery of questions. "Mommy, what's wrong?

Why are you so sad?" And the one that wrenched her heart the most: "Why don't you ever smile anymore?"

Passing the Atlantic Superstore, she had an idea. Buy Connor some sweets, maybe even some ice cream, and a few toys. She knew she hadn't been giving him the love and affection he needed lately and a little spoiling wouldn't hurt. Besides, she wasn't living paycheck to paycheck anymore. Along with chocolate bars and ice cream, she purchased a coloring book and crayons, a Tonka pickup truck (Connor loved trucks of all shapes and sizes) and two bubble blower kits, something she thought they could do outside in the backyard together. On a whim, she stopped at the liquor store next to the supermarket and bought three bottles of Chilean white wine. She still relished the occasional drink to numb her emotions when debilitating negative thoughts began to get the upper hand.

She arrived home. She was unlocking her front door when Jeff, her ex, pulled into the driveway in his blue pickup. Connor was in the passenger seat. She tried her best smile, but thought it came off as politician plastic at best. Jeff climbed out of the truck, but Connor stayed inside.

Jeff stopped about ten feet in front of her, their unspoken but understood personal space perimeter since the divorce. He eyed her curiously. "You've been crying. Are you okay?"

"I was... I was at the cemetery. I'll be fine. What's Connor doing still in the truck? Come on, son."

Jeff motioned for the boy to stay put. He did. "I know you haven't been feeling that well lately. I just thought, maybe it'd be a good idea if I take him this weekend. You can take some more time to, you know, recover."

Anisa was going to object, but the expectant smile on Connor's face changed her mind. Respecting the Anisa-Jeff personal space perimeter, she approached the pickup truck, leaned in, and kissed him on the cheek. "You be good now."

"I'm always good, Mommy. Daddy's gonna take me fishing tomorrow."

"Take care of him," she told Jeff as he backed out of the driveway, Connor waving cheerfully.

"I will. Take care of yourself."

Inside the bungalow, Anisa realized with a frown she'd forgotten to give Connor the Tonka truck. Oh well. It would have to wait. She put the toys and sweets away and sat down in the living room with a bottle of wine. Her eyes focused first on the main feature of the room, the fireplace, its oak mantel decorated with glass-encased photos of her dead family members, a photo of Franklin the most recent addition. She sighed. *A wall of death. I should put those away. Bad memories.*

She gazed around the room at the clutter and disarray and frowned. Connor's clothes and some of his toys were strewn around the room—on the floor and on the furniture—and a few dirty dishes and a half-eaten grilled cheese sandwich cluttered the coffee table. The floral-patterned wallpaper on one feature wall, matching the curtains covering the bay window, did nothing to brighten her mood. Except for a few inherited PEI seascape and landscape paintings hanging on the white walls, they were otherwise barren. A long time ago, she'd lost interest in decorating. Only recently, she'd lost interest in housekeeping.

Two glasses of wine later, her thoughts drifted to Saint Death. Recent traumatic events had left her fearful of the Bony

Lady's vengeful powers and she'd stopped all prayer and worship. She also feared any further tampering with Saint Death might result in a lynch mob of lunatic Christian fundamentalists coming after her. If she was losing regard for her own life, the least she could do was take steps to insure Connor's safety. She had conveniently dismissed the very real possibility that Saint Death had saved her son's life. Alienating herself even further, she'd put space between herself and her friends Manuel and Helen. And since no Saint Death-connected murders had occurred in the town for three months, and no lynch mobs had been unleashed, she assumed Manuel was taming Helen's hateful and vengeful tendencies.

She stood, closed the curtains, lit a candle, and placed it on the coffee table. She poured a third glass of wine, sat down on the couch, and tried to tell herself she wasn't alone. She was simply spending much-needed recovery time by herself.

Two hours passed in relative silence. Dusk descended on the house. Anisa was oblivious to the hissing sound of the odd car passing on the two-lane highway fronting the residence. As her mind became pleasantly numbed, she wasn't sure why, but she picked up the candle, followed the small flame to a hallway closet, and opened the door. Months ago, she'd removed it from Connor's bedroom, cloaked a black towel over the Bony Lady, and hidden her in the closet.

She fished around the top shelf. Two pairs of gloves, a hat, and scarf; but no Saint Death. *Where did she go?*

She checked two bedrooms. Nothing. She felt a small jolt of adrenaline surge through her body as she moved silently toward the third door, Connor's bedroom. Before opening it, she stopped, feeling her heart rate beginning to accelerate. She was suddenly thrown back in time and space.

She was no longer in her house in her hallway on the first day of fall. She was standing on Franklin's balcony and sliding the door open, a flashlight in hand. The DR bloodbath flashed before her in all its macabre goriness. Franklin, propped up against the wall. Covered in blood. His black eyes looking at her. In the eyes, an eerie calmness. His lips pursed in a small satisfied smile. Natalie, her head resting sideways on his chest; her face, beautiful in death, a picture of peace and calm, her eyes locked on Franklin's eyes. And she was... she was hugging him. An embrace of death. Francisco's mangled corpse was lying on the shattered remains of a coffee table, large spears of glass protruding from his chest, hundreds of tinier fragments embedded in his face. Blood everywhere, his dark eyes wide with horror; his mouth agape in what at one time must have been a painful scream. The last thing she saw, imprinted graphically in her mind's eye, was a blood-spattered Saint Death statue grinning mockingly at her.

Just as she'd done then, Anisa started screaming and fled. By the time she realized what had happened, she was slouched over in the middle of her backyard, gasping for breath and waging a war with a wave of nausea. She tried to force it back to the pit of her stomach but it was no use. She coughed twice and spewed partially digested bits of wine-soaked grilled cheese sandwich onto her lawn. She finished puking and sat down on a plastic lawn chair, trying to regain her composure.

After a few minutes, the nausea passed and she started to feel a little better. She looked up into the sky and noticed a dark bank of clouds surrounded by bright white moving steadily closer. Bowling balls of thunder rolled in the sky, intensifying as the clouds neared. The wind whipped up, swirling and hissing around her. An empty plastic lawn chair flew into the fence and shattered.

The rain came, first in a drizzle and then in sheets. Anisa stayed on the lawn chair, terrified yet mesmerized by Mother Nature's fury. Even her breathing reached something approximating normal. But in a short time, she was soaked to the bone and reason asserted itself in a traumatized mind. She remembered the Environment Canada weather warning she'd seen online this morning. "When thunder rolls, get indoors."

What the hell am I doing? She hurried inside and fought with the intensifying wind to close the screen door. She won that battle and clicked it shut, noticing the chair she'd been sitting on lift off. It swirled around like a hovering helicopter, and sailed over the fence, vanishing into the tree line. She thought for a second about retrieving the other two chairs and a few of Connor's toys, but quickly changed her mind. By now she was shivering with cold and besides, it was far too dangerous. The house had already begun to groan and creak from the ferocity of the thunderstorm.

She threw her wet clothes into a laundry hamper and changed into a pair of loose-fitting jeans and a white cotton t-shirt. She went into the kitchen and retrieved a flashlight from a junk drawer. She poured a glass of water, rinsed the puke from her mouth, and spat it into the sink. She rinsed and refilled the glass, went into the living room, and sat down on the couch, trying to work up the courage to check Connor's bedroom for Saint Death. About five minutes later, she felt calm enough to investigate, even though the thunderstorm was probably at the height of its ferocity by now. Halfway down the hall, she noticed the candle lying on a hallway rug on its side. She realized she must have dropped it during her panic-stricken exodus. She flicked on the hallway light and bent down. *Thank God—or do I thank Saint Death?—it went out. I could've burned the house down.* Some wax had spilled out onto the rug and hardened. She pulled the candle free, placed it on the hallway closet shelf, and continued down the hall.

Thunder boomed in the heavens. The house trembled and creaked. Lightning flashes flickered in the windows.

The lights went out.

Oh no. Tensing, she turned the flashlight on, thought about returning to the relative safety of the living room, and changed her mind. Suddenly it was as if she were being guided by some ethereal force, and her only choice was to open the door. She reached it and slowly turned the handle. The door creaked open. She shone the beam on the wall, moving it over the pictures; the fearless lion, the blue smiling elephant, the determined rhinoceros, the jumping giraffe. A flickering candle on a small table in the corner of the room caught her eye. The flame lit the black eye sockets of Saint Death. The skeleton saint grinned at her. The intermittent lightning flashes bursting in from the window cast a large, menacing shadow above and behind Saint Death, making her and her deadly scythe appear larger than life, larger than Anisa.

Her first emotion was fear and a rising sense of panic that aimed to send her once again bolting out the door. So much for the ethereal force. She took a few deep breaths, and after a moment the panic passed. Her second emotion was anger at her son. *The lit candle. He could've burned down the house.*

Connor must have dug Saint Death out of the closet and returned her to his bedroom. The anger slowly dissipated as logic prevailed. How could she blame the child for that? He must have realized on some level Saint Death had not only saved his life, but brought him back from the dead.

Precipitously Anisa's apostasy of Saint Death made no sense to her. *What the hell was I thinking? Screw what the neighbors say. Fuck the townsfolk. I can't abandon my holy savior.* She approached the statue. "Okay, Most Holy Death. I'm sorry. Please forgive me." She picked her up along with the candle, carried them into the living room, and put them both on the coffee table. Guided by the flashlight beam, she went into the kitchen and returned with a bottle of Bacardi white rum and two shot glasses.

Thunder rolled, lightning cracked, wind-battered trees writhed sibilantly like vengeful serpents, and sheets of torrential rain pounded the windows. Anisa rummaged through her bedroom dresser until she found what she was looking for—the red votive candle, the symbol for love and passion. Returning to the living room, she lit it and placed it in front of The Lady of the Night, alongside the other candle, which she suddenly realized was black—representing protection and harm. She didn't recall ever owning a black candle, but evidently one had mysteriously found its way into her son's possession and subsequently inside his bedroom. Was her ex giving their son accoutrements for Saint Death worship? She didn't know. She'd never mentioned Saint Death to Jeff. But surely Connor must have. That statue had stayed in his room for how many weeks after he was resurrected from the dead? She pushed the thought away and concentrated on the task at hand—a prayer for love and passion and for protection from harm, since she would no longer be abandoning her miracle-working saint; not now, not ever.

She brought the shot glass to her lips and dipped her tongue inside the clear liquid. It tasted strong and slightly sweet and oaky. She raised the glass. "Sorry, Most Holy Death. No tequila. Here's to having you back in my life." She drained the shot glass, smacked it down on the oak coffee table, and studied the statue. Both candles cast a giant black shadow of Saint Death on the white "wall of death" above the fireplace. The larger-than-life Bony Lady danced and swayed in rhythm to the lightning flashes, the flickering candles, and the thundering storm. Her shrouded skeleton head and gigantic scythe hovered above the fireplace mantel as if protecting all the framed images of dead people perched on top. She watched the Bony Lady in action. *Maybe I shouldn't put those away.*

She went into the kitchen and returned with a bottle of Coke and a glass of ice. She was jumpy tonight. She felt a prescient knowledge that something was going to happen. Something good, she kept telling herself as she mixed a rum and Coke. She sat back, sipped, and studied the dark shadow of Saint Death dancing on her wall, the scythe now descending and rising in synchronicity with the rolling thunder. The earlier nausea was slowly being replaced by a kind of euphoria, mixed with a deep connection, admiration, and love for the Bony Lady.

She was silent for a long time, trying to construct the perfect words, the perfect petition, the perfect prayer. The words formed, gelled in her mind, and began flowing like a river.

"Oh Most Holy Death, I beseech you, please provide happiness, passion, and love in my life. Protect me from... "

So deep was her mind focused on her mission, it was after the third ring that she finally realized her phone was ringing. Recognizing the number, she answered it.

"Are you okay?" Helen said, skipping the social niceties even though it had been almost a month since they'd spoken.

"I'm better now."

"You sound drunk."

"I've had a few."

"Is Connor with you?"

"No. His dad has him this weekend."

"Do you have power?"

"No. The storm knocked it out."

"Are you sure you're okay?"

"Yeah, how about you?"

"I'm at my sweetie's. The storm knocked the power down here but we have a back-up generator. We're drinking Scotch."

"Good for you. Say hi to Manuel."

"I will." There was an uncomfortable silence, then Helen said, "Are *we* okay?"

"I hope so."

"You hope so?"

"We are, Helen."

Helen's words tumbled like an avalanche. They were tinged with sadness. "It's just that you don't call me anymore. You seem to go out of your way to avoid me at work. We used to be such good friends. I know you're going through a lot right now, Anisa. Maybe you just need your own space, but I'd like to help you. I love you, girl. I miss you. I miss our friendship. I want you back in my life."

"I'm sorry. I haven't been myself lately."

"Listen, we'd like you to come to a barbeque tomorrow at Manuel's. It'll be great. We'll have a bonfire, enjoy the amazing ocean view, and get all caught up. It'll be just like old times. And I have some very good news for you, but I won't tell you over the phone. I want to tell you in person. Will you come?"

It was as if her decision to reembrace the Bony Lady had infused her with a new enthusiasm for life. "I'd love to, Helen. Thank you."

"We'll pick you up at six-thirty tomorrow, okay?"

"Sounds good."

"Okay, I gotta run. Dinner's ready. One more question. What were you doing when I called?"

Anisa had never lied to Helen before, and she saw no reason to start now. "Praying to Saint Death."

"I knew it. Awesome. Me too."

CHAPTER TWENTY-ONE

The Lady of the Night stood guard inside the entrance door to the lavish mansion, her hollow black eye sockets focused intently on her guests. Larger than life, she was cloaked in red and held the scythe in her left hand proudly. In the middle of a massive gold room decorated with plush black couches and shimmering white granite tables, a fire blazed inside of an ornate fireplace, its oak mantel decorated with a large slithering red serpent. One wall was entirely glass and the black of night was spotted with a million shining stars and an ominously glowing full moon. The other walls were dotted with candles burning in decorative wall-mounted candle holders. Seven in all, representing the multiple miracle-working powers of the Holy Saint. On the floor in front of the blazing fire, a luxurious throw rug set the tone for relaxation. It was streaked with brown, white, black, red, gold, purple and green, the seven colors of Saint Death. In the middle of it, the flame of a seven-color votive candle flickered on a black granite table. Beside it stood two golden goblets and a bottle of red wine.

Lounging in front of the fire in a black robe, his black hair grown out and slicked back, Franklin picked up a goblet and gazed thoughtfully out at the stars. His eyes drifted over to the love of his life; or in this case, the love of his death. Dressed in a sheer white negligee that complimented her beautiful body perfectly and left little to the imagination, she lay beside him, her deep blue eyes mesmerized by the fire. Her long brown hair shimmered in the dancing lights: orange flickering flames, flickering yellow candlelight, twinkling stars and glowing moon.

"I think this calls for a toast," Franklin said. "Could it be more perfect?"

Natalie looked at Franklin, smiled, and picked up her wine goblet. "I think you're right, baby. And no, it couldn't be more perfect."

"Let's toast Saint Death for bringing us together."

"That's always a good one. To our holy savior."

They clinked golden goblets and drank.

"You know, honey," Natalie said, getting up and leisurely strolling over to the expansive window, "When I first met you, I thought you were a freak. Freaky Franky, I thought to myself."

His eyes were riveted to her moving form. "You're not the only one. I thought that about myself. People used to call me that as a kid."

She reached the glass wall and stared out at the magnificent view for a moment. Off in the distance, the abstract pattern of dark blue, gray, and white—Earth—shimmered from space. She turned around, faced him, and took a sip of wine. "But you're not Freaky Franky at all. You're an angel. You're my angel in heaven."

Drink in hand, Franky rose and joined her at the window. "Thank you for saying that, my dear. Things could have gone a lot differently. I was on a dark path. But I'm so happy Saint Death showed me the light. She saved me, answered my prayers, and brought us together." He moved closer, putting a hand on her slim waist. "You're *my* angel in heaven. And I love you to death."

She stroked his smooth chin gently. "I love you, too."

Locked in a tight embrace, they kissed long and passionate. When they released, Natalie returned her gaze to Earth. "Isn't it beautiful?"

"It is. But I think I'm happier up here. I like the afterlife better than the other life."

"Me too. But sometimes I wonder how our friends are doing on Earth."

"Same here. But we pray for them regularly."

"We do. Should we do it again? Tonight?"

"Of course," Franklin said. "Let's do a preliminary toast-prayer combination now."

"Okay. You do the words. You're good at that."

"Here's to Anisa and Terry finding love and happiness in whatever form that takes. May they experience the best that life has to offer."

"Here-here," Natalie said as they toasted. She gave Franky a wry grin. "Now don't go praying for any bad stuff. You know what happens when you do that."

Franky considered this. "Well, I can't die a second time. I don't think so, anyway."

The red serpent on the fireplace mantel slithered and hissed, flicking its long tongue at the two lovers.

The life-sized Saint Death statue suddenly came to life and floated across the room, its black eye sockets glowing, its mocking grin tightening into a look of consternation. They backed away as it hovered closer. Saint Death spoke, her tone terse and authoritative. "Maybe you can't die a second time, but you can be separated and sent to the bowels of hell."

Franky pulled Natalie toward the seven-colored carpet as the skeleton saint's form grew and spread across the spectacular view, shrouding it in darkness. He almost tripped over the seven-colored votive candle in his panic and haste.

"I'm sorry, Most Holy Death," he said. "I didn't mean anything by that comment. I promise. It was a joke."

"It was a bad joke," the Holy Saint said. "Mere mortals must not entertain; or worse, act out on evil thoughts. To do so brings forth harsh punishment. You know this."

"I do. Please forgive me."

There was a momentary silence as the skeleton saint considered this. "Okay. In the future watch your tongue, please."

They were both kneeling now, their hands clasped together in prayer before their holy savior.

"Thank you, Saint Death," Franklin said.

"Thank you, Saint Death," Natalie said.

Saint Death's grin returned, not mocking at all this time, but kind and gentle. "It's nothing, my children. Everyone needs a little guidance sometimes. Now, if you'll forgive me, speaking of guidance, I have much work to do on Earth."

Her majestic form shrank. There was a hissing sound, followed by a pop, and she vanished.

Natalie and Franklin returned to lounging and drinking in front of the blazing fire. Franklin caressed Natalie's arm. His hand found her breast and slowly massaged it, gently tugging and teasing her erect nipple.

She moaned softly. "You said you love me to death?"

"I did. I do."

"Then fuck me to death."

Waking up, Anisa was sure it wasn't a dream at all. It had felt incredibly real, although her efforts to speak to her brother had fallen on deaf ears. "Franky, it's me. Over here." But her voice didn't find voice, except in her mind. She had been just a pair of eyes looking in at a fishbowl of life, somehow attached to it yet somehow far removed. She'd even panicked at one point, trying to pinch herself awake. But she was all eyes and no body.

She looked at the battery-operated bedside clock. 10:36 am. Wow. She had slept in. Big time. She remembered the night clearly enough. After the conversation with Helen, she'd finished her prayers, blown out the votive candles, carried Saint Death into her bedroom and placed her on a dresser, and gone to bed. By that time, shortly after midnight, although the power hadn't returned, the storm had passed and the night was dead calm.

Her eyes drifted to the dresser and found the statue of Saint Death. A ray of sunlight poked in from the partially open black velvet window coverings, casting a yellow angelic circle above the statue and giving her face a warm glow.

She went into the adjoining bathroom and flicked on the light. Good—power had been restored. Looking at herself in the mirror, she realized for the first time in a long time how beautiful she was. Her long, flowing black hair gave her black eyes an exotic, captivating, and magical quality. She smiled, admiring her perfect teeth, and realized it was her first real smile in a long time. She removed her panties and t-shirt and climbed into the shower, luxuriating in the warm water as it cascaded off her naked body.

It came to her in an instant. What Terry had said in the DR. He'd had an epiphany. He'd sworn it was real. This wasn't a dream at all. It was real, and somehow Saint Death had transported her there to show her that Franklin and Natalie were not only perfectly fine, but madly in love. The thought infused her with joy, energy, and a renewed sense of self-worth.

After showering she dressed quickly, made some coffee, and sat at the kitchen table to make a list of today's chores. Text Jeff about Connor. Clean house. Laundry. Clean backyard. Cut grass. Make grocery list. Pay bills. Call Terry about epiphany.

Four hours later, she sat at the kitchen table again, crossing items off the list. She'd completed everything (Connor was safe and sound, enjoying his time with his dad) except call Terry. She picked up her cell phone, found Terry's number, and began pressing numbers. But she chickened out on the last digit.

Terry had been madly in love with Natalie. To be sure, he was probably still mourning her death. To tell him about the epiphany would also mean telling him that Natalie and Franklin were living happily ever after in the afterlife. How would he handle that? Anisa sighed and put down the phone. She needed to think things through.

CHAPTER TWENTY-TWO

The sound of a barking dog, followed by the roar of a motorcycle engine, woke Juana. She opened her eyes with a smile. In three months, she couldn't believe how much her life had changed for the better. Her parents, although sometimes she wondered if they really were her biological parents, had taken her advice and started daily worship of Saint Death. Although Santiago had steadfastly opposed the skeleton saint in the beginning, even going so far as to call it a "devil-worshipping cult," over time he just couldn't ignore the miracles. When he'd gotten a new and better-paying construction job, Juana had said it was in answer to her prayers. When Marta got a job as a waitress in an upscale restaurant in the popular tourist district of Zona Rosa, Juana steadfastly maintained it was in answer to her prayers. Maybe Santiago had still been on the fence regarding the second miracle, but when the mysterious old man who'd given her burritos that one day reappeared last week at the Tepito Saint Death shrine and handed her $100,000 in cold, hard American cash, Santiago could no longer ignore the miracle-working supernatural powers of the skeleton saint. Now the entire family of three embraced the skeleton saint with all their devotion, loyalty, love, and affection. They never prayed for revenge or bad things to happen to people. They only prayed for good things.

Juana rolled off the air mattress onto the dusty dirt floor and went into the bathroom, washing herself up as best she could in the trickling drops that flowed from the rusted shower head. She put on her best and cleanest white dress, tied her hail in a ponytail, and pushed aside the blue, hole-filled blanket that served as her bedroom door.

She saw Marta and Santiago sleeping side by side on a weathered mattress on the floor of a room that served as bedroom, living room, dining room, and kitchen. She smiled. Not for long.

That morning, a realtor was picking the family up in a fancy car and taking them on a tour of nice rental apartments in much better barrios than where she currently lived. They were moving up. Things were getting better. This was the happiest day of her life.

She pulled the strapless wristwatch from the pocket of her dress and realized it was eighty-thirty am. In another half hour, the realtor would arrive. Time to wake them.

She touched Marta's arm. "Mommy, wake up."

Marta opened her eyes. "Is it time, my dear?"

"A half hour."

Marta got up and passed through the blue blanket, through Juana's bedroom, and into the bathroom.

Santiago snored.

Juana made coffee and lowered a steaming hot cup to Santiago's nose. It never failed.

He opened his eyes and sniffed the strong acrid aroma. He wiped sleep from his eyes, smiled at Juana, and took the black coffee. "You're such a Godsend, honey. Or should I say, an angel of Most Holy Death?"

She grinned. "That's better, Dad."

Twenty-seven minutes later, the family was in a navy-blue Audi Quattro driven by Mateo, a young, enthusiastic realtor wearing a black suit, a crisp white shirt, and a gold tie. "I thought we'd look at apartments in Zona Rosa first," he said. He turned to Marta. "It's close to your work, and also pretty close to your husband's new construction site."

"That's a nice area," Marta said. "I'd like that."

"Sounds good to me," Santiago said.

"By the way," Mateo said. "Some of these places you may have to furnish. They might even need appliances. You might want to add your own colors and your own window coverings. You can afford that?"

"I don't know," Santiago said. He squeezed Juana's arm gently. "Can we afford that, angel?"

Mateo frowned.

"We can afford that for sure," Juana said. "And we can afford lots more. Pretty soon we're gonna have more money than we know what to do with. We're gonna be rich."

"Pretty confident little girl," Mateo said as they pulled into the secure underground parking lot of a gleaming metal, glass, and concrete high-rise, expansive balconies affording spectacular city views.

"I'm not so little anymore," Juana said. "I'm gonna be sixteen soon."

"You're growing up to be a fine young woman," Santiago said.

"And we're gonna put you through university," Marta said.

"I'd like that very much."

"What do you want to study in university?" Mateo asked as he parked.

"I want to study medicine. I want to be a doctor. I want to devote my life to helping people. It's the greatest thing people can do with their lives."

They entered an elevator, ascended eleven floors, and stopped. Down the hall, Mateo opened the door to apartment 1101 and they entered.

Marta was speechless at the beauty and modernity of the suite. According to the feature sheet she held in her hard, it was 1300 square feet with three bedrooms and two full baths. Even the brand-new stainless steel appliances were included, along with living room and dining room furniture. The walls were painted a warm desert sand color. Even though she was in the heart of Mexico City, one of the biggest cities by population in the world, it was so quiet she could almost hear a pin drop. What a contrast to the noisy, dilapidated dump they lived in. She went out to the balcony, took in the expansive city view, and was overcome with emotion. She couldn't stop the tears of joy.

"We'll take it," she said to Mateo when he appeared.

Juana grabbed her hand. "What's wrong, Mommy?"

She hugged Juana tightly. "Nothing's wrong, angel. I'm overjoyed at our good fortune."

As they toured the rest of the apartment, Marta wondered if she'd ever tell Juana, whom she loved as a daughter, about her true parentage—that she had the blood of violent cartel members coursing through her veins. *No, she's too young for that. It's gonna have to wait.* She decided that revealing the true source of the $100,000 gift would also have to wait, given their interconnectedness. While two of the recent financial miracles were certainly Saint Death's doing, at least one—the $100,000 gift—was from one Doctor Manuel Ricardo.

CHAPTER TWENTY-THREE

It was a starlit fall evening, a balmy twenty degrees Celsius, and barely a breeze to be had. Anisa and Helen had just arrived. Helen had picked her up in Doctor Manuel Ricardo's repaired navy-blue Audi Quattro.

She and Helen watched the flames dance in the fire while the dead calm water of the Atlantic Ocean glittered and gleamed under an almost full moon. A dock anchored to the sandy shoreline spread out into the water. A speedboat was tied off at the end of it.

Behind Helen and Anisa, Manuel barbequed steaks, potatoes, and onions, expertly manning the food with one hand while sipping a beer with the other. After picking Anisa up, Helen had remarked on how beautiful Anisa looked, claiming she "positively glowed." Helen had pressed her about the reason, but Anisa had remained tight-lipped, saying she wanted to hear Helen's news first, and only once they got to the fire and had drinks in their hands.

Helen handed Anisa a glass of white wine. "Well, you've got no excuse now," Helen said. "What's your news?"

"Do you think I forgot? I told you earlier, you first."

"Should I tell her, honey?"

"Of course," Manuel said.

Helen reached into her pocket and pulled out a gold ring with a large diamond. She put it on her finger.

Anisa gasped.

"It's an engagement ring," Helen said. "We're getting married next summer."

Manuel had left the barbeque and stood at Helen's side, both of them beaming with ear-to-ear smiles.

Anisa rushed into Helen's arms so fast she almost knocked her off her chair. Her eyes welling with tears, she gave Helen a big hug. "Congratulations. I'm so happy for you." She unhooked herself and gave Manuel a warm hug. "Really, Manuel, I wish you guys all the happiness in the world. Congratulations."

"Thank you," he said, returning to the barbeque. "Someone's gotta keep her in line."

"Of course you're invited to the wedding," Helen said. "I'd like you to be my maid of honor."

"I'd be honored," Anisa said, raising her glass. "A toast to the happiness of you and Doctor Ric—I mean, Manuel. Cheers to you guys."

Manuel didn't miss a beat, rushing over to touch glasses before returning to the barbeque and flipping over some sizzling steaks.

"I guess it's my turn now," Anisa said. "It's pretty heady stuff compared to what you guys just announced."

"Is it bad?" Helen said.

"No. It's quite good actually. It made me see things a lot more clearly. Should I begin?"

"Not yet."

"What, you mean after dinner?"

"No, I mean after my other surprise."

"What? You have another surprise?"

Helen approached Manuel at the barbeque. He handed her the tongs and opened the back door. "You can come out now."

A man stood in the doorway.

"Surprise," Helen and Manuel said in unison.

At first all Anisa saw was a black silhouette, and she couldn't make out who it was. But when he emerged into the moonlight and the deck lanterns, she recognized him instantly. Her eyes moistened for a second time. She leapt from the lawn chair, dropping her wine glass on the grass, and ran into his arms.

They hugged warmly, and finally Anisa pulled away and looked into his deep green eyes, which still reflected some of the pain of Natalie's passing. But there was something else. His hair had grown out, and there were dark sockets under his eyes. How he must have grieved her death. Maybe he'd lost a lot of sleep.

But she also saw a new humbleness about him; something less proud, more vulnerable and sensitive. For the most part, she liked the change. "Terry, my God. It's really you. I wanted to call you so many times but couldn't. I don't know why. I'm sorry."

He wiped a moist eye. "It takes two to tango. I wanted to call you but couldn't. I guess, you know, we were hurting too much and needed time to heal."

"That's it," Anisa said, leading him by the hand to a vacant lawn chair beside her. "Come. Sit. Have a drink."

"One right here," Manuel said, popping the cap off a bottle of Budweiser and handing it to Terry.

Helen joined them and explained she'd found Terry on Facebook. He'd accepted an invitation to pay a surprise visit to Anisa to help cheer her up. "You spoke of him highly," Helen said. "And you were in such a funk I thought it was the least we could do."

"Thanks," Anisa said. "I don't know what to say. You're a much better friend than I gave you credit for. And I shouldn't even be admitting that."

"Don't thank just me," Helen said. "It was actually Manuel's idea."

"Thanks Manuel," Anisa said. "You're much more than just a great doctor."

"Don't mention it."

Conversation ensued. Terry told Anisa about his recent promotion as bank manager of a Scotiabank in downtown Toronto. Cecil Schmidt, the man originally chosen for the promotion, had inappropriately touched some female staff members, and it had finally caught up to him. He was now facing six sexual assault charges. He had not only been passed up for the promotion, but fired on the spot. "Now I'm the bank manager. Funny, it used to be such a big thing on my bucket list, and now it feels so small compared to the things that really matter."

"It's a major accomplishment," Anisa said. "Congratulations." Some of the old chemistry was coming back, and she didn't want to ruin it by bringing up her epiphany. She hoped Helen had forgotten about it.

"Thank you," Terry said. "I suppose you're right. What are your career plans?"

"Wait a minute," Helen said. "I'm not trying to be rude, but she can tell you her career plans later, maybe over dinner." She looked at Anisa. "You think I forgot, don't you?"

Anisa didn't answer. It was obvious Terry was still smarting from Natalie's death, and she didn't want to ruin it by tearing off scabs on wounds that were not yet properly healed.

"Oh no, girl, you promised," Helen said. "I've delivered two surprises, and now it's your turn. Did you know Terry was coming? Is that why you were so radiant when I picked you up?" She looked at Terry. "Isn't she beautiful?"

He nodded with a smile. "Stunning."

Helen continued. "Indeed she is. She glows. She positively radiates joy and happiness. I have to tell you in all the years I've known her, I've never, ever seen her like this. Come on, Anisa, come clean with me. Someone told you about Terry coming, didn't they?"

"No, this is a complete surprise, and I'm thrilled."

But Helen wouldn't let it go. "Well, what happened? Inquiring minds want to know."

"Dinner's almost ready," Manuel said. "Five minutes."

"After dinner, then," Anisa said, thinking she had an out.

"No, now," Helen insisted.

Anisa thought for a moment. She could tell the story but omit the hurtful parts. That wasn't lying. It was omission, selective truth. The justification was enough. "Okay."

By now, Manuel had joined them. "Everything's warming in the oven. But I wanna hear this first."

"I had a vision last night in my sleep," Anisa said. She looked at Terry. "Remember in the DR when you told me about your epiphany?"

He nodded. "It changed me and made me a better person. But it wasn't a dream. It was real."

"So was mine," Anisa said. "I don't want to bring up old wounds, but I saw Natalie in my epiphany. And Franklin. They're both very happy."

"I know," Terry said.

"You know?"

"Yeah, and I know they're together, if that's what you're afraid to tell me. I had possibly the exact same epiphany."

Anisa was incredulous. "Wow, when?"

"Last night. And, yeah, at first I was, you know, madly jealous. But later I realized that it feels right. Isn't it exactly as it should be? Since Natalie tried to save his life, isn't it fitting that Franky's looking after her in the afterlife?"

But wait a minute. In the DR. Terry's suspicions. That must have been it. There was a question of possible infidelity prior to Natalie's death that Terry wasn't addressing, or didn't want to address. Anisa decided that he'd obviously found some way to reconcile or ignore or dismiss it. So would she. "Knowing there's an afterlife has given me a new joy," Anisa said. "I guess I'd considered it before, but never really thought it through. I didn't think that when I died, I'd end up in some palatial abode far off in space with the man of my dreams." *Maybe that wasn't quite the right way to put it.*

"Man of your dreams?" Terry said. "You dating?"

"No."

"Can we take this conversation into the dining room?" Manuel said. "Dinner's ready."

Manuel's dining room—soon to be Manuel and Helen's dining room—was painted a warm and inviting dark green. It was decorated with paintings of pyramids and assorted hand-carved wooden masks. Sliding-glass doors featured a spectacular ocean view. An oval oak dining room table was set with red silk napkins. Seven seven-colored votive candles provided soft, romantic lighting. Six high-back black leather chairs stood at the table.

They took their seats, Terry at one head of the table and Anisa to his right. Manuel occupied the other head of the table with Helen to his left.

Food, drink, and conversation flowed smoothly. Terry and Anisa discussed their recent epiphany. Anisa, uncertain if Terry had seen exactly the same PG-13 version as she had, was careful not to reveal too much. After all, Franky was her brother and frankly, details about his sex life were just too much information. She thought the same would apply to Terry, probably more so, since Natalie and Terry had been engaged to be married. *Don't rub salt in the wound.*

"Could you pass the salt, please?" Helen asked Anisa. "Don't give me that look. It's just salt."

Anisa laughed and, as if everyone had a secret psychic knowledge of her thoughts, the other three burst out laughing. "What's so funny?"

"I don't know," Helen said. "Your laugh. It's cute. And I don't think I've ever seen you laugh so freely like that before. I'm glad you're enjoying yourself."

It was true. Anisa was enjoying herself. Truth be told, she didn't ever remember being this happy. She almost had to pinch herself to make sure it was real. To keep the conversation light, she decided to change the subject. She was sure Terry didn't want to discuss Natalie all night, and she sure as hell didn't want to discuss Franky all night, although he had indirectly become a source of her happiness.

She pointed to a painting of a pyramid on the wall. "What is that, Manuel?"

He sliced through a bite-sized piece of rare sirloin steak. "It's the Pyramid of the Sun, located in the ancient city of

Teotihuacan, just outside Mexico City. It's one of the largest pyramids in the world."

"It's beautiful. Have you been there?"

"Oh yes. I've climbed it. The entire site is interesting. The Pyramid of the Sun is near the Pyramid of the Moon, along the Avenue of the Dead... "

The *rat-tat-tat* of gunfire shattered the sliding-glass door, raining shards of glass on the four.

Two balaclava-masked men burst inside. One took aim at Manuel and fired. Manuel took a bullet in the chest but quickly drew his 57 Magnum and shot the man twice in the head as his chair tipped over. He slammed into the wall and melted down it, leaving a squiggly red streak. The other man looked at his dead accomplice, paused, and pointed his handgun at Helen. But the momentary distraction gave Terry a small window of opportunity and he leapt from his chair, grabbing the man's gun hand.

Kneeling down and attending to Manuel, Helen screamed, "No, God, no, please no."

As Terry twirled around the dining room with the armed man, wrestling for control of his weapon, Anisa jumped up and said to Helen, "Get his gun. Get Manuel's gun. Shoot him."

As the twirling attacker neared her, Anisa picked up an empty wine bottle and smashed it over his head. It shattered and dazed him for a second or two, but he pulled Terry outside and the dance of death continued under an almost full moon.

Anisa grabbed another wine bottle and followed the dancers outside.

The masked attacker pushed Terry to the grass and they rolled toward the fire, still wrestling for control of the weapon.

Raising the bottle, Anisa moved closer. With the frenetic movement in the darkness, it was hard to tell who was who.

Clutching the 57 magnum, Helen, her face twisted with rage, stepped through the shattered remains of the door and onto the lawn. "Where is that son of a bitch?"

The masked man kneed Terry in the groin and he doubled over, clutching his aching nuts. The man stood up, kicked him in the face, and pointed the gun at his head.

Anisa seized the opportunity and clobbered the man over the head with the wine bottle. "Who says social drinking isn't good for your health?"

The man groaned and spun around with the weapon.

Helen fired. The bullet narrowly missed the man's head and zinged into the forest. "I'll kill you, you fucking bastard." She fired again, and the bullet grazed the attacker's arm.

He brought the gun barrel closer to Anisa's head. She tried to strike him a third time with the wine bottle, but he brought an arm up fast and knocked it loose from her grip. The wine bottle rolled along the lawn.

Helen fired again. The bullet whistled into the ocean, plunging into the water with a plop.

From the ground, Terry kicked the man's knee hard as he fired at Anisa. The attacker lost his balance and the trajectory of the bullet changed, smashing through a window of Manuel's house. The attacker fell on the grass.

Terry mounted him and punched him in the face twice. Then he hammer-fisted his gun hand and the attacker dropped the gun.

The mob mentality took over, that inexplicable groupthink that causes humans to riot, loot and destroy businesses and commit all kinds of heinous acts. Anisa picked up the wine bottle and approached. "Stand back," she ordered Terry. He raised his fists long enough for her to smash the man in the head with the bottle twice before it shattered to smithereens.

Terry had the man's wrists pinned to the ground, but Anisa realized he was still conscious and struggling.

Then he spoke. "Go ahead and kill me. It won't matter. There'll be more, and they'll kill all of you fucking devil-worshippers."

It was Helen's voice Anisa heard next, tight with tension but ringing with authority. "Stand back. Both of you."

They did.

Holding the gun, she approached the man as he tried to get up, and planted her knee hard on his chest. He groaned loudly as two of his ribs snapped like twigs. She pulled the balaclava off his face. Even through the bloody cuts and bruises, she recognized him instantly. Her voice was filled with hatred and rage. "Randy Safferty. You killed my fiancé." It didn't matter to her that it was his partner in crime who had pulled the trigger. In her eyes, and in the eyes of the law, they were both guilty of murder. An eye for an eye.

He spit out two blood-soaked front teeth and grinned at her. "Nice fucking breasts."

She jammed the barrel of the gun into his mouth.

Anisa and Terry watched silently.

"You're no fucking diamond in the rough," she said. "You're nothing but a murdering, sex-assaulting loser. At least that's what you were."

He struggled to grab the gun, but it was too little, too late. She plugged one bullet into his mouth and out spewed a fountain of blood. She removed the gun, plugged two bullets between his eyes, stood up, and wiped blood spatter and brain matter from her chin.

She got up and started to walk inside. Halfway there, she covered her face with her hands, doubled over, and began balling her eyes out, convulsing violently with wracking sobs.

Pastor Paul Bishop led fifteen-year-old Peter Matheson into his bedroom. "Just take your pants off and lie down. I'll just be a minute."

The young boy looked at him, worry wrinkles scrunching his brow. "I don't know. This doesn't feel right anymore."

Pastor Paul turned around at the door. "What do you mean? You want to be in God's good graces don't you?"

"Is this what God wants? I don't know anymore."

"Don't you want God to prevent your father from beating your mother?"

"Yeah. I love my mom."

"Of course you do. And God will protect your mom if you do what I say. I'm a man of God and God allows me certain benefits for keeping people in His good graces. This is one of them. Are you okay with that?"

"Yeah." But Peter's tone was unconvincing, and he looked sad.

"Just put on a happy face," Pastor Paul said. "This won't take but a minute."

He closed the door, went into the living room, and picked up the disposable cell phone. He punched in Randall's number and got voicemail. He frowned. *They should have been done by now. Something's wrong.*

The cut was clean, precise, and fast. Pastor Paul Bishop's head flew through the air as his body gyrated and spewed blood. He staggered back and crumpled to the floor. His head hit the wall, thudded along the carpet, and landed at his feet.

Saint Death grinned. *Sick fuck. Not bad handiwork, if I do say so myself.* She crossed his arms on his chest, picked up his head, and placed it neatly inside his folded arms. *You lost your head, but now you found it. Rot in hell.* Then she laid the bloody scythe at his side and vanished into thin air.

Through an alcoholic haze, Riley Hock studied the young couple across the table at Juan's Calmado in the Dominican Republic. "What did you say?"

"I was just introducing ourselves," the young man said. "I'm Danny, and this here's my wife, Lila."

Riley's drunken eyes squinted. He saw two couples where there was only one. "No, you didn't. You just called me a smartass. Did you just call me a fucking smartass?"

Danny stood. "You don't have to be rude. I was just introducing myself."

"Fuck you," Riley said. "I know people around here. I have connections. Do you know I can have you and your ugly wife killed for four thousand pesos?"

Danny grabbed his wife by the hand. "Let's go, sweetie. We don't have to listen to this smartass's bullshit. Why don't you go fuck yourself, you ugly drunk loser."

As they left, Riley shouted at their backs. "You'll pay with your lives. Fucking dumb tourists. You'll pay with your lives. Wait and see."

A half hour later, he staggered up the hill to his condo behind Juan's. A dark shadow descended from the cloud-covered sky and touched down in front of him. Saint Death grinned and raised the scythe.

"Who are you?" Riley said. "The fucking Grim Reaper or something?"

The cut was executed with lightning speed and surgical precision. Riley's blood-dripping head launched in the air. The rest of him danced around in what Saint Death fancied was a poor attempt at the mambo for a few seconds before staggering into the road and dropping like a sack of bananas.

"That's the first true thing you've said all night, you fucking smartass. Rot in hell."

She watched as his head rolled down the hill and stopped in the middle of the road fronting Cofresi beach. She thought of retrieving it, but a five-ton service truck roared down the street and ran over it, squashing it into the asphalt like a grapefruit. *Oh well. They can't all be the same.*

She laid the scythe carefully at Riley's side, placed his left hand around the handle, and stood back to admire her spontaneous creativity. *There you go. Now you're the Grim Reaper.* She couldn't help a small chuckle.

Then she disappeared with a pop and a flash.

EPILOGUE

December 21, the first day of winter. Dusk. Anisa gazed out the window and saw the first snowflakes drifting lazily down. Carpeting the lawn, blanketing the trees, melting and disappearing as they landed on the ocean. *How cleansing and purifying a white world looks,* she thought. *How innocent.* She smiled, realizing it had been many years since she'd enjoyed the changing of the seasons. But now, once again, she had every reason to be happy.

On that ill-fated night at Manuel's, she had seen how quickly happiness could be shattered. Now she felt much more confident that it would establish a more lasting permanence in her life. It could have been a lot worse, she thought, turning her gaze away from the winter wonderland and slumping into her new black leather couch. She could be dead, Helen could be dead, Terry could be dead, and Doctor Manuel Ricardo could be dead. But he had been spared. Miraculously, the gunshot wound to the chest had missed all vital organs. When he crumpled into the wall from the blast, he'd slammed his head and knocked himself unconscious. In her panic, Helen had assumed the worst.

While Helen sobbed over Manuel, she and Terry had dragged the two dead bodies into the forest and found a suitable burial site. They had no intention of calling the police, too afraid were they of the possible ramifications. They'd returned for shovels and had decided to check in on Helen. And, lo and behold, Manuel was not only sitting at the dining room table, very much alive, he also had a glass of Scotch on the rocks in his hand. He'd agreed with their decision to leave the police out of it, and was in the process of getting sufficiently drunk, anesthetizing himself so he might instruct Helen on how to remove the bullet. So Terry and Anisa had delayed the funeral of the unidentified assassin and one Randall "Saphire" Safferty, and instead assisted with Manuel's successful operation.

After that, Manuel had another idea before burying the thugs. They'd filled glasses with Scotch, cleaned up some of the evidence of the assassination attempt, and placed the statue of Saint Death front and center on the dining room table. After anesthetizing themselves from the shock and horror of the attack with two more glasses of Scotch, they'd prayed to the Holy Saint.

Anisa remembered Manuel's words now as if they had been spoken yesterday. "Please, Most Holy Death. Preserve our innocence in this act of self-defense. Help us dispose of the bodies and cover our tracks. I beseech you to end this terrible witch-hunt—an affront and an insult to the goodness, love, and joy that you not only represent, but so readily provide to your worshippers. Please, do it peacefully and bring no harm to those who have disrespected you. End it now and end it forever."

Maybe the Skinny Lady didn't have the word *peacefully* in her vocabulary, but she'd definitely ended the witch-hunt. After the prayers, they'd all gone out to the impromptu cemetery, and there was no sign of the bodies. It was like they'd vanished into thin air. Another search around the thirty acres didn't produce any signs of a vehicle or a boat. They had no idea how the men had arrived at Manuel's house. Maybe, along with the bodies, Saint Death had miraculously airlifted a car or a boat off the property.

Anisa knew one thing for certain. She was out of harm's way. Even though she no longer lived in Montague, when she did travel there to run errands, townsfolk went out of their way to be nice to her. Montague, the scenic little riverfront town, was living up to its slogan, "Montague the Beautiful."

She reached for the bottle of wine, uncorked it, and filled her glass. It was only eleven am, but it must be noon somewhere in the world. *Beautiful. Montague is beautiful once again. Just like my house.*

After Terry had announced his feelings for Anisa and she'd expressed the same feelings for him, it seemed prudent that they start fresh with a new home. Call it luck, or holy intervention: a bank manager position opened up at Scotiabank in Montague, and Terry applied for and received the transfer. Anisa had sold her house, and together they bought a modest-sized oceanfront bungalow on five acres, about twenty minutes south of Montague.

Terry walked into the living room wearing a white apron that said *Kiss the Chef.* "Connor really likes that racetrack we bought him."

"You mean the one *you* bought him."

"Right. Call it an early Christmas present. He hasn't left his bedroom all day. Only problem is, he always wants me to race him and I'm supposed to be cooking dinner. Had a hard time getting away. Men aren't very good multi-taskers, I'm afraid."

"Come over here, Mister Chef," Anisa said.

He sat down beside her.

"You ask me, you're a great stepfather and a great cook. That makes you a great multi-tasker in my mind."

"Compliments will get you everywhere," Terry said.

Anisa kissed him full on the lips. "I'm just obeying your apron."

He kissed her back. "Don't mind if you do."

"How's dinner?"

"The potatoes are almost ready. The steak is marinating and the Caesar salad is ready. I'm gonna do onions, potatoes, and steak on the barbeque, but I thought I'd get the potatoes started in the oven first." Terry poured himself a drink using the spare glass Anisa had put aside for him. "You talk to Helen?"

"Yeah. They'll be here any minute. They only live next door, remember."

"That's convenient."

"It sure is. Honey, I know we've only lived together for just under a month, but how do you like it? You know, how do you like me?"

He sipped his wine. "I don't like you."

"I didn't think so."

"I love you, Anisa. I'm crazy about you."

She felt her eyes begin to moisten. It was an effort to hold back the tears. "You're so good to me... so good with Connor. I don't know what I would've done without you. I love you, Terry. I never thought I'd say this, but I love my new life with you."

She leaned over and kissed him long and hard. They hugged tightly.

Terry released her and stood. "I better check the potatoes." He stopped halfway to the kitchen and turned around. "I'm so proud of you, baby. Having the courage to quit your job at Sobeys. Getting accepted at the university to complete your doctorate in psychology. All your dreams are coming true. We really do have a reason to celebrate."

The doorbell rang.

Anisa stood, wiping her eyes. She finally lost the battle, and two tears snaked down her cheeks. "Let me help you, baby. Our guests have arrived."

As the sun sank on the ocean horizon, five people sat around a dining room table and, over much laughter, many jokes, and a few glasses of wine, they all enjoyed a delicious pre-Christmas dinner.

Manuel raised his wine glass. "To our hosts. Dinner is delicious. Friends are gifts to be cherished and we should never forget that."

"Cheers," they said, almost in unison, before toasting and sipping.

"That reminds me," Anisa said. "We have something else to celebrate. I have an announcement to make."

"I love surprises," Helen said.

Raising her wine glass, Anisa stood. "Terry has proposed to me. I've accepted. We're getting married next summer."

Everyone stood and toasted the upcoming union. Even Connor grinned and raised his glass of apple juice.

"I wish you all the happiness in the world," Manuel said. "When's your wedding day?"

"On the first day of July," Anisa said.

Helen's jaw dropped. "That's *our* wedding day."

"I know," Anisa said. "That's the other surprise. We can do a double wedding. If you want to, that is."

"I think that's a great idea," Helen said.

"Agreed," Manuel said, beaming.

A comfortable silence descended on them as they resumed dining. Manuel pointed to a painting of a pyramid on the wall. "Hey, that's almost identical to the one in my dining room."

"Well, you never finished your story," Anisa said. "The first time I had dinner at your place. You left off saying, 'The Pyramid of the Sun is near the Pyramid of the Moon, along the Avenue of the Dead...'"

A crashing sound outside startled them. Drawing his gun, Manuel leaped out of his chair in an instant. But Anisa was one step ahead of him. She slid open the sliding-glass door and looked outside into an opaque darkness. She turned around with a grin. "False alarm. A raccoon tipped over a garbage can. See, there he goes now."

Also by William Blackwell

Phantom Rage, Poison Rage, Infected Rage
Nightmare's Edge
Resurrection Point
Brainstorm
Rule 14
Assaulted Souls
Assaulted Souls II
Assaulted Souls III
Blood Curse
Black Dawn
The Strap
The End is Nigh
Orgon Conclusion
Freaky Franky
The Witch's Tombstone
The Dark Menace
Tales of Damnation
In Your Dreams
Macabre Alley
A Head for an Eye

In Your Dreams Preview

"On the surface, it's a gripping horror thriller with brutal, shocking twists. But beneath that, it's a thought-provoking exploration of obsession, loneliness, and the terrifying power our subconscious holds over us. The writing is bold, cinematic, and immersive—it reminded me of a cross between Clive Barker and early Stephen King, yet with a unique, modern edge." -Amazon

"I have finished reading In Your Dreams. WOW, just WOW! What an amazing tale. You are one hell of a gifted writer." -Amazon.

"This is an amazing book. Great ending." -Goodreads

Alienated from humanity, Oliver Gimble is a self-indulgent sloth who finds vicarious comfort in binge-watching horror movies and gorging on junk food. During sleep, he escapes into a meticulously constructed dream world where he discovers carnal delight with an enigmatic woman called Stella.

His bizarre lifestyle begins to unravel when he meets Carmen Weathersby, a lonely woman, who in Oliver's mind's eye mysteriously transforms into Stella, the woman of his dreams.

But soon Oliver realizes Stella is actually interfering with his new relationship and will go to any lengths, even murder, to possess him.

When Carmen's elderly mother suffers a heart attack, fingers point to Stella. Suddenly, people close to Carmen start dying—brutally and inexplicably.

Careening helplessly down into a cryptic and otherworldly realm somewhere between reality and perception, Carmen and Oliver struggle to try and solve the macabre mystery before it's too late.

A multi-layered, horrifying journey of self-discovery, *In Your Dreams* examines the powerful and shocking connections between our conscious and subconscious worlds—boldly questioning the very nature of reality.

About the Author

Canadian dark fiction author William Blackwell studied journalism at Calgary's Mount Royal University and English literature at Vancouver's University of British Columbia. He worked as a journalist for many years before pursuing his passion for storytelling. His novels have been characterized as graphic, edgy, and at times terrifying. Currently living on a secluded acreage on Prince Edward Island, Blackwell finds much of his inspiration from Mother Nature, odd people, bizarre nightmares, and traveling around the world.

Author Comments

Thank you for reading this book. I would be eternally grateful if you would post a book review on your favorite book retailer website. A positive review is the highest compliment a writer can receive. Reviews are crucial to the success of any author and also help readers discover new books. You don't have to say much. A few sentences will suffice.

In other news, I have a gift for you. Complete the signup form below with your name and email address and download a FREE copy of *Resurrection Point*, a dark tale about the horrifying consequences of experimenting with death and resurrection. You're only agreeing to be kept up to date on blog posts, new releases, and freebies. I promise I won't spam you and you can unsubscribe at any time.

Thanks again for your support.

http://www.wblackwell.com/free-ebook/

.

9 7 8 1 0 6 9 7 3 1 8 6 9